F   Cassidy, Carla (Carla
CASSIDY Bracale)
            Are you afraid?

ARE YOU AFRAID?

Carla Cassidy

A SIGNET ECLIPSE BOOK

SIGNET ECLIPSE
Published by New American Library, a division of
Penguin Group (USA) Inc., 375 Hudson Street,
New York, New York 10014, USA
Penguin Group (Canada), 90 Eglinton Avenue East, Suite 700, Toronto,
Ontario M4P 2Y3, Canada (a division of Pearson Penguin Canada Inc.)
Penguin Books Ltd., 80 Strand, London WC2R 0RL, England
Penguin Ireland, 25 St. Stephen's Green, Dublin 2,
Ireland (a division of Penguin Books Ltd.)
Penguin Group (Australia), 250 Camberwell Road, Camberwell, Victoria 3124,
Australia (a division of Pearson Australia Group Pty. Ltd.)
Penguin Books India Pvt. Ltd., 11 Community Centre, Panchsheel Park,
New Delhi - 110 017, India
Penguin Group (NZ), cnr Airborne and Rosedale Roads, Albany,
Auckland 1310, New Zealand (a division of Pearson New Zealand Ltd.)
Penguin Books (South Africa) (Pty.) Ltd., 24 Sturdee Avenue,
Rosebank, Johannesburg 2196, South Africa

Penguin Books Ltd., Registered Offices:
80 Strand, London WC2R 0RL, England

First published by Signet Eclipse, an imprint of New American Library,
a division of Penguin Group (USA) Inc.

ISBN 0-7394-6509-0

To the two Lauras in my life, Laura Peterson and Laura Cifelli—thanks for the support and encouragement. You're just what a writer needs, a great agent and a great editor.

Chapter 1

"Hi, Barry, you're on eleven-fifty AM. Are you afraid of the dark?" Dr. Jessica Langford checked her watch. 11:45. Fifteen minutes more and she would be finished with her nightly radio show and could go home.

"No, it isn't the dark that scares me," Barry, the caller, said. "It's bugs."

"Any particular kind of bugs?"

The call went the way all the calls that came in to the show went; the caller talked about his fear, and Jessie gave advice and coping mechanisms.

If anyone had told her two years ago that she would spend two hours a night on her own radio show, she would have laughed.

She'd been perfectly satisfied with her life, enjoying a thriving private practice specializing in helping people with fears and phobias. She'd had a marriage she thought was perfect and a four-year-old son whom she thought hung the moon.

Eighteen months ago that had changed when her

husband, Larry, had taken her to a lovely dinner and over appetizers had told her he'd fallen in love with his secretary and had filed for divorce.

Within six months she had moved out of her lovely home and into a condo, was sharing custody of Charlie and mourning the death of her marriage.

She'd met Henry James, the owner of the radio station, when he'd come to her office to seek treatment for fear of public speaking. After six weeks of therapy he felt confident enough to attempt a speech in front of a local high school senior class. The speech had been successful and he had broached the topic of a nightly radio show with Jessica.

The two-hour show had been a surprising success and there was talk of syndication in the near future. For Jessica the talk show fit well into her schedule. She worked her private practice from ten to three five days a week, then didn't have to be at the radio station until ten at night.

These hours allowed her to be home in the mornings to put Charlie on the school bus and be there when he returned home from school. They shared their evenings together, then she tucked him into bed and left for the radio station. She'd hired a live-in babysitter, who had quickly become part of her little family.

As far as Jessica was concerned she had the best of both worlds. She was able to pursue her own career goals and at the same time be, for all intents and purposes, a full-time mom to six-year-old Charlie.

She finished the call with Barry and looked through the glass partition at her producer, Chris Mathison, on the other side. He held up one finger and spoke into the earpiece. "Cameron."

She nodded. "We have time for one more caller." She punched one of the buttons on the console before her. "Cameron, you're on the air with Dr. Jessica. Are you afraid of the dark?"

"Not me." The voice was deep and smooth. "I love the dark. In fact, I'm not afraid of anything. I'd find it far more interesting to talk about your fears, Dr. Jessica."

Jessie stifled a sigh. A smart-ass. There was always one a night. "I don't think our listeners would find my fears very interesting," she replied.

"On the contrary, I think they'd be fascinated." The deep voice that had moments before sounded smooth now sounded strangely ominous. "I think your callers would be very interested to know that you have a fear of cemeteries."

Jessie froze as a roar resounded in her head. Her heart hammered frantically. The scent of damp earth filled her nose. The black of night swallowed her. Air—she needed air. Her throat constricted. Her mouth filled with the taste of dank dirt.

Hands bound. The sound of a shovel hitting dirt. Help me.

Help me. She was lost, lost in a horrifying memory as terror suffused her.

"Jessie! Jessie, what's wrong?"

The familiar voice came out of the darkness and pulled her up from the grave of memories that had momentarily overwhelmed her. Chris stared at her worriedly through the glass partition, his voice whispering through the tiny speaker in her ear.

"I'm sorry, we're out of time for this evening." Her voice sounded reedy and thin as she flipped the switch to disconnect the last caller. "Join us on Monday night for another two hours of *Are You Afraid of the Dark?* Good night."

As her theme music began to play, Jessie ripped off the earphones and reached, with trembling fingers, for her coffee cup.

Chris opened the door and stepped into the booth. "Are you all right?" He plopped down in the chair that was sometimes occupied by live guests.

With tousled brown hair and clad in jeans and a T-shirt, he looked like a teenager who should be out skateboarding or hanging with his buddies at a high school football game.

She forced a smile to her lips, although it felt stiff and unnatural. "I'm fine. I guess I zoned out for a minute."

He raised an eyebrow. "You sure? You looked sick. I thought you were about to throw up or something."

"I'm fine. Really. Just tired." She took a sip of her coffee, hoping the hot brew would burn the chill out of her body. "I'm just glad it's Friday night and

I have the weekend to catch up on some sleep." She stood and grabbed her cup.

"Leave it," Chris said. "I'll clean up. You get out of here and go home."

She smiled at him gratefully. "Thanks, Chris. You're a doll." She grabbed her coat and pulled it on, then said good-bye to her young producer.

At midnight the offices of the KTKC radio station were dark except for the one Jessie worked from. As she walked down the long hallway toward the front entrance she was aware of the hollow echoing *click* of her heels against the tile floor.

She'd never noticed before tonight the absolute, profound silence of the hallway or just how dark it was with no lights flowing from the doorways she passed.

She focused her gaze straight ahead to where she saw the figure of Daniel, the security guard, seated by the front entrance. No question, the last caller had spooked her.

Daniel stood as she approached, and a wave of relief swept through her. "Evening, Doc," he greeted her. "Good program tonight."

"Thanks, Daniel." He jingled his keys as he stepped toward the door to unlock it for her. "Uh . . . Daniel, would you mind walking me to my car?"

He looked at her in surprise. In the three months he'd been on duty, she'd never requested an escort. "Sure."

She was grateful he didn't ask questions, but

simply unlocked the door and stepped outside just behind her. "I think we're going to have an early hot summer," he said as the damp night air embraced them.

"That's what the weathermen are saying," she replied. It was only the last day of April, and it had been a mild winter. The signs of spring were already beginning to take on the blooms of summer. None too soon, as far as she was concerned. She'd always hated spring.

As they reached her car she pulled her keys from her purse and smiled up at the tall, beefy older man. "Thanks, Daniel. I appreciate it."

He shrugged. "That's what I'm here for, Dr. Langford. I hope you have a good weekend."

"I'll see you Monday night." She got into her car and locked the doors, eager to get home.

It was just a coincidence, she told herself as she pulled out of the parking lot. The fact that the last caller of the night had been named Cameron and had mentioned cemeteries was nothing more than a crazy coincidence. There must be a hundred men named Cameron in Kansas City, and a fear of cemeteries was fairly universal.

She stifled a yawn with the back of her hand, grateful that the radio station was only a ten-minute drive from her condo.

As she pulled into her driveway she punched the remote button that opened the garage door. A good night's sleep would banish the last of the bad taste the call had left in her mouth.

She parked in the garage and closed the door behind her, then got out of the car and entered the house through the door that led from the garage into the kitchen.

As usual Maria had left the light on over the stove to illuminate the kitchen. For the millionth time Jessie thanked her luck in finding Maria Vernon and hiring her on as a live-in housekeeper and nanny.

She'd just shrugged out of her coat when Maria appeared in the kitchen. The fifty-five-year-old woman was clad in a brushed cotton nightgown, but it was obvious she hadn't been sleeping.

"Evening, Dr. Jessie," she said, her plump face wreathed in a smile as she stepped forward to take Jessie's coat.

"Hi, Maria. Any problems tonight?" Jessie relinquished her coat to the grey-haired woman.

Maria shook her head. "None. He got up once for a drink of water, then went right back to sleep. I enjoyed the show tonight."

A cold fist of fear clenched Jessie's stomach as she thought of that last caller. She consciously willed it away. "It was okay. All I want now is the luxury of my bed."

"Go. I'll lock up."

Jessie smiled. "I don't know what I'd do without you, Maria."

Maria's eyes darkened. "I'd have been dead by now if it wasn't for you. I can never thank you enough for what you've done for me." She cleared her throat. "Now, off with you. Get to bed. You know that little boy will be up early and wanting his mama."

"You're right. Good night, Maria. I'll see you in the morning." Jessie left the kitchen, walked through the living room and down the hallway. The first doorway led to Maria's room. The second was Charlie's.

She stepped into her son's room, the area around the bed illuminated by a night-light. Charlie slept on his back, sprawled out as if proclaiming himself king of the mattress.

She leaned down and pulled the sheet up to his chest, fighting the impulse to kiss his freckled face clean off. He was the best of her, this little boy, with his bright blue eyes and equally bright mind.

Sometimes she thought Charlie was her gift from God, a magnificent first prize for living through an unimaginable nightmare when she'd been younger.

There had been a time when she'd thought that her husband, Larry, had been the prize for despair. He'd been the man who'd made her see possibilities when she thought none had existed, the man who had healed scars she'd believed would never be healed.

But Larry had become a cliché of middle-age stupidity, leaving behind his wife and child for a twenty-one-year-old secretary named Tammi who had a tongue piercing and fake boobs.

Jessie had come to terms with her husband's defection. The divorce had been remarkably civilized, and she was willing to do whatever it took to make sure that she and Larry stayed on good terms for Charlie's sake.

She leaned down and kissed her son's forehead, then drew in a deep breath of the scent of him. Nothing in the world smelled like a little boy sleeping, the fragrance of big dreams and body heat, of bubble gum toothpaste and adventure. She left his room, her heart filled as only Charlie could fill it.

Bed beckoned, but Jessie knew from experience it would take her a while to unwind. Normally she curled up in bed with a book and read until she fell asleep, but tonight her nerves were too jangled to focus on a book.

She undressed and pulled on her favorite navy nightshirt. As much as she tried to forget it, that last call of the night remained in her mind, bringing with it that cloying, suffocating feeling she knew rationally was nothing more than a case of post-traumatic stress.

Before leaving her walk-in closet, she reached up to the top shelf and pulled down a shoebox that had once held a pair of bright red knee-high boots. The boots were long gone, but the box contained pieces of Jessie's soul.

She carried it to her bed and stretched out, then with trembling fingers removed the lid. The box contained her life in paper detail: her birth certificate, a life insurance policy, marriage and divorce papers. There were photos as well—graduation from Kansas University, her wedding day and the first photo of Charlie, red-faced and squealing with displeasure.

Beneath were news clippings of the event that had shaped her life, chosen her career path and nearly killed her.

It had been a long time since she'd looked at them, and she now steeled herself for the emotional drain of remembering that distant past.

Eighteen years had yellowed the clippings and made them brittle. Carefully she pulled one out, her fingers still trembling as she unfolded it and spread it on the bed next to her.

LATEST T&B VICTIM SURVIVES, the headline screamed. The accompanying grainy black-and-white photo depicted Detective Adam Cappa with his arm around an unidentified young teenage girl whose face was hidden in the big man's chest.

It had been front-page news. The T&B serial killer that had traumatized Kansas City for almost a year had already killed five young women. The killer had been nicknamed T&B by the news media because he tortured his victims, then buried them alive in graves in area cemeteries.

Jessie drew a breath, realizing she'd stopped breathing for a moment. She pulled out the next clipping and stared at the photo of the Hillside Cemetery. It had been spring, and she could almost smell the scent of honeysuckle and lilac that had permeated the air on that particular day in late May.

The photo showed a single gravesite, the dirt in

front of the stone disturbed by crime-scene special-
ists and their shovels and picks. The headstone
read CAMERON JACKSON—1934–. There had been no
end date because Cameron Jackson was still alive.
He was a resourceful old man who had prepared
his gravesite for his eventual demise, leaving only
the date to fate.

On a spring night eighteen years ago, for endless
moments of terror, in a state between life and death,
Jessie had been in Cameron Jackson's final resting
place as damp earth had been shoveled on top of
her and a killer whistled "Amazing Grace."

She drew another ragged, gasping breath and
shoved the clippings back in the box and slammed
the lid down tight. That's where it all belonged—in
a box, in the past.

She got up from the bed and returned the box to
the top shelf in the closet, but before going back to
bed, she stood in front of her dresser mirror and
looked at her reflection.

The thirty-four-year-old dark-haired woman
who stared back at her was a survivor. She'd not
only endured hours of torture at the hands of a
madman, she'd also come through the aftermath
reasonably well-adjusted, thanks to a good therapist and loving parents.

She raised her nightgown, exposing her black
lace panties and above that the crisscross scars left
from that night of terror so long ago.

Ugly. Deep, dark ridges of scarred tissue rode
her belly like leeches.

She was the last known victim of the T&B killer, the only victim who had survived. The T&B killer had never been caught, nor had there been another murder attributed to him. She dropped her nightgown back into place and turned away from the mirror.

Had the phone call tonight been nothing more than a coincidence, or after all these years had the killer from her past returned to finish the job?

She turned off her bedroom light, but the room wasn't plunged into total darkness. A small nightlight burned in a wall socket near the bed, illuminating the room with a comforting glow.

Climbing into bed she thought of the irony and wondered what her callers would think if they knew that Dr. Jessica Langford was afraid of the dark.

Chapter 2

Detective Jake Merridan sat in the dark bedroom, his gaze focused on the open window, the screen propped against the wall beneath the sill.

Dual emotions warred inside his head. As a cop he supposed he should have been worried, and he might have been if the screen had been ripped or torn and flung to the outside of the house.

But the cop in him had played second banana to his role as father, and as a father he was pissed. You put your kid to bed and you expect them to be there thirty minutes later when you check on them.

It was obvious Jimmy hadn't been abducted by aliens or kidnapped by a crazed killer. He'd carefully removed the screen on his window and had sneaked out into the dark of night. To do what? And with whom?

Was this normal behavior for a twelve-year-old boy? Jake leaned back in the chair and rubbed a hand across his whisker-stubbled jaw. If Jake would have pulled this particular stunt when he'd been twelve, his old man would have met him at the window with a fist in the face and locked him out of the house for a week.

However, Jake wasn't his father. The problem was, Jake had no idea how to handle this. They'd been doing so well over the past year, when they'd suddenly found themselves alone.

Then three months ago something had changed. Jimmy had become withdrawn, alternating between sullen silences and belligerent outbursts. Was it just normal stuff that marked the transition between boy- and manhood?

Jake leaned his head back and closed his eyes. Damn you, Colette, he thought. Damn you for leaving me, for leaving us to muddle through all this alone.

As if his problem with Jimmy wasn't enough, he had a new murder case on his desk that was giving him nightmares. The woman, Terri Sinclair, had been a twenty-four-year-old single parent. It appeared that she'd been abducted from a shopping mall parking lot, her six-month-old baby left unharmed in a stroller next to her car.

A representative from the mall had contacted the police when somebody had reported the baby abandoned. The officer who'd responded to the call had run the plates of the car beside which the stroller had been found. The plates on the five-year-old Honda Civic came back as registered to Terri Sinclair.

Officers had gotten her address from the motor

vehicle department and had gone to her house, to find her boyfriend waiting for her return from the store. He'd been frantic when they'd explained the situation and had insisted they file a missing persons report. The fact that the woman had seemingly disappeared into thin air, leaving her baby behind, had prompted the officer to do just that.

Jake hadn't gotten involved in the case until the morning when Terri Sinclair's body had been found in a drainage ditch. She'd been bound with duct tape, beaten and stabbed to death, a plastic white lily left on her chest.

The sight of that lily had sickened Jake, sickened him in a way nothing else had in a very long time. He'd thought he'd become inured to the cruelties that people were capable of, both physical and emotional. He'd been wrong.

He froze as he heard a sound just outside the window. He sat up as a sneaker-clad foot came into the window, followed by Jimmy's upper body.

"About time," he said.

Jimmy's head shot up and connected with the bottom of the window with a *thunk*. "Jeez, Dad. You scared me."

He tumbled into the room as Jake reached out and flipped on the desk lamp, illuminating the room enough so he could see his son.

Clad in a pair of sweatpants and a shirt, with his dark hair tousled boyishly, Jimmy looked no worse for his nighttime foray.

Jimmy sat on the edge of the bed and began to

take off his sneakers, his gaze studiously refusing to meet his father's. Jake sat close enough that he could smell the night air that clung to his son, air untainted by the scent of cigarette or marijuana smoke.

So Jimmy wasn't smoking any dope, but that didn't mean drugs hadn't become an issue. That's the first thing Jake had thought of when he'd noticed the change in Jimmy's behavior. It was the first thing any parent should consider in this day and age.

"Where have you been?" he asked.

"Nowhere." In that single word Jake heard the familiar rise of belligerence in his son's voice as he stretched out on his back on the bed.

Jake stood, a bone weariness sweeping through him. Once again he silently cursed the woman who had left him alone and ill equipped to deal with raising a preteenager.

"Jimmy, talk to me. Tell me what's going on, where you went tonight." He tried to keep any pleading tone from his voice.

Jimmy kept his gaze focused on some distant point beyond his father's shoulder. "There's nothing going on and I didn't go anywhere. I just went out to the backyard and sat for a while. It's not a big deal."

The kid had turned off, tuned out, and Jake knew from past experience there was no talking to him tonight. Once Jimmy put up his walls, nothing was able to tear them down. "Sneaking out is a

very big deal. In this house we use the doors to
come and go, not the windows. You got it?"

"Got it," Jimmy replied, and turned on his side
away from Jake.

Jake stood for a long moment next to his son's
bed, then turned and left the room. Getting into a
murderer's head and solving a crime suddenly
seemed far easier than dealing with the son who
had become a stranger, the son whom Jake loved
more than any other person on the face of the earth.

Chapter 3

Jessie studied the new patient form on the desk in front of her. Mark Smith would be her last patient of the day. According to the form he'd filled out he was a fifty-two-year-old man who worked as a mechanic at a local garage.

The space under REASONS FOR YOUR VISIT had been left blank. That wasn't necessarily unusual. Many people were reluctant to put down in writing why they were seeking the help of a psychiatrist. It sometimes took two or three visits before even they knew exactly what had brought them to her.

She slipped the new patient file into her top drawer, then got up from her desk and went to the coffeemaker on a small table in the corner and poured herself a cup of the fresh brew.

She returned to her chair, sipped her coffee and took a few minutes to clear her mind and prepare for the new patient.

Jessie's office didn't contain the traditional psychiatric sofa. Although she had a desk, the real heart of the room were two wingback chairs separated by a teakwood table bearing a Tiffany-style lamp.

The sitting area, with its muted lighting, gave an aura of comfort, of intimacy that was conducive to opening people up, allowing emotions and fears to surface.

The fear she'd gone to sleep with on Friday night after the strange phone call to the radio station had dissipated over the weekend. She had chalked it up to nothing more than a crazy coincidence.

Besides, it was impossible to hang on to painful memories and fear from the past when Charlie so filled her present. They'd spent the weekend doing the usual things, time in the park, a movie, then sorting through the clothes Charlie had outgrown and dropping them off at a charitable foundation.

She took another sip of her coffee, then punched a button on the intercom. "Sarah, would you please see Mr. Smith in?"

"Right away, Dr. Langford," Sarah replied.

A moment later a knock fell on the door and it opened to admit Sarah and a tall, muscular man with dark hair just beginning to gray at the temples, and even darker eyes. Jessie stood and left her chair behind her desk to approach them.

"Dr. Langford, this is Mark Smith," Sarah said.

Jessie held out a hand. "Mr. Smith, nice to meet you."

He grabbed her hand in a tight, almost painful

grasp and nodded, then released her hand and shoved his in his pockets.

"Thank you, Sarah." As Sarah left and closed the door behind her, Jessie motioned her new client into one of the chairs. "Please, sit down, Mr. Smith."

He took the chair closest to the door, a muscle ticking in his jaw. Jessie sat in the other chair, aware of an almost palpable tension rolling off the man.

"Beautiful afternoon, isn't it?" she said, hoping a bit of small talk would alleviate his obvious uneasiness.

"I guess it's all right." He had a deep voice that might have been pleasant if it hadn't been filled with a timbre of something dark. . . . Something barely suppressed.

"Would you like a cup of coffee? Or maybe a soft drink?" she offered.

"No." He sat on the edge of the chair as if poised to run.

Patients came in all shapes and sizes, with all kinds of problems, big and small, but they generally fell into two groups, as far as Jessie was concerned. Those who eagerly embraced the idea of exploring inner feelings and traumas, and those who were forced to come through the courts, through a spouse or through some dramatic turn of events. She had a feeling Mark Smith fell into the latter category.

There was a moment of awkward silence as Jessie gave him time to open up a dialogue. He sat with lips compressed as the seconds ticked by. Apparently he didn't intend to make this easy.

"What brings you to my office this afternoon, Mr. Smith?" Jessie finally asked when it became apparent he wasn't going to offer anything unsolicited.

"Don't you psychiatrists usually write down notes?" he asked. For the first time since he'd entered the office he gazed at her. His eyes were not friendly, but rather reminded her of cauldrons of simmering anger. It was her job to get to the source of that anger.

"Actually I prefer to tape record our sessions," Jessie explained.

"Are you taping me now?" His dark brows shot up in alarm.

"No, I wouldn't tape you without your permission. The first time I meet with somebody the session is usually a get-to-know-you kind of thing." She paused a beat to let him digest this. "Is there something you'd like to ask me?"

He frowned down at his feet. "I can't think of anything right now. I heard you're good at this sort of thing. I've listened to your radio show before."

"Is that what made you come in? Something you heard on my show?"

"Not really. My wife told me it was time."

"You're having problems in your marriage?"

He stood suddenly, fists clenched at his sides.

Jessie tensed. There were three panic buttons in the room, buttons that when pushed would not only summon Sarah, but also would ring building security. One of the buttons was at her desk, one was in the private bathroom and one was on the underside of the teak round table that separated the two chairs.

Since hanging her shingle for private practice, she'd never had to punch one of those buttons, but if Mark Smith made the slightest aggressive move toward her she prepared to do so now.

He took a step backward, toward the door and flashed a taut smile. "I'm sorry, Doc. This was a mistake." Without waiting for her reply, he turned and flew out the door.

Jessie was still seated in the chair when Sarah opened the door and peeked in. "You okay?"

"I'm fine."

The middle-aged receptionist stepped into the room. "What did you do? Threaten him with a lobotomy?"

"He got cold feet." Jessie frowned, thinking of the darkness she'd seen in his eyes. "If I was to guess, he'll be back."

"Your ex called a few minutes ago. He wants you to call him back when you get a chance."

Jessie stood. "Thanks. You can go on home, Sarah."

"Are you sure? Officially I'm on the clock for another forty-five minutes or so."

Jessie smiled. "Since when do we do anything officially around here? Go, get out of here. I'm just going to make a few notes, then I'm headed home myself."

"I'll lock up," Sarah said, then closed the door and left Jessie alone.

She walked over to the desk and sat down. From the bottom desk drawer she pulled out a new notebook, the kind of spiral theme book most students used. She opened the cover and on the first page printed the name Mark Smith.

She never took notes when with a patient, but immediately after a session she wrote her thoughts and impressions and anything else that might be important.

When she'd been in therapy years before, the therapist had sat with pad and pencil in hand and every time Jessie spoke a thought or a feeling she'd scribble something on the pad.

Jessie had never forgotten the sound of the pen against the paper, the curiosity about what the therapist had been writing, the fear that perhaps she'd said something wrong or thought something horrible.

It was during that time she'd decided if she ever had a job like that she would do things differently. She took notes, just as her therapist had done, but the difference was she did it when patients weren't around to worry or wonder what was being memorialized on a sheet of paper.

On the second blank page Jessie wrote her initial impressions of Mark Smith. Defensive posture, possibly coerced to seek help by spouse, suppressed anger. There wasn't much else she could write after so brief a time with him.

She closed the notebook, filed it in a locked cabinet, then returned to her desk and picked up the phone. It was rare for Larry to call during the week. The upcoming weekend was his with Charlie. It wouldn't be the first time he'd had to cancel plans.

She punched in his work number, then waited for the call to be connected. "Willow, Bail and Langford," a pleasant female voice answered.

"Mr. Langford, please."

"May I ask who is calling?"

"Jessica Langford." Jessie sighed. The law firm seemed to change receptionists as often as she changed her underwear.

"Jessie," Larry's deep voice filled the line. "Thanks for getting back to me so quickly."

"What's up?" she asked.

"I was wondering if you and Charlie wanted to meet me tonight for pizza. You know, just the three of us, kind of like old times."

"Can you get a babysitter for Tammi on such short notice?" She bit her lip, knowing her comment was catty.

Larry laughed. "You're bad, Jessie. So what do you say? Tonight at five at Pepper's?"

"All right," she agreed after a moment of hesitation. "We'll meet you there."

Fifteen minutes later as she drove home she wondered what had prompted Larry's dinner invitation. Although she and Larry had managed to maintain a friendship, the three of them hadn't shared a meal together since the divorce more than a year ago.

Her feelings where Larry was concerned were complicated. There was a part of her that would always love the man who had helped make her whole, encouraged her to seek her dreams and who had fathered her child.

There was also a part of her that still harbored a bitter resentment, an ache of heartbreak whenever she thought of his infidelity and how easily he'd thrown away what she'd thought they had together.

She might have been able to swallow his dalliance with Tammi if she hadn't been fairly certain that the young, sexy blonde wasn't the first of his infidelities, but rather the latest in a long string.

She'd made her peace with the divorce and with the fact that Larry wouldn't be a part of her future except as her son's father.

Three hours later she and Charlie sat in a booth in Pepper's Pizza, waiting for Larry to arrive. Pepper's Pizza was a neighborhood joint. A back room sported two pool tables and a jukebox that played nothing but oldies.

The main area was filled with red leather booths and several pinball machines that buzzed and clicked and rang when played. The ambience might be terrible, but the pizza was world-class.

"Jeffrey Cook threw up today in math class," Charlie exclaimed. "It was awesome." Jessie sighed. Only a six-year-old boy would find vomit awesome. "His face got all green and he raised his hand, but before Mrs. Cantor could talk to him he spewed. . . . "

"Enough," Jessie said with a laugh. "I do not want to talk about this before we eat."

Charlie grinned at her. "Okay, but after we eat I'll tell you how Megan cried because some of Jeffrey's puke got on her shoe."

Thankfully at that moment Larry breezed through the door. Jessie never thought about how much her son looked like her ex-husband until she saw them together.

Larry had a broad, freckled face that implied a friendly, boyish quality, one that often made his opponents in the courtroom underestimate him. Charlie had gotten his sandy-colored hair and freckles from his father.

"Sorry I'm late," Larry said as he squeezed into the booth next to his son and across from Jessie. "How's my favorite kid?" He nudged Charlie with his elbow.

"Fine." Charlie nudged him back and giggled.

"Hi, Jess." His warm smile curved his lips. "You're looking good, as always."

"Thanks," she replied, again wondering what had prompted this family meal. Larry had rarely made time for meals together when they had been married.

The waitress appeared at the table and they ordered. Once the waitress had departed, Charlie asked for quarters to play the pinball machine while they waited for the food to arrive.

"How's work?" she asked Larry once Charlie had left the booth.

"Busy. As long as people continue to get married, there will always be a demand for good divorce lawyers. So, how have you been?"

"Good . . . busy. Between Charlie, the practice and the radio show I sometimes feel like I'm meeting myself coming and going, but I like being busy. I'm even doing a seminar next Wednesday night at Maple Woods Community College."

"Sounds terrific. I've caught the show a couple of times. It's good. You're good."

His words of praise swept a swift warmth through her. "The powers that be seem to be happy. There's some talk of syndication."

"That's great."

She shrugged. "If it happens. If it doesn't I'm fine with things the way they are." She picked up her glass and took a drink of soda. "Did you happen to catch the show Friday night?"

"No, why?"

"I got a strange caller. It freaked me out just a little bit."

"What kind of call?"

As she told him about the caller named Cameron she fought against a dark wave of apprehension that threatened to possess her.

Larry's brows raised in alarm when she'd finished. "Jesus, Jess, did you tell somebody? Go to the police?"

"And tell them what? That I had a caller named Cameron who wanted to talk about the fear of cemeteries?" She shook her head. "I've pretty much decided it was nothing more than a crazy coincidence. It will take a lot more than a phone call to force me to go to the authorities and dredge up the past."

To her surprise he reached across the table and grabbed her hand. "Jessie, promise me you'll let me know if anything else like this happens."

His reaction surprised her. One of the things that had attracted her to Larry in the first place was his seeming inability to overreact to any situation. His hand around hers was warm and familiar, but it wasn't her hand to hold any longer, and she pulled away.

"I'm sure it's nothing to worry about—just one of those crazy coincidences life sometimes serves up." She offered him a smile. "Besides, I have a feeling Tammi would protest if I suddenly started calling you every time I got a nutty phone call at the station."

He unfolded his paper napkin and placed it in his lap. "Tammi isn't in a position to protest anything anymore. I kicked her out last week."

At that moment the waitress arrived with their pizza, and Charlie ran back to the booth. For the remainder of the meal the conversation revolved around Charlie and school and the merits of pizza instead of vegetables.

It was close to seven o'clock when the three of them walked out of the pizza place and into the cool spring night. "'Night, Dad. See you this weekend," Charlie said.

"Saturday morning at nine o'clock," Larry replied. "Don't worry, I'll be there."

As Charlie ran for Jessie's car, Larry turned to Jessie, his features earnest in the last gasp of daylight. "Call me, Jessie. Call me whenever you need to talk."

He loosened his tie, and Jessie realized it was the same red paisley tie he'd been wearing when he'd told her he wanted a divorce. He gazed at her car where Charlie had gotten into the passenger's seat, then looked back at her once again.

"Every day I deal with clients seeking divorces and wonder how many of them will eventually live with regrets. I've been entertaining some regrets of my own recently."

She couldn't have been more shocked if he'd said he was considering a sex-change operation and loved wearing women's panties. "Larry . . . " she began, knowing she needed to say something but unsure of what to say.

"I know, I know. Now isn't the time or the place," he said smoothly. "We'll talk soon, okay?"

She nodded and watched as he walked toward his little sports car parked nearby. A reconciliation?

Although the word hadn't been spoken, she had to wonder if that was what he had in mind.

Minutes later as Charlie chattered about his day, Jessie considered her feelings where Larry was concerned. Certainly there was a comfortable familiarity there.

Larry knew her history; he knew her scars, both the emotional and the physical ones. When he'd walked out she'd known there would never be another man in her life. She couldn't bear the thought of showing those scars to any other man.

Thankfully she didn't have to make any decisions tonight where Larry was concerned. He hadn't said the *R* word out loud, and there was no guarantee he would ever say it.

For now nothing had changed. She had a son to tuck into bed and a radio show to do. Again a sense of disquiet whispered through her. And hopefully tonight there would be no strange calls to evoke any memories of her past.

He sat at the small dinette table, a cup of coffee before him. Outside the early morning sun peeked over the horizon, promising another beautiful spring day.

A miniature tape recorder was set within easy reach of him, but for the moment he ignored it and focused on the sharp, bitter taste of strong coffee.

There was nothing better than a jolt of caffeine after a long night. And it had been a long but satisfying night. Not perfect, but satisfying.

He didn't know her name, but he did know that she'd been standing alone at closing time outside of Pudgie's Bar. It had taken him exactly three minutes to get her gagged and bound and into the trunk of his car.

He didn't know her name, but he knew that her long dark hair had been soft as silk, that she'd smelled like vanilla beans and that when he'd taken her pants off, her blue eyes had rolled into the back of her head.

With the memory still fresh in his mind he got up from the table and poured himself another cup of coffee. He should sleep, but knew from experience that sleep wouldn't come until he'd relived in his mind every moment of his time with the woman.

She'd thought it was over after he'd finished raping her. They always did. He'd seen the hope that lit her eyes as he'd gotten off her, the hope that rape was all he had in mind, the hope that she might survive the night after all.

His first blow to her jaw had squashed the hope, replacing it with frantic terror, then that strange glaze of resignation that always happened when he took out his knife.

It had been too soon. Two women in three days. He hadn't planned it that way; it had just happened. Both women had been at the wrong place at the wrong time. Right for him, but deadly wrong for them.

He returned to the table and sipped his coffee, noting how the sunrise shot pretty pastel colors across the early morning sky. He loved the spring, the scent of green everywhere, birth bursting forth from the earth.

Earth. Dark, rich earth. For a brief moment his head filled with the scent of it. His fingers clenched around the coffee mug as a slow rage built up inside him.

He'd wanted to bury them. He'd needed to bury them, but he couldn't. He couldn't finish the ritual of death properly. It had all been ruined years ago.

It was like doing a jigsaw puzzle and having one piece left to put into place before moving on to the next puzzle. A piece was missing from the puzzle and he couldn't move on until he completed the first.

His fingers trembled with the force of his emotions as he placed his cup on the table, then punched the play button on the tape recorder.

"We have time for one more caller. Cameron, you're on the air with Dr. Jessica. Are you afraid of the dark?"

"Not me," the deep male voice responded. "I love the dark. In fact, I'm not afraid of anything. I'd find it far more interesting to talk about your fears, Dr. Jessica."

There was a moment of silence, then, "I don't think our listeners would find my fears very interesting."

"On the contrary, I think they'd be fascinated. I think your callers would be very interested to know that you have a fear of cemeteries."

There was a gasp, barely audible but there nevertheless. That faint, almost nothing sound shivered through him, momentarily stilling the rage.

He punched the stop button and hit rewind, then played it again.

Gasp.

He punched the stop button and hit rewind, then played it again.

Gasp.

Over and over again he played and replayed, listening to her voice, relishing that gasp. She'd been afraid. He relished her fear. He wanted her to spend the rest of her numbered days in terror.

The rage returned without warning, red sheets falling in front of his eyes, the scent of rich, dark earth filling his head. With a roar he shoved the tape recorder off the table. It hit the floor, and the plastic casing shattered.

It was her fault that the ritual hadn't been completed. She was the one who had ruined everything. She was the missing piece. She was the one who had made everything change.

She was the one who had gotten away.

Chapter 4

The interrogation room was hot. Bo Westerly was hotter. "You can keep me in here for hours, but I'm not going to confess to nothing I didn't do." He glared at Jake as if the detective was personally responsible for every ill that fate had blown his way.

Something in that sullen glare reminded Jake of his son. "Just tell us what happened and maybe we can work something out," he said, barely hanging on to his patience.

Bo slammed his hands down on the tabletop. "There's nothing to tell. Don't you two get it? I'd never hurt Terri. I loved her."

"But you were angry with her." Monica Gallagher, Jake's partner, rose from her chair. She was an impressive woman, big boned and almost six feet tall. With her brown eyes narrowed into menacing slits and her hands balled into fists at her side, it was obvious she intended to play bad cop.

That was fine with Jake, who was functioning on too little sleep and with the sting of an early morning fight with his son.

He just wanted this interview to be over with. The room was stifling and Bo wasn't big on personal hygiene. Even the rose-scented crap Monica wore couldn't mask the sour scent of body odor that wafted from good old Bo.

"Yes . . . no." Bo leaned back in his chair and crossed him arms defensively over his chest, a sheen of perspiration on his broad forehead. "All right, we had a fight before she went to the store, but it wasn't a big deal."

There was a whine to his voice that grated on Jake's nerves. Bo Westerly was a two-bit criminal with a rap sheet as long as Jake's arm, mostly petty theft and drug possession charges. He seemed far more interested in keeping himself out of trouble than helping to find out who might have wanted his girlfriend dead.

"It was a big enough deal that your neighbors heard you yelling at her," Monica exclaimed.

"It wasn't any bigger deal than usual," Bo protested, the whine more pronounced. "Me and Terri, we always argued loud, but that doesn't mean I'd ever hurt her."

"Somebody beat her half to death before they finally put her out of her misery with a knife," Monica said. "A beating like she took, that looks personal. That looks like somebody was in a rage."

Bo drew a deep breath, his nostrils nearly pinching closed. "You people are wasting my time, wasting your time. I told you, I didn't kill her. Jesus, she was the mother of my kid."

The patience Jake had barely maintained until now snapped and he slammed his hands on the table and half rose from his seat and glared back at the man who was their best suspect for the murder of Terri Sinclair. "You were pissed off because she refused to marry you. She'd had your baby, but she wouldn't have you."

"That's not true. . . . We was going to get married. I loved her, man. I didn't do this. I swear I didn't." He looked at Monica, then back at Jake, beseeching them to believe him.

"She didn't want to marry you, that's what all her friends have told us," Jake yelled. "She didn't want you, and that pissed you off. You fought and she took off for the mall and you sat there and stewed about it, getting more and more angry until you couldn't stand it any longer."

Jake was vaguely aware of Monica touching his arm, but he ignored her and leaned closer to the stinking, sweating Bo Westerly. "You got into your car and drove to the mall. Fucking bitch, right? That's what you thought. Fucking bitch was good enough to have your baby, but she didn't want your name. She didn't want any kind of real commitment to you, so you grabbed her and tried to beat some sense into her."

Someplace in the back of his mind he knew he

was out of line, but for just a moment the lack of control felt wonderful.

He slammed his hands on the table once again, the force causing Bo to jump. "You beat her until she couldn't tell you no."

"Jake," Monica said in a low voice. "Back off."

As quickly as the anger had come, it left him. Jake stepped back and took a deep breath.

"Man, you're crazy," Bo said softly, genuine fear in his eyes.

"I'm going to get a cup of coffee," Jake said. "Detective Gallagher, you can finish up here."

He left the interrogation room and went directly to the men's room, grateful to find himself alone. He walked to the sink and wet a paper towel and raked it over his face, the coolness soothing.

He rarely lost his cool and wasn't sure why he had now. Hell, he didn't even think Bo was their perp. His gut instinct told him Bo had told them the truth. The man was a loser, but Jake didn't think he was capable of murder.

Sliding the paper towel across the back of his neck, he closed his eyes for a moment and remembered the angry words he'd exchanged with his son that morning before he'd left for work and Jimmy had left for school.

He tossed the paper towel into the trash and left the bathroom, bumping into Monica. "You okay?" she asked, her dark eyes worried.

"Yeah. What did you do with Bo?"

"Cut him loose. We've got nothing to hold him

on. Are you sure you're all right? You usually don't get so crazy."

Jake pulled a hand through his hair. "Too little sleep and too much attitude from a certain young man."

Together they walked toward the back of the squad room, where the coffeepot was always full. "So Jimmy is giving you a hard time?"

Jake poured his partner a cup of coffee, then poured one for himself. "As of this morning he's decided he's too old for a babysitter. We went round after round before he left for school." He took a sip of the hot brew, then continued. "I told him there's no way with my hours I'm going to let him stay alone, that Mrs. Crawford would continue to be in the house when I wasn't there."

"I take it he took it badly?" Monica raised a perfectly plucked eyebrow.

"I didn't know a front door could be slammed three times before somebody got out of it," he said dryly.

Monica laughed. "Try not to get too tense about it. He's growing up, and trust me, there's nothing worse than male adolescence." Monica was the single parent of three teenage boys.

"I don't remember being so difficult when I was that age."

Monica's smile fell away. "From what you've told me about your old man, it's a good thing. If you'd been too difficult, you'd be dead."

"You got that right."

"Merridan . . . Gallagher," Captain Broadbent yelled above the din in the room. He motioned for them to join him in his office.

Captain Broadbent was in charge of the detective division. Broadbent was a tough guy who rode his people hard, but was well liked by his men because he rode himself hard and had a reputation for fairness.

"We got another one," he said before they'd gotten into the door of his office. "Ninety-fifth and North Maple. Body of a female found in a ditch. The responding officer said there's a plastic lily on her chest."

Jake's own chest knotted with tension as he and Monica exchanged glances. One was a murder. Two was something else entirely.

Within minutes they were in Jake's car, he behind the wheel and Monica in the passenger's seat. "Jesus, and I thought it was going to be a nice spring," she said. "Just what we need, a—"

"Don't even say it," Jake cut her off. "Don't even think it," he said, knowing she'd been about to say a repeater, a serial killer. "Maybe it's not a lily. Maybe it's not the same at all." He felt Monica's gaze on him. "And stop looking at me like that."

She stretched out her long legs and worried a hand through her brown hair. "I've got a bad feeling about this, Jake. I've got a real bad feeling."

Half an hour later as Jake looked at the victim, he had a bad feeling as well. She lay in a shallow drainage ditch behind the Rosewood Methodist

Church. A church employee had spotted her when he'd come outside to do some yard work on the property.

They didn't have her name, had found no identification anywhere around the body, but they didn't need to know her name to know how she had died. She'd died badly.

She'd been beaten and one eye was completely swollen closed; the other wide in a sightless death stare. Jake didn't need to be a medical examiner to know she'd probably died from multiple stab wounds to the chest, but not before enduring hell.

Duct tape covered her mouth and bound her hands together. She was naked from the waist down and her blouse lay against her chest in bloody shreds. On top of her blouse rested a plastic white lily.

"Just like Terri Sinclair," Monica said softly from next to him.

"Yeah, don't remind me." Jake surveyed the area. It was obvious this was just the dump site, that she'd been killed someplace else. There wasn't enough blood for this to be the killing place.

"We need to find out who she is, trace her last footsteps and find out where she was killed." He said the words aloud even though Monica knew what needed to be done.

"I've already called it in and have Taylor checking on missing persons to see if we get a hit," Monica replied. "Martin has initially established death between two and six this morning. Hopefully he'll have something else for us when he does the autopsy."

Jake wasn't optimistic. The Sinclair autopsy had yielded nothing specific other than the fact that the knife used to kill Terri had been approximately six inches long. Nothing unusual or identifying about the blade width and condition. Nothing for the cops to gnash their teeth on.

"We need to find out if this woman and Terri Sinclair have any connections, any common friends or acquaintances. They appear to be the same age. Maybe they hung out at the same places."

Monica gazed at him soberly. "It looks like you're going to be functioning on too little sleep for a while longer."

"Looks like," he agreed grimly. "Looks like it's going to be one hell of a spring."

Chapter 5

It was just after nine o'clock on Saturday morning when Larry arrived to pick up Charlie for his weekend with his son. "Is that fresh coffee I smell?" he asked as he stepped into the front door.

Jessie looked at him in surprise. Usually when he looked to collect Charlie he didn't even bother to come inside the house, but rather honked from his car in the driveway. "Sure, come on in," she said, not letting her surprise show. "Charlie, your dad is here," she called down the hallway.

She led Larry through the living room and into the kitchen, where she gestured him to the table while she poured them each a cup of coffee.

"Ah, you always made the best coffee," Larry said after taking a sip. "Where's Maria?"

"On the weekends when Charlie goes to your house, Maria goes to stay with her sister," Jessie explained.

"Dad!" Charlie flew into the room, lugging a large canvas bag.

"Whoa, what did you do—pack your whole bedroom in that bag?" Larry asked. "Why don't you take it out to the car and store it in the backseat."

"Okay, be right back." Charlie flew out of the room, and Larry directed his attention back to Jessie.

"He's such a good kid. You've done a great job with him."

"Talk to me again when he's a teenager," she replied.

His gaze held hers with intent. "You know, I was thinking this morning before I got here that it would be nice if you and I would have dinner one night, just the two of us."

Jessie took a sip of her coffee and eyed her ex-husband over the rim of her cup. He was dressed casually this morning in a short-sleeved sports shirt and jeans. He'd gained weight since the divorce, although the extra pounds didn't detract from his all-American appearance.

There had been a time when just the sight of him had made her heart stutter in her chest, when his warm smile had made her feel as if she were the most important woman on the face of the earth. But that was a long time ago, before she'd learned that his smile wasn't just a gift to her, but shared with others as well.

She lowered her cup. "What are you doing, Larry?"

He frowned. "What do you mean? I'm having coffee with you and thinking maybe it would be nice if we had a night together, kind of like old times."

She studied him for a long moment. "You know what I think? I think Tammi has been gone a week and you're feeling a little lonely, and I'm handy."

"That's not true," he protested. "I was thinking about you long before Tammi left." He looked down into his cup, a thoughtful frown creasing his broad forehead. "I keep wondering how things might have been if I hadn't screwed it all up."

He looked at her again. "What do you say, Jessie? Dinner, that's all I'm asking." He leaned forward, bringing with him the familiar scent of his minty cologne. "I was a fool and I'm willing to admit it. We used to be good together. Don't we owe it to each other, to Charlie, to see if we could still be good together?"

At that moment Charlie bounded back into the room, eager impatience dancing all over his lively features. "Come on, Dad. Isn't it time to get rolling?"

Larry laughed, then drained his cup and stood. "You heard the man, it's time for us to get rolling."

Jessie walked them to the front door and got a hurried kiss on the cheek from her son as he raced toward Larry's car in the driveway.

"Think about what I said, Jessie, and we'll talk more tomorrow night when I bring Charlie back."

She nodded, then watched as the two of them got into the car and the car disappeared down the block.

There had been a time in the days immediately after Larry had left that she'd prayed he'd suddenly come to his senses, declare that he'd been a fool and wanted their marriage more than anything else in the world.

She returned to the kitchen to finish her coffee and had just sat down at the table when another knock fell on the front door. Before she could get up the door opened and a female voice called out.

"Jessie, it's me."

"In the kitchen." She smiled at the blonde who was clad in a blue bathrobe and fuzzy slippers.

"I saw the ex leave with the munchkin, so I figured it was time for a little girl talk." Kayla Warren made herself at home, going to a cabinet to grab a cup and pour herself coffee.

Kayla was the next-door neighbor, a thirty-seven-year-old divorced real estate broker with no children. She and Jessie had hit it off from the moment they had met on the day that Jessie and Charlie had moved in.

"So with Charlie away, why don't you join me tonight for an evening of drinking and dancing and general debauchery?" Kayla asked as she sat in the chair Larry had so recently vacated. "Me and a couple of my friends are going to Night Life tonight. Why don't you come along?"

Jessie shook her head. "You know nightclubs aren't my thing. I have a date tonight with a good book, a cup of tea and my favorite nightgown."

Kayla raised a pale eyebrow. "You're a bore, Dr.

Jessica. How are you ever going to meet Mr. Right if you don't put yourself out there on the market?"

"I'm not looking for Mr. Right."

"Then what about finding a Mr. Wrong for a few nights or weeks of fun?"

Jessie laughed. "Finding Mr. Wrongs seem to be your expertise," she said teasingly, then sobered. "Besides, Larry's making some noise about possibly getting back together."

"Really?" Kayla took a sip of her coffee and eyed her over the rim of the cup. "And how do you feel about that?"

Jessie leaned back in the chair and gazed at the woman who over the past year had become a good friend. "I haven't decided how I feel about it," she confessed. "Larry is relatively safe, familiar, and if you catch me on a lonely night, I'd say the idea of getting back together with him is rather appealing."

"But?"

Jessie flashed Kayla a quick smile. "But I haven't forgotten what caused the divorce in the first place, and to be honest, I fell out of love with Larry a long time ago and I'm not sure it's possible to love him in that way again."

"Then what you need to do is find a Mr. Wrong to fill up those lonely nights so you don't make a stupid mistake where Larry is concerned," Kayla replied.

"No, thanks. For the most part I'm very content with my life as it is right now."

"Boring? You're content with boring?" Kayla asked with another arch of her eyebrows.

"Just because I don't have a man in my life doesn't mean my life is boring," Jessie replied dryly. "Between Charlie and work, most of the time I'm too busy to be bored or lonely."

"Speaking of work, how's the syndication deal coming along? Will we be hearing Dr. Jessica Langford on radio stations across the country?"

Jessie finished her coffee and stood to pour herself another cup. "Who knows? Chris told me last night that a couple of bigwigs are coming into town next weekend and want to meet me for dinner. I try to stay as uninvolved with the business end of things as possible. I'll go to dinner, make nice, then we'll see what happens." She returned to the table and sat once again. "What about you? How's the real estate business?"

The two women visited for another few minutes, then Kayla finished her coffee and looked at the clock on the wall. "I'd better get out of here. If I want to look good enough to pick up a twenty-something hottie tonight, I'd better start my beauty regimen now."

Jessie walked her friend to the door and told her good-bye, then went back to the kitchen to make herself breakfast.

Although Jessie adored spending time with her son, there was also a small part of her that enjoyed the two weekends a month Charlie spent with

Larry, leaving Jessie alone to attend to nobody else's needs but her own.

The day flew by. She cleaned, made a trip to the grocery store and fixed fresh salmon for dinner, which Charlie hated. After dinner she carried a glass of white wine out onto the deck and sat to watch the sunset.

This was the time of evening she both loved and hated. She loved the hues and beauty of the sunset but wanted to cling to the last spark of day and keep the darkness of night at bay.

Night had not been her friend for many years, not since before the attack that had nearly taken her life. Thankfully she hadn't passed on her fear to Charlie. A night-light burned in his bedroom because she wanted it, not because he needed it. The last thing she'd ever want to do was taint Charlie's innocence by sharing any piece of the destruction of her own.

Her thoughts turned to Larry. Her parents hadn't lived long enough to see her and Larry divorced. They had died in a car accident when Charlie was a baby. They'd been so happy that Jessie had managed to put her past behind her and make a life with Larry, whom they had positively adored. Of course, at that time nobody had known about Larry's affection for women other than his wife.

She remained on the deck until her wineglass was empty and the deep purple of twilight had nearly faded, then she went back inside.

By nine o'clock she was in bed, classical music playing softly from her clock radio and a book by her favorite author in hand.

She thought about her conversation with Kayla. There were nights and odd times of the day when a deep loneliness pierced through her, a loneliness that her son couldn't fill.

She was thirty-four years old, quite young to decide to live the rest of her life alone, and yet that's what she had done when Larry had left her.

The very idea of playing the dating game, exposing her past to a man, allowing anyone to see the physical scars that marred her body, was repugnant. She had trusted Larry with all her secrets, all her darkness, but she couldn't imagine ever trusting any other man.

The phone rang and she picked up the cordless on the nightstand next to the bed. She'd been expecting a call before bedtime.

"Hi, Mom."

Jessie smiled at the sound of her little boy's voice. "Hi, Charlie."

"I just called to tell you good night," he said.

"Did you have a good day with your dad?"

"Yeah, it was okay. He was on the phone a lot, but we played catch for a while, then we drove through McDonald's for supper."

"What have you got planned for tomorrow?"

"Dad said maybe we'd go to the zoo. I've got to go to bed now. Dad's yelling at me to get off the phone."

"Good night, honey. I'll see you tomorrow night." She hung up with a smile on her lips. Having Charlie's voice be the last one she heard before going to sleep was just fine with her.

Stifling a yawn, she placed her book on the nightstand and shut off the lamp, plunging the room into the semidarkness of her nights.

She must have fallen asleep almost immediately, for the next thing she knew the shrill ring of the phone split the silence of the house and shattered the last of a distant dream.

A glance at her clock radio let her know it was just after midnight. Who would be calling at this hour? Charlie! Had something happened to Charlie?

She fumbled for the cordless phone and turned it on at the same time she sat up and shook her head to clear it of sleep.

"Larry?"

No response, although she could tell somebody was on the line. "Hello? Is somebody there?"

Silence. She pressed the receiver more tightly against her ear. "Is somebody there?" she repeated.

"Somebody's here," a voice whispered in a barely audible tone. There was a click, and all Jessie heard was the pounding of her own heartbeat, and she knew she was alone on the line.

She fumbled the phone back on the base.

Light. She needed light.

Somebody's here.

She turned on the lamp on the nightstand, but that wasn't enough. *Somebody's here.*

On trembling legs she got out of bed and stumbled across the room and flipped on the bright overhead light. She sank to the floor next to the light switch, afraid her legs wouldn't carry her back to the bed.

She gulped deep breaths of air, fighting the feeling of suffocation that threatened to overwhelm her. *Somebody's here.*

Stop it, Jessie, she commanded herself. You're overreacting. But telling herself that didn't help. Tingling shot through her hands and feet and adrenaline pumped through her in a fight-or-flight response.

Someplace in the back of her mind, she knew she was experiencing a full-blown panic attack. She'd had them before, but it had been years since she'd had her last one.

Get it under control, Jessie. For God's sake, she counseled people who suffered from panic attacks.

Still, knowing physiologically what was happening and trying to control it were two different things. An overwhelming sense of impending doom slithered through her, blurring her vision with tears as her heart banged in a painful, frantic rhythm.

She pulled her knees up to her chest and lowered her head to her knees, drawing in slow, steady breaths until the panic attack finally passed.

Her legs were still unsteady as she pulled herself

from the floor and sat on the edge of the bed. It was just a prank, she told herself. A prank phone call on a Saturday night, probably made by some kid looking for a little fun.

Forget it, she told herself. You're overreacting to a stupid prank phone call. As soon as she could breathe normally again she'd feel completely stupid about the whole thing.

What she wanted to do was pick up the phone and call somebody, connect with somebody and stay on the line with them until dawn broke in the horizon and chased away the dark of night.

She could call Larry. He'd said she could call him anytime. He was the only person on the face of the earth who could understand how a phone call in the middle of the night might send her crashing into a panic attack. He was the only person on the face of the earth who could provide a voice of reason in the miasma of irrational thoughts going around in her head.

And what would he tell her? That it was nothing more than a crank call? He'd be calm and patient as he reminded her that she'd been sound asleep when the phone had rung, that sleepiness might have made her only imagine that voice on the other end of the line.

Somebody's here.

Had the voice been real or had she imagined it?

Somebody's here.

She couldn't shake the feeling that she'd heard that voice before. She'd heard that voice a million years ago when she'd been blindfolded and bound and gagged by a madman. She'd heard that voice when she'd been blind and helpless as he'd raped her, then carved up her stomach, then buried her alive.

Chapter 6

One murder was a problem. Two was a task force. Captain Broadbent had assigned Jake as lead detective in charge of three others on the murders of Terri Sinclair and Millie Walker.

Identifying the second victim had been easier than Jake had initially thought it would be when he'd seen her body in the drainage ditch. Fingerprints had yielded her identity, along with the information that she'd had an arrest and conviction for shoplifting two years before.

In the two years since that time, twenty-three-year-old Millie Walker appeared to have kept her nose clean. She worked as a nurse's aide in a facility for the elderly and lived in a small studio apartment that had yielded no clues as to who might have wanted her dead.

According to her friends, Millie was a lively young woman who worked hard and enjoyed playing equally as hard. She had no steady boyfriend, nor did she have any ex-boyfriends who had been a problem.

She loved the clubs, and Pudgie's had been one of her favorite hangouts, as it was in walking distance from her apartment. It was also the last place she'd been seen.

For the past week Jake and his team had worked to try to find some intersecting point between Terri's life and Millie's. But so far they could find nothing that the single mother had in common with the nurse's-aide party girl.

The tiny office that had been designated as the war room for these particular murders was made even smaller by the bulletin board that held crime-scene photos and the table beneath the board that held stacks of files, reports and transcripts of interviews.

At the moment Jake was alone in the room. Monica had gone to grab some lunch, and Terrance Jackson and Sam Barrett, the other two detectives working the case, were out in the field, conducting more interviews of friends and family of the victims.

It was a well-known fact that the first forty-eight hours of a homicide investigation were crucial, but those hours had passed long ago and they had garnered nothing to help them solve these crimes.

Jake was still hoping to find a connection between the two women—a favorite store, the same dentist, some intersecting point that might lead them to a killer.

If they were connected, then the odds of them solving the crime was much better than if the two women had been nothing more than random selections of a serial killer.

He opened the file folder in front of him and fanned out the crime-scene photos that had not made it to the bulletin board. These photos depicted the lilies that had been left behind at each crime scene, a fact that was not being made public.

The plastic flowers could be found in most chain discount and arts and crafts stores. There were no identifying marks on the lilies, no way to trace where they might have been bought.

A dead end.

Like this case.

He looked up as Monica came into the room, carrying with her a brown paper bag from the closest hamburger drive-through. She set it on the table in front of him. "It's like a morgue out there. Everyone must be out on calls."

"What's this?" He gestured toward the bag.

"A deluxe with fries. You have to eat and keep up your strength if you want to catch a killer."

"Unfortunately we've got no suspect for me to tangle with," he replied as he opened the paper sack. The scent of the food made his stomach grumble and reminded him he hadn't eaten since the night before.

"Sure we do. We know our perp is male and probably between the ages of twenty-five and fifty.

We know he's highly organized and probably above average in intelligence."

"Yeah, yeah, we've got the usual profile to work with, a profile that narrows our search down to half of the Kansas City and surrounding area population."

"Eat your burger, Mr. Pessimistic," Monica said.

He grinned at her and stood. "I'm going to get a soda. You want one?"

"No, thanks. I'm good."

"I'll be right back." He left the small office and walked through the squad room toward the vending machine area. Monica was right. The squad room was like a morgue; only a couple of officers were at their desks, talking on phones.

"Ma'am, we generally don't take reports about disturbing phone calls," the desk sergeant said to an attractive dark-haired woman who stood at the counter that separated the public area from the squad room.

"Please, you don't understand. If I could just speak to somebody." Although her voice was low and controlled, Jake sensed an underlying emotion that momentarily distracted him from his quest for a soda.

"Most of my men are busy right now. Why don't you leave your name and number and I'll have somebody call you as soon as possible," the sergeant said in an obvious attempt to get her out.

"Sarge, I got a minute. I'll take the lady's report," Jake said.

She looked at him then, her eyes a shade of blue that flirted with more than a hint of gray. He'd thought her attractive, but as she flashed him a grateful smile attractive transformed into stunning.

"Knock yourself out, Detective Merridan," Sergeant Wilks said, and opened the gate to allow the civilian through.

"Detective Jake Merridan," he said in introduction. "If you'll just follow me, we'll go to my desk and I'll take your report," Jake said, then turned on his heels and headed for his desk.

What in the hell was he doing? As if he didn't have enough on his mind. He had a serial killer to catch, a burger and fries getting cold and he'd decided to take a report from a woman because she had pretty eyes.

He gestured her into a chair next to his desk, then took a moment to search through his drawers for a proper miscellaneous incident form. As he searched he was conscious of her on several different levels.

She was small in stature, slender but with obvious curves. Her perfume was light and flowery, and something about her made Jake aware of the fact that he hadn't shaved that morning and his white shirt sported the wrinkles of a man who didn't understand the fine art of ironing.

A nervous energy radiated off her as she clutched her hands together tightly in her lap. The tailored navy suit she wore looked crisp and professional and let him know she probably wasn't a housewife but rather held some sort of job outside the home. He noticed she wore no wedding ring.

He found the appropriate form and placed it in front of him, then met her gaze once again. "We'll start with some basic information. Your name?"

"Jessica Langford."

Jake frowned as he carefully printed the name on the form. Her name sounded very familiar, but he was certain if he'd met her before he'd have remembered her. She was the kind of woman men remembered.

"Jake." Jackson and Barrett entered the squad room. "We located Millie Walker's sister, and we think we've found a link between the two vics."

Jake held up a hand to the two detectives. "We'll discuss it when I'm finished here." He flashed Jessica Langford an apologetic smile as the two men nodded and disappeared into the war room.

"Sorry about the interruption. Your address?"

She lived not far from the police station, in a neighborhood of upper-middle-class condos and town homes. Jake had looked at one of the condos before he'd bought his house years ago.

"Tell me what brings you here today, Ms. Langford," he said, and looked at her once again.

The tension on her well-defined features was obvious. "I've received some strange phone calls." She broke eye contact with him and instead stared down at her hands in her lap.

"Strange how?"

"For one thing, they come in the middle of the

night. My caller ID shows them as anonymous calls."

"And what does the caller say?" Jake asked, even though he knew this was a waste of both their time. The police rarely got involved in phone calls unless a terrorist or death threat was made. Even then, with the advent of prepaid cell phones, anonymous calls had become almost impossible to trace.

She looked at him once again, a frown etched across her forehead. "I'm sorry, this was a mistake." She stood, and Jake hurriedly pushed back from his desk and stood as well. "I'm sorry to have wasted your time, Detective Merridan, but I realize I'm being silly."

She turned to leave but stopped and faced him as he called her name. "You know, the best way to deal with unwanted phone calls is to work with your phone company or change your number."

"Thank you. I'll do that."

He watched her leave, noting the sway of her hips beneath the navy skirt, the shapeliness of her slender legs. It had been a very long time since a woman had stirred him on any level, but the pretty brunette had reminded him just how long it had been since he'd had sex.

Too damn long.

He tossed the incomplete report in the trash can, then headed back to the war room, where his burger and fries and perhaps a break in the murder case awaited him.

*   *   *

Jessie sat in her car in the police station parking lot, her fingers wrapped tightly around the steering wheel. She'd been foolish to come here to make a report.

After the phone call Saturday night she'd been on edge, and despite her training, despite her education, the insidious unwanted emotion of fear had haunted her. Then Sunday night she'd received another call, the same as the night before, and she'd decided to file a report.

She leaned her head back and relaxed her fingers from around the wheel. The police had far more important things to investigate than a couple of middle-of-the-night phone calls. She read the papers; she'd seen the reports of the two latest murders.

It wasn't until Detective Merridan's dark eyes had gazed at her expectantly that she realized she was behaving like one of her patients.

She spent half her time teaching her patients about the difference between rational and irrational fear. Rational fear was based on real circumstances that created the potential of danger. Irrational fear was based on a pure emotional level that had little to do with reality.

The moment she'd walked into the police station she'd been struck with the gut-wrenching memory of the last time she'd been in a police station. At that time she'd been a shell-shocked victim forced to relive her horror again and again as she was questioned and questioned about what had happened to her.

She never wanted to answer those kinds of questions again. She never even allowed herself to think about the horror of that night.

Starting her engine, she drew a deep breath. Maybe it would have been easier to make a silly, hysterical-woman report if the detective she'd spoken to had been older, balding and with a paunchy spread around his middle. Detective Jake Merridan had been none of those things.

As she pulled out of the parking lot to head back to her office, she thought of the detective. Rarely did the mere act of gazing at a man cause a little kick of a hormone rush, but that's what she'd felt when she'd looked at Jake Merridan.

Even though she'd been nervous and reticent about being in the station, on some level she'd noticed him not as a law enforcement official, but as a man.

How could she not notice his thick-lashed dark eyes or rugged features? With his handsome features and broad shoulders and slim hips, he'd looked more like a cover model than a cop.

It had been obvious that whatever information the other detectives had was important, because once he'd said they'd located a possible link between two victims, the energy level that had wafted off Merridan had increased tenfold.

The other detective had mentioned the name of Millie Walker, a name that Jessie had seen in the paper that morning. The headline had read NO NEW LEADS IN WALKER MURDER.

Certainly Detective Merridan had more important things to do than talk to her about some stupid phone calls, calls that couldn't even be characterized as threatening or dangerous.

Yes, it had been foolish to rush in to the police station. She'd been driven by irrational fear, fallen into the trap of allowing her fear to control her.

It was time she get a grip. When she got back to the office she'd call the phone company and have her number changed. It was the first step in regaining control.

"What did you do—get lost on the way back from the vending machine?" Monica asked as Jake reentered the small office.

"Yeah, got lost in a hot little number with big blue eyes," Terrance Jackson said with a smirk.

"They were more gray than blue," Jake replied as he sat at the table with the others. Monica looked at him curiously. "Some woman named Jessica Langford came in to make a report about weird phone calls."

"Jessica Langford? Dr. Jessica Langford?" Monica asked.

Jake shrugged. "Maybe. She didn't tell me if she was a doctor or not."

"But you'd let her examine you any day of the week," Terrance said.

"Not unless he wants his head examined," Monica replied. "She's a psychiatrist. She has a call-in radio show and talks about phobias and fears. I saw someplace that she's doing some sort of semi-nar this week at Maple Woods Community College."

Jake thought about the woman who had just flown from the station. She might talk about phobias and fears on the radio, but he knew from looking in her eyes that, at least in that moment that she'd spoken to him, she'd been experiencing a fear of her own.

A psychiatrist. Too bad he hadn't been able to talk to her about Jimmy. He frowned and shoved thoughts of his son to the back of his head and instead concentrated on the task at hand. "You said you found a link between our two vics. What kind of link?"

Sam Barrett leaned forward, his bald head gleaming in the overhead light. "Both Millie Walker and Terri Sinclair got their nails done at the same place." Sam pulled a small notepad from his pocket and flipped it open. "A place called Lovie's Nails. Terrance and I went by there, but apparently they were closed up for lunch."

"We'll head back over there this afternoon and see what Lovie can tell us about the two women," Terrance said.

"Maybe this is the break we need," Jake said, more to himself than the others. They needed a break on this case. He needed a break with his son, but he had a terrible feeling that things were about to spiral completely out of control on both fronts.

Chapter 7

Maria Vernon knew fear.

Intimately.

For thirty-five years of her marriage she'd awakened every morning with the crushing weight of fear seated on her chest, the taste of despair in her mouth and the terror of wondering if today would be the day that her husband would finally kill her.

Her husband, Craig, had celebrated their thirty-fifth wedding anniversary by getting rip-roaring drunk and breaking her arm. She'd celebrated by waiting until he'd passed out, then she'd left him. She'd been certain he would kill her if she left, but equally certain that he'd kill her if she stayed another day.

She had no family except her sister, who suffered from MS and was in a wheelchair, so she'd ended up in a shelter, where she'd lived for six weeks. It was while there that she'd met Dr. Jessie, who had donated some counseling to the women in the shelter.

That had been three years ago, and when Dr. Jessie had asked her if she wanted the job as housekeeper and nanny almost two years ago, Maria had jumped at the chance.

Dr. Jessie had not just given Maria a job, she'd given her back her respect, given her a reason to get up in the mornings and had given her people to love.

One of those people sat across from her at the dinner table, a frown tugging his childish lips downward. "What's the matter, Charlie? You don't like your dinner?" she asked the little boy. "I thought macaroni and cheese was one of your favorites."

"It is." He used his fork to trace a path through the mound of macaroni on his plate. "I just wish Mom was home. I like it when the three of us eat dinner together."

She smiled at him. "I like it too. But you know she had to talk to a bunch of college students tonight. I'll tell you what, after you eat your dinner we'll put in *The Lion King* and watch it together. By the time the movie is over maybe your mother will be home."

Charlie's frown disappeared. "Okay," he agreed.

Maria's heart expanded with her love for Charlie. She'd decided in the first year of her marriage that there would be no children. For years she'd sneaked a birth control pill every day to ensure that a child would never be part of her unholy marriage.

That tiny act of defiance had robbed her of the opportunity to be a mother, but had also assured her that no child of hers would know the horrors she lived.

Her sister asked her often why she'd stayed with Craig for so long, and Maria didn't have a good answer, at least not one that would make sense to a rational, reasonable adult. Fear had been a powerful motivator for her to leave and change her life, but it had been just as powerful in keeping her paralyzed and afraid to make a change.

Battered-wife syndrome, that's what the counselors had said. She'd been a textbook case of a wife who'd been systematically isolated from everyone, utterly dependent on her abuser and twisted into thinking her life would be over if she left the very man who posed the biggest threat to her life.

To this day she didn't know why she'd finally made the decision to leave. There had been no epiphany, no sudden bolt of lightning, just a weariness that had finally outweighed the terror.

Charlie finished eating, and as she cleaned up the kitchen he got the movie ready to watch. Minutes later she sank down next to him on the sofa and they began to watch the cartoon adventures.

There was nothing better than sitting next to a child and watching a Disney movie. Charlie's laughter filled the living room as the movie played. Unlike many kids his age, Charlie wasn't given to chatter during a show, but rather stayed focused on the story being told on the screen.

They were halfway through the movie when the phone rang. Maria reached for the receiver on the end table. "Hello?" There was no reply, but she could hear somebody breathing, knew somebody was there. "Hello? Who's there?"

"Somebody's here." The voice was deep but whisper soft.

"Who is this?" Maria kept her tone level, not wanting to transmit to Charlie the edge of apprehension that tightened her muscles. "Please, who is this?" She held her breath, waiting for an answer. "Craig, is that you?"

There was a click and she knew she was alone on the line. She hung up the receiver, rich, raw fear trekking through her. Had it been Craig? After two years had her ex-husband found her once again?

She wouldn't tell Dr. Jessie about the phone call. She couldn't tell her. After all, there was no guarantee the call had been from Craig.

She leaned back against the sofa cushions and placed an arm around Charlie's shoulder. He cuddled against her like a pup curling up to sleep against his mother's belly.

No, she wouldn't say anything about the phone call. It wasn't that she was afraid that Craig would kill her. Rather she was afraid that somehow he would manage to destroy the happiness she'd found here with Charlie and Dr. Jessie.

*   *   *

"Fear and intuition is an evolutionary tool of survival," Dr. Jessica Langford said from the podium on the stage in the community college's theater.

He shouldn't have come, but when he'd heard the announcement of the seminar she was giving he'd been unable to fight the need to see her once again.

He sat in the back row, his anonymity assured by the darkness and the crowd that surrounded him. And there was a crowd. It seemed like everyone in the Northland area of Kansas City had come to see Dr. Jessica Langford talk about fear.

"We use fear to navigate our way through life and we use it to make important decisions," she continued.

She had a nice speaking voice, low and kind of sexy. She'd been a pretty teenager and she'd grown up to be a beautiful woman. Tonight she wore a tailored royal blue dress that looked classy. Her dark hair was pulled back and contained in some sort of clip at the nape of her neck.

He shouldn't be surprised that so many people had shown up this evening. Her radio show was popular, as there seemed to be more fear in the world than at any other time in history.

The crime rate was up, wars were being waged and people went to bed each night with the unsettling feeling of potential danger lurking nearby. Every evening the news was filled with stories of pedophiles and identity theft, of terrorists and murderers.

But it certainly wasn't fear that had brought him here tonight. He needed to know so many things about her, wanted to know so many things.

Had her life been good since the night she'd been pulled out of that grave? He knew from public records that she'd married, had a child and divorced, but he needed to know more.

She'd become his obsession, and he knew he couldn't go forward until he addressed the issues from the past.

Chapter 8

The audience had been wonderfully receptive. As Jessie gathered up her notes at the lectern, the pleasure of a job well done filled her. The theater was emptying quickly as the audience filed out, eager to get home after their evening outing.

"Great job, Jessie," Chris said, his boyish face beaming with pride. The radio station had sponsored the seminar, and Chris had not only handled all the details with the community college, but he'd also sat on the front row to lend her moral support.

"Thanks. I always enjoy these kinds of things." She placed her notes in her briefcase. "And at least you're not making me come in to do the show tonight." The station was running a prerecorded show for that night's time slot.

Chris flashed her a grin. "You deserve the night off. I just wish the guys from Five Star Syndication had been here to see you in action."

Jessie smiled at her young boss. "It will happen, Chris. We just have to be patient."

"Patience has never been my strong suit," he replied. "I'm still aggravated that they canceled their plans to come into town to meet you. Want me to carry that for you?" He gestured to her briefcase, then looked at his watch. "I need to get back to the station."

"No, I've got it. You go ahead. I'll see you tomorrow night," she replied.

"Okay." He was running for the nearest exit before the word was completely out of his mouth.

Jessie checked her own wristwatch. Eight thirty. It was possible Charlie would still be awake when she got home and she could at least kiss him good night. She closed her briefcase and headed for the exit.

The scent of spring flowers filled the night air as she stepped outside of the building. To the south the dark night sky lit with a flash of lightning. The weathermen had forecast a storm moving in sometime over the night hours. It looked like they'd predicted accurately.

"Dr. Langford."

Jessie jumped at the deep voice coming from just behind her. She gasped and whirled around, then relaxed. "Detective Merridan."

"Sorry, I didn't mean to startle you. I found your seminar very interesting. You're a good public speaker."

A flush of pleasure swept through her and she didn't know if it was caused by his kind words or the fact that just looking at him quickened her heartbeat.

Even with the night shadows clinging to him, emphasizing the angles of his face, something about him appealed to her on a physical level.

"Thanks. I enjoy speaking. Do you often attend seminars here?" she asked, curious as to why he had come.

"Never. But my partner told me about yours this evening and I decided to check it out. It's an interesting topic, fear."

"Needless to say, I find it fascinating," she replied. There seemed to be a crackling electricity in the air between them, and she wondered if he felt it as intensely as she did. Maybe it was simply the approach of the storm, she thought. Some atmospheric disturbance that had nothing to do with him or her.

"Look, would you like to go someplace and get a cup of coffee?"

The invitation surprised her. It came out of the blue, like his presence here before her. Why was he here? What did he want from her? Was it possible he'd learned about her past?

"There's a Perkins over on Oak Street. They usually serve a good cup of coffee." She had no idea why he'd issued the invitation, but if nothing else she was curious enough to meet him at the restaurant.

"Okay. I'll meet you there in just a few minutes." He didn't wait for her reply, but rather turned on his heels and disappeared into the darkness of the night.

Jessie hurried to her car, trying to figure out why Detective Merridan had sought her out this evening. She hoped it wasn't her past as a victim.

Part of what had made her walk out of the police station on Monday was because she hadn't wanted to go there. In the weeks following the crime that had almost taken her life, her world had revolved around living and reliving what had happened.

She'd seen the pity in the officers' eyes, felt the curious stares of her parents' friends. Even though she'd been a minor and her name had been kept out of the newspaper reports, people around her had known.

She'd talked about the crime for the last time when Larry had asked her to marry him. That night she'd painfully recounted some of the events that had led to her being found half alive in a cemetery. She'd sworn at that time that she'd never discuss it again.

At this time of the evening the Perkins on Oak Street wasn't busy. She walked into the front door and saw the detective already there in a booth near the back.

As she approached she noticed how his black dress shirt pulled across the width of his shoulders and how his dark hair shone beneath the artificial light. A whisper of warmth knotted in the pit of her stomach, a tingling warmth she hadn't felt for so long she almost didn't recognize it as what it was. . . . Physical attraction.

She also couldn't help but notice that his gaze swept the length of her and she felt his gaze like a physical touch on her breasts, on her waist and on the length of her legs.

She offered him a tentative smile and slid into the booth across from him. "It looks like there's a storm brewing outside."

"Yeah, I heard we were supposed to get rain."

He looked ill at ease, and once again she wondered what had prompted his invitation to join him for coffee. At that moment the waitress arrived to take their orders.

"We'd like two coffees, and I'd like a piece of caramel apple pie." He looked at her. "What about it, Dr. Langford—a piece of pie?"

She nodded. "Caramel apple sounds wonderful."

"Two coffees, two pieces of pie," he said to the waitress, who departed, leaving them alone once again.

"And please, make it Jessie," she said. "Dr. Langford makes me feel as if I'm somehow on duty."

"Only if you call me Jake," he replied. "Like you, when somebody calls me Detective Merridan I feel as if I need to make a report or something."

Jessie felt her cheeks warm slightly with a touch of embarrassment. "I'm sorry about the other day at the station. I wasted your time."

Once again the waitress returned to serve their

orders. "Did you talk to the phone company about those calls you were getting?" he asked when the waitress was gone.

"Yes. As of next Monday I'll have a new phone number. That should take care of the problem." At least she hoped that would take care of the situation. There had been no new phone calls since Sunday night, and she hoped the weekend calls had been nothing more than the work of bored teenagers.

Jake picked up his fork and cut into his piece of pie, and Jessie did the same, wondering again why she was here, why he was here. His dark eyes gave nothing away. Was it morbid curiosity that had prompted him to seek her out? A desire to take a look at, talk to the only known survivor of the T&B killer?

He took a sip of his coffee, then looked at her once again. "I would imagine that weird phone calls would be one of the negative aspects of your work, especially since you're so publicly visible with your radio show."

"We definitely get more than our share of strange phone calls at the station," she replied. "Chris, my producer, does his best to screen the calls, but at least once a night some smart mouth gets through either to try to disrupt the program or try to get under my skin."

"And do they succeed?" His lips curled up in a smile. God, he had a great smile, and she responded to it like a giddy teenager overwhelmed by hormones.

"In disrupting the program? Never. In getting under my skin? Sometimes." She reached for her coffee cup and told herself that he was probably married with five children, that he might look good but he probably belched or scratched himself in public or was a control freak, all things she abhorred.

"So, you have a radio program and you give seminars. What else occupies your time?"

"I have a private practice and I'm a single parent of a six-year-old son, Charlie. He definitely occupies a lot of my time."

"We have that in common. I'm a single parent too, although my son, Jimmy, is twelve."

She was ridiculously pleased that he was single, although she didn't know why it pleased her. She certainly had no intention of indulging in any kind of a relationship with him. She had no intention of indulging in a relationship with any man.

He shoved his empty plate aside and leaned back in the booth. "Why psychiatry? Any particular reason why you chose that field?"

For the first time since she'd sat down across from him she relaxed. So apparently he didn't know about her past. Unless he was being coy, and Detective Jake Merridan didn't strike her as the kind of man to play coy.

"The workings of the human mind have always intrigued me."

"The mind can be a scary place," he replied.

"Yeah, it can be," she agreed. "And I'm sure in your line of work you see what people are capable of when the mind doesn't function properly."

This time his smile was grim. "You've got that right. I guess we approach things a little differently. You want to know why a killer kills. I don't care why they do it—I just want to make sure we get them off the streets."

"The longer I'm in this business the less I understand about what drives people to do the things they do," she said. "But I do get a lot of satisfaction from helping people deal with their fears and phobias."

"And I get a lot of satisfaction slapping cuffs on a perp." He smiled again, and in that smile Jessie knew it was time to leave. His smile was far too engaging, his physical attractiveness too enticing and the keen intelligence that shone from his eyes was too appealing.

"I've got to get home," she said, feeling the need to escape his presence. She opened her purse.

"Please, let me get it," he said. "After all, I invited you."

She closed her purse. "Thank you. Maybe sometime I can return the favor and buy you a piece of pie and a coffee," she said, although she had no intention of following through on the offer.

"Before you go I want you to have this." He reached into his shirt pocket and withdrew a business card. "It's got my work number on it and my cell phone number. If you have any more problems with those phone calls, let me know and I'll see what I can do to help."

She took the card from him, and the brush of his fingers against her own once again caused a wave of heat to course through her.

"Thanks, Jake. I appreciate it."

"Good night, Jessie," he replied.

She turned to leave, but paused as he called her name once again. She turned back around to face him. "I just wanted to tell you that blue is definitely your color."

She nodded, then headed toward the exit, acutely conscious of his gaze following her. His compliment rang in her ears as she got into her car.

While she had enjoyed the novelty of sitting across the table from a man who could easily be described as eye candy, she still had no idea why he'd sought her out.

It hadn't been an accident that he'd shown up at the seminar, nor did she have the feeling that the invitation for coffee had been purely spontaneous.

He was single, handsome and caused more than a touch of sizzle in her. Kayla would tell her to spread him on a cracker and eat him right up.

But Kayla didn't know about Jessie's past. She didn't know about monsters in a box on a shelf in a closet. She couldn't understand that if Jessie pursued a relationship with any other man she'd have to take those monsters out of the box, and she simply wasn't willing to do that.

*   *   *

Jake motioned the waitress for a refill on his coffee. He should head home. Tonight had been one of the few nights he'd had off since Terri Sinclair's body had been found.

Instead he decided to have one more cup of coffee and try to figure out exactly what had prompted him to go to the seminar this evening.

He tried to tell himself that he'd thought it would be educational to listen to Dr. Jessica Langford speak. Even though Jake tried to keep himself in good physical shape, he knew that most criminals were caught on brain power, not brawn.

The truth was he hadn't come to the seminar to hear her speak. He'd come because he hadn't been able to get her out of his mind since the moment she'd left the police station.

Her perfume had lingered in his head long after she'd gone, and her fear-filled eyes had haunted him. Tonight there had been no fear in her lovely eyes.

He nodded his thanks to the waitress who refilled his coffee, then wrapped his fingers around the warm cup, his thoughts still consumed by the woman who had recently sat across from him.

Something about Dr. Jessica Langford drew him as no woman had done in a very long time. He liked the way her dark hair looked clean and silky, that her complexion was flawless. He liked that this evening her eyes had reflected intelligence and confidence.

The blue dress she'd worn hadn't only made her eyes appear blue, but had also emphasized her slender waist and the thrust of her full breasts.

Face it, my man, what you're suffering is a little case of the hots for the lady psychiatrist. But the coffee they'd shared this evening would be the beginning and the end of it.

The last thing he wanted to do was get involved with a woman who had the capacity to shrink his head, to look inside his mind. He would be afraid she might see something in his head, something so dreadful, so awful it had caused his wife to leave him and their son and never look back.

He pulled up to the curb in the quiet residential neighborhood and stared at the house where minutes before Dr. Jessica Langford had gone inside.

He'd known where she worked, where her private practice was located, but he hadn't known for sure where she lived. Now he knew.

Lightning slashed across the sky and the air was heavy with the scent of the approaching storm. He loved spring storms, had missed the wildness of nature in conflict when he'd lived on the sunny West Coast.

He'd had to leave Kansas City all those years ago. Another bolt of lightning lit the sky, followed by a crack of thunder. Like a roar of anger, he felt the thunder deep in his bones.

Everything would have been fine if that bunch of kids hadn't chosen the Hillside Cemetery as their party place on the same night he'd tried to bury Jessica Clinton. Not only had he been unable to finish what he'd started, but over the next couple of days he'd worried about what she might remember, what she might have heard. He had no idea what clues he might have given to her that could be used by the police to find him.

A change of scenery, a change of his signature had been necessary to ensure his survival. The West Coast had proved to be fertile ground, but he'd never forgotten Jessica Clinton, who had survived and lived to marry Larry Langford.

Dr. Langford's home was a brick condo, attached to the next-door neighbor by a common wall. The yard was neat, and a flower border next to the sidewalk leading up to the door sprouted red and purple tulips.

A soccer ball rested on the grass beneath the front picture window. Charlie's ball. He knew all about her six-year-old son.

The boy would miss her when she was gone. He felt bad about it. He liked kids. He believed that children were the epitome of innocence, possessed the purest souls.

When he'd taken the woman from the shopping mall, she'd had a baby in a stroller. A little boy in a navy sailor suit, a hat at a jaunty angle on his little bald head.

As he'd grabbed the woman from behind and slapped duct tape across her mouth, the little boy had given him a goofy, toothless grin. When he'd shoved the woman into the trunk of his car, the baby had clapped his hands together as if finding the whole thing wonderfully entertaining.

He'd known somebody would find the baby, that he'd be taken care of and not harmed. He'd never intentionally hurt a child unless it was absolutely, positively necessary.

Yes, little Charlie would miss his mother, but children were wonderfully resilient. Nothing and nobody was going to keep him from finishing the job he'd begun eighteen years before.

A light came on in a window at the left of the house and he wondered if it was her bedroom light. Was she preparing for bed? Changing out of her pretty blue dress and into a pair of pajamas?

He imagined her brushing that long dark hair of hers, hair he remembered being silky soft and smelling of fruity shampoo.

Did she linger in front of her mirror, staring at his mark on her belly?

He'd left a piece of himself with her in the form of the scars she'd wear for the rest of her life. Of course, he'd never intended for her to live another eighteen years. She was supposed to have died that night, sucking in cemetery dirt.

He could have taken her half a dozen times already, but he hadn't. He'd waited eighteen years. He could wait a little bit longer.

Every woman he'd ever taken had been surprised. They'd had no warning that danger was near, no forewarning that their lives were about to be extinguished by a man they'd never met.

But he wanted Dr. Jessica Langford to see him coming. He wanted the psychiatrist who specialized in fear to know the deepest, most profound fear before he buried her deep in the ground and completed the ritual he'd begun so long ago.

Chapter 9

"Hey, partner."

The voice pulled Jake from his dreams, and he shot up from his prone position on his living room sofa. He stared at Monica, who sat in a chair nearby, for a moment disoriented as to what day, what time it was.

Thursday. It was Thursday morning. Last night he'd attended the seminar and had spent the remainder of the night tossing and turning and chasing sleep.

"How did you get in?" he asked, grateful that his briefs-clad body was covered by a sheet.

"Jimmy let me in. He said to tell you he'd see you whenever you got home tonight."

Jake raked his hands through his hair. "What time it is?" Jesus, what kind of a loser was he? His kid had left for school without so much as a good-bye, his partner had arrived to drive him to work and he still had bed head and the memory of disturbing dreams.

"It's almost eight." Monica frowned. "I didn't know you were still sleeping on the sofa." There was a tiny note of censure in her tone. "You know, I'd come over any time and help you pack up her things."

"I know." He swung his feet to the floor and stood, careful to keep the sheet wrapped around his lower body. "When I'm ready I'll let you know. I'd better get a fast shower, then we need to get to the station."

It had been almost two years since Jake had slept in his own bed in the master bedroom. Initially when Colette had disappeared he'd moved to the sofa because he couldn't stand sleeping in their bed while not knowing if she was dead or alive.

In those first days of her disappearance, he'd done everything he could as a cop, everything he could do as a man to find her. When she'd left the house on a warm June evening she'd told him she was running to the nearest convenience store for a loaf of bread and a gallon of milk and would be right back.

But she hadn't been right back. Two hours later he'd gotten Mrs. Crawford to stay with Jimmy and he'd gone looking for Colette. He'd found the car parked at the convenience store, but no sign of his wife.

As a cop who had seen the horrors of life, he was certain that something awful had happened to her. But there had also been a little edge of doubt in his mind, as he remembered her long silences, her distance, the unspoken discontent he'd sensed in her.

She'd called him three days later and confirmed that his cop's instincts had been wrong, but his instincts as a man had been right. She'd been having an affair, was in love with another man and was moving to Florida. She wished him well, told him divorce papers would be in the mail and she wouldn't fight him for custody of Jimmy.

He now sat on the edge of the king-sized bed he'd once shared with his wife, to pull on a clean pair of socks. He wasn't sure why he hadn't cleared out her things and reclaimed the bedroom as his own.

He knew she wasn't coming back, nor would he allow her back in his life. Maybe he kept her things in the room to remind himself that you never really knew anyone, even the people closest to you. Maybe he kept the room as it had been to remind himself that even the people you loved most dearly had the capacity for betrayal.

He pulled on a pair of slacks, his thoughts going to Jessica Langford. He'd always been attracted to blondes. Colette had been a blonde. But there was no denying that something about the dark-haired psychiatrist had kicked up a healthy dose of lust inside him.

For the first time since he'd been a teenager what little sleep he'd gotten had been filled with erotic visions. He'd dreamed of her dark hair splayed against a white pillow and her shapely legs wrapped tightly around his hips. Her mouth had been hot against his as she moaned his name and he buried himself in her.

He grabbed a shirt from the closet, dismissing thoughts of his dreams. If he dwelled on it for too long he'd have to get back into the shower, this time with the cold water running at full blast.

He left the bedroom to find Monica standing at the front window, peering outside. Funny, they'd been partners for four years and even though she was an attractive single woman, he'd never had any desire to hit on her. He trusted her more than he'd ever trusted anyone in his life, had shared a lot of personal history with her, but had never wanted to take the relationship to any other level.

She whirled around as if she sensed his presence. "Ready?"

"Yeah." Together they left the house and got into her car. A couple of days a week they shared a ride to the station, using the twenty-minute ride to discuss cases, analyze theories and pick each other's brains about pertinent crimes.

Lately they'd done more bitching about their personal lives than talk about their jobs. "Jimmy was pleasant this morning," she said as she pulled out of his driveway.

"Lucky you. I guess he saves all that preteenager angst and rage just for me," Jake said dryly.

"Things still that bad?"

Jake sighed. "Actually the last couple of days haven't been too bad. He still wants me to fire Mrs. Crawford and let him stay home alone while I work, but he seems to have realized that's not happening anytime in the near future."

Monica was silent for several minutes. "You two ever talk about her?"

Tension snapped inside Jake. "No, never."

She cast him a quick sideways glance. "Because he doesn't want to or because you don't want to?"

Jake frowned, not sure he wanted to have this conversation before he'd at least had his first cup of coffee. "I don't know. It's just never come up."

Again she gave him a quick look, then returned her attention back out the front window. "And you don't find that odd? That his mother goes out for a loaf of bread and never comes back and Jimmy doesn't talk about her?"

"She's gone. He knows that, I know that. What's to discuss?"

Monica shook her head. "I'll tell you something, Jake, for an intelligent cop there are times you can be a real dumb ass."

Jake sighed once again and stared out the window. "Mind your own business, Monica," he said irritably.

She laughed. "Like that's really going to happen."

Even though she'd irritated him, her words haunted him throughout the day. Was it possible that what Jimmy needed from him was a conversation about Colette?

He'd told Monica that they'd never discussed her, but that wasn't exactly true. On the day that the divorce papers had arrived in the mail Jake had sat down with his son and explained that they were getting a divorce and Colette was marrying another man.

Jimmy had seemed to accept his mother's defection without emotion. He'd never asked any questions, had never cried for his mother and he and Jake had simply gotten on with life.

Did Jimmy need some sort of explanation for his mother's actions? The problem was Jake had none. How could he explain something he didn't understand?

Oh, he understood that Colette was apparently not happy with him, but how did a woman walk away from her son? There were dark places in his thoughts that made him wonder if Colette's hatred for Jake ran so deep it had somehow spilled over onto Jimmy. That she'd seen something so terrible in Jake she'd just wanted to get away and cut all ties.

Certainly Jake had the personal history that might frighten a woman away, but he'd worked all his life to make sure he never became the kind of brutal, hateful man like his father.

It was just after seven when Monica dropped him off back at his house that evening. It had been another frustrating day on the job. No new leads in the murder cases. Nothing to help them identify any particular suspect.

When he went inside the house he found Mrs. Crawford and Jimmy seated on the sofa, watching a reality show. "Who's getting voted off this week?" he asked.

"It's gonna be Adam," Jimmy replied. "He needs to go. He's a real snake."

Betty Crawford stood, a smile wreathing her wrinkled face. The widowed woman had been a godsend since Colette had left. She'd struggled financially since her husband had died three years before, and when Jake had approached her about sitting with Jimmy she'd jumped at the opportunity. She liked Jimmy and needed the extra money that working for Jake brought in.

"He's already done his homework, and there's leftover meat loaf in the refrigerator," she said.

"Thanks, Betty. Why don't I walk you home?"

"Nonsense. Take your shoes off and relax. I'm old, but not too old to walk next door under my own steam." It was what she said every night when Jake offered to accompany her to her door.

It took only a minute after Betty left to recognize that Jimmy was in a good mood. He smiled at his dad and patted the sofa. "Why don't you sit and watch the rest of this with me?"

Jake eased down on the sofa next to his son, who immediately started filling him in on who the players were and what was happening on the television.

He savored the moment of camaraderie. Jimmy's happy animation filled him up, soothed his heart. The last thing he wanted to do was bring up the subject of Colette and ruin this moment with his son.

"Who do you want to see win?" Jake asked.

Jimmy grinned. "Julie. She's hot."

"She's hot?" Jake laughed and reached to tickle his son. "She's hot?" he repeated, as Jimmy giggled and tried to scoot away from his dad. "You are way too young to think any woman is hot."

Jimmy managed to evade Jake's tickling fingers, his face flushed with laughter and his eyes shining brightly. "I might be young, but I know hot."

Jake would beg to differ with his son. Hot wasn't a skinny woman running around a beach in a bikini. Hot was a brunette with blue-gray eyes in a royal blue dress. Hot was a couple of buttons left unfastened to give a man just a hint of cleavage.

The mood between Jake and Jimmy remained upbeat and positive for the remainder of the evening. Jimmy sat at the table and talked about school and baseball while Jake ate a meat loaf sandwich. He'd slathered the sandwich with extra ketchup to kill the taste of the meat. Mrs. Crawford loved to cook for them. Unfortunately she wasn't much of a cook.

It was a perfect night, and at eight thirty when Jimmy went to bed, Jake was grateful he hadn't taken Monica's advice and broached the subject of the woman who had disappeared from their lives.

They were fine, Jake told himself as he made up his own bed on the sofa. Jimmy was fine. There was no reason to pick at wounds.

He watched the ten o'clock news, then turned off the lights and the television and settled into the lumpy sofa for the night.

As he tried to chase sleep his thoughts turned back to the cases that had been dealing them fits for the past two weeks. Terri Sinclair and Millie Walker, their names, their personalities and lives were imprinted in his brain. He knew the only way to exorcise them from his mind was to solve their murders.

No matter how hard Jake tried to maintain an objective, unemotional relationship with the victims of crimes he investigated, he never quite succeeded.

Investigation yielded personal information that exposed intimate details that made the victims come alive despite their deaths.

He now knew that Terri Sinclair had suffered a tragic miscarriage before giving birth to her son, Bobby. He knew that Millie Walker had not only worked at the nursing home but had also volunteered time to speak to middle-school children about the crime of shoplifting.

Both women had loved chocolate, fake nails and romantic comedy movies. Both had died terrible deaths, and their cries for justice echoed in his head.

Jake and his team were still chasing down the lead that both women had had their nails done at the same shop, but so far it was taking them nowhere. The women had come in on different days of the week, and all the shop employees' alibis had checked out.

He was in that twilight stage between consciousness and sleep when he heard Jimmy's door creak open. The tug of sleep fell away as in the moonlight streaking through the front window, he watched his son move silently across the living room toward the kitchen.

A drink of water? A little snack? Jake tensed as he listened to find out what his son was up to at eleven o'clock on a school night.

When he heard the click of the back door opening, Jake shot up. He'd told his son that going out his bedroom window was taboo, had said that in this house people left by the doors. But that didn't mean he wanted his son sneaking out of the kitchen door in the middle of the night.

He swung his feet to the floor and stood, then moved across the living room as silently as his son had done moments before. Just as he thought, the kitchen door that led to the backyard was open, the night air sliding in on a faint breeze.

Jake stepped outside, his gaze instantly locking on the figure of his son silhouetted in the moonlight. Jimmy sat on a small stone bench that rested in the center of what had been a flower garden, but in the last couple of years had surrendered to weeds.

The flower garden had always been Colette's hobby, and Jake's heart clenched as he realized it was this place, her place, that his son came on the nights he sneaked out of the house.

Jimmy saw him coming and Jake sensed him straightening his shoulders in a posture of defensiveness. "I'm not doing anything wrong," he said as Jake approached. "I never leave the yard."

Jake sat next to him on the stone bench and tilted his head back to look at the three-quarter moon overhead. "It's a nice night," he said.

Even without the benefit of full light Jake could tell that the gaze his son cast him was suspicious, as if he was certain a shoe was about to fall directly on his head. "Yeah, it's all right," he replied grudgingly.

"Maybe sometime next week we should go pick out a couple of flats of flowers and plant them out here."

Jimmy relaxed, his shoulders sagging forward just a touch. "That would be cool."

"Your mom always spent a lot of time out here." There, he'd finally broached the topic of Colette.

"Yeah." Jimmy sighed, a sigh far too deep for a twelve-year-old. "I always kind of thought she liked her flowers better than she liked me."

Again Jake's heart clenched, and he placed an arm around his son's shoulder and pulled him closer, grateful that Jimmy didn't pull away, but rather seemed to melt into Jake's side. He fought to find the words to assure his son.

But how could he assure Jimmy of how much Colette loved him when she'd walked away and left him behind like a piece of clothing no longer in style? How could he protest Jimmy's words when he'd been at work and not around to see how his wife related to their son on a daily basis?

"Jimmy, whatever problems your mother had, they were her problems, not yours."

"I know," Jimmy said, but Jake wasn't sure that he did understand. Hell, Jake didn't understand it himself. "I just wish . . ." His voice broke.

"Wish what, son?" Jake asked, and tightened his arm around him. Whatever Jimmy wanted, whatever he needed to make his world right, Jake would do it.

"I just wish things would get back to normal."

Jake frowned. "What do you mean, normal? I thought we were living a fairly normal life."

Jimmy straightened up and eyed his father, a frown dancing across his boyish features. "It's not normal for a dad to sleep on the sofa every night, and it's not normal that you've got all her junk in your bedroom. She's been gone a long time and she's never gonna come back to get her stuff."

Jimmy's words stunned Jake. He'd never have guessed that it bothered Jimmy that he slept on the sofa, that it had taken him so long to pack away Colette's things and return to the bedroom.

"I think it would be cool if you'd get married again, this time to somebody who likes boys, somebody who likes being a mom."

Again Jake was surprised, but he did his best to

hide it. "You mean marry somebody like Julie, the bikini-clad babe?"

Jimmy giggled, and the sound shot a welcome swell of pleasure through Jake. "No, just somebody nice who likes kids."

"I'll keep that in mind," Jake replied. "Now, it's late. You have school in the morning. I think we should both get some sleep."

"Okay," Jimmy replied. "Dad?" he said as he stood.

"Yeah?"

"I love you."

If nothing else in his life ever went right again, Jake knew he'd hold this moment in his heart forever. And tomorrow he'd take back the bedroom he'd abandoned when his wife had left him.

Chapter 10

"Even though I know it's irrational, I get into bed each night and I'm certain there's somebody hiding under the bed." The young woman twisted her hands together in her lap, her pretty face etched with lines of stress.

This was a first visit for Rhonda Leewood, but Jessie was grateful that the tall, dark-haired woman didn't seem reticent about discussing her personal life and easily admitting what had brought her to see Jessie. It was so much easier to help people when they were more than willing to help themselves.

"So when you're lying there in bed, what exactly happens?" Jessie asked.

She frowned and ran a hand through her boyishly short brown hair. "I lie there and try to tell myself that there's no way anyone is hiding under the bed, that the doors are locked and my partner, Darlene, would know if somebody had sneaked into the room to hide. But no matter how hard I try to convince myself of that, it doesn't work. My heart starts to pound and I break out into a sweat and feel like I can't breathe."

She broke off and took a deep, steadying breath. "Then I finally manage to get up and turn on the light and look under the bed."

"And there's nobody there," Jessie said.

Rhonda nodded. "And there's nobody there. But that doesn't stop me from turning on the light again fifteen minutes later and checking once again. . . . And again . . . and again."

"And how does Darlene react to this?"

Rhonda frowned. "She tries to be understanding, but she's starting to lose her patience. I can't blame her. I'm not getting any sleep and she's not getting any sleep and it's making both of us pretty irritable."

Jessica smiled sympathetically. "Well, the good news is I have a couple of ideas to help you." Although Jessie had no idea what might have brought on this particular fear, hadn't learned enough about Rhonda's history to understand all the dynamics at work, she did know that what Rhonda needed at the moment was an immediate fix. They'd have time to delve into the underlying cause later.

Rhonda leaned forward, her brown eyes lighting with hope. "What?"

"What do you have under your bed at this very moment?" Jessie asked.

Rhonda frowned again. "Nothing but dust bunnies."

"I recommend you go out and buy enough of those flat plastic storage units to fill up the space under the bed. That way you'll know it's physically impossible for anyone to be hiding there."

"I never thought about doing something like that," Rhonda exclaimed.

Jessie smiled. "Sometimes we're too close to the problem to see the easy fix. If this doesn't help the panic attacks you're suffering, I can write you a prescription for a mild tranquilizer. In any case I'd like for you to make an appointment for next week and let me know how you're doing."

"Thank you, Dr. Langford." Rhonda stood with a grateful smile.

"I'll see you sometime next week," Jessie replied. As the young woman left the office to return to the reception area, Jessie moved to sit at her desk.

It took her only minutes to write down in the appropriate notebook her impressions of Rhonda Leewood; then she leaned back in her chair and stared at the bright bouquet of flowers that adorned one corner of her desk.

The bouquet had been delivered that morning with a card from Larry. He certainly knew her well enough to know what buttons to push. He not only knew she'd always loved to get flowers, but he'd apparently made certain the bouquet contained her favorites, the hybrid Summer Sunshine roses.

The cheerful bright yellow roses had been the same kind her father had bought her mother every year on their anniversary. Gazing at them had never failed to shoot a wave of warmth through Jessie.

She frowned thoughtfully and leaned back in her chair, her gaze remaining focused on the lush blooms. In the past week Larry had stepped up his campaign toward a reconciliation. He'd called every night and continued to try to persuade her to have dinner with him, just the two of them alone.

So far she'd resisted, unsure if she wanted to encourage him or not. There was a part of her that longed to have a partner again, to share glances across the kitchen table over a morning cup of coffee or to snuggle with in the darkest hour of the night. She just didn't know if she wanted those things badly enough to trust Larry again.

She reached out and touched one of the velvety yellow blooms, then dropped her hand back on the top of the desk. The problem was, it wasn't just herself she had to think about. There was Charlie.

Even though Jessie would have preferred her son to be raised in an intact family, she hadn't wanted him to be raised with the stress and unhappiness that had marked the end of her relationship with Larry.

Charlie had adjusted remarkably well to the divorce. What frightened Jessie was the idea of going back into a relationship with Larry, getting Charlie accustomed to the idea of that intact family, then discovering that Larry hadn't changed at all.

She didn't want to put herself in that position

again, nor did she want to put Charlie in the position to have his family torn apart for a second time.

A knock fell on her office door and thoughts of Larry scattered to the wind. The door opened and Sarah stuck her head in. "Mark Smith is here. He doesn't have an appointment. Do you want me to make one for him for next week?"

Jessie checked her watch. It was still early. She had a full hour before she absolutely had to get out of here to meet Charlie as he got off the school bus. "No. Why don't you go ahead and send him in?"

Sarah disappeared, and a moment later Mark Smith came through the door, looking as uncomfortable and tense as he had the last time she'd seen him.

"Mr. Smith, it's nice to see you again." She gestured him toward one of the two chairs.

"I wasn't really expecting to see you today," he said as he sat in the chair closest to the door.

"It worked out perfectly," Jessie said as she walked to the chair next to his and sat. "I just happen to have a little free time." She smiled at him and waited.

He focused his gaze across the room at some indefinable point, his shoulders rigidly straight as he leaned forward on the chair in a position conducive to a quick escape. "I went and saw you last week at that seminar you gave at Maple Woods," he said.

It had been a full week since Jessie had lectured at the college, a full seven days since she'd had coffee with the darkly handsome Jake Merridan. For some reason the tall detective had been in her thoughts far too often in the past week.

She focused her concentration back on the man beside her. "And what did you think of the seminar?"

He shrugged his stiff shoulders. "It was kind of interesting. Do you like doing stuff like that?"

"Stuff like what?"

"Talking in public."

"Yes, I enjoy it."

"What else do you like to do?" He finally looked at her, his eyes dark, deep with some emotion that instantly sent a sharp edge of apprehension through her. "I mean, what do you like to do in your spare time?"

There was something in his tone of voice that intimated the question wasn't just an idle one, but rather one of great importance to him.

There had been several patients in the past who had developed an unhealthy attachment to Jessie, and it was that kind of energy she felt wafting off Mark Smith.

"I prefer not to discuss my personal life," she said with a light tone. "But why don't you tell me what brings you to see me?"

Once again he broke eye contact with her and stared at the wall opposite them. He was silent for several long, tense moments, then he released a deep sigh. "I lost a family member and I'm having trouble coping."

"I'm sorry for your loss. How long has it been?"

He frowned, forcing deep slashes across his forehead. "Long enough that I shouldn't be feeling like this."

"You said you lost a family member. Was it a parent? A child?"

"My brother."

"You were close to your brother?" Each answer came from him as if forced out past enormous strain, but she couldn't help him if she didn't have enough information.

"Apparently not close enough." He ran a hand across his jaw and she saw the tremble of his fingers. "He committed suicide."

Guilt could be as devastating as sorrow, sometimes more so. Jessie waited to see what else he'd share about the death of his brother. Once again long moments passed in silence, and she realized he didn't intend to share anything without prompting.

"Tell me something about your brother," she said.

He gripped the arms of the chair and propelled himself up. "I'm not ready to do this today. I . . . I just came in to make an appointment. Maybe next week." As he talked he edged toward the door. "Today just isn't good for me."

She didn't stop him when he left. One thing Jessie knew for certain was that therapy wouldn't work if the patient wasn't ready, and it was obvious Mark Smith wasn't ready.

She'd just finished making brief notes when

Sarah knocked, then came into her office. "I'm not sure how to bill Mr. Smith," she said, and plopped into the chair the man had vacated moments before.

Jessie looked at her watch. The man had been in her office for less than ten minutes. "Don't bill him for today. Did he make an appointment for next week?"

Sarah nodded. "Next Thursday at two o'clock."

Jessie wouldn't be surprised if sometime in the next week he'd call to cancel the appointment. She hoped he showed up. Even though he made her slightly uncomfortable, she saw the rage and pain in his eyes and knew he needed help.

She stood from behind her desk. "I'm out of here. I've got a bus stop date with the man in my life."

Sarah smiled and stood as well. "And I've got a date with some insurance forms. I have a feeling your date is going to be a lot more fun than mine."

Jessie laughed and grabbed her purse. "Before you leave for the day, would you mind putting a little extra water on the flowers?"

"Sure, but don't you want to take them home?"

"No, I'll just enjoy them here at the office for as long as they last," Jessie replied. She didn't want them at home. As beautiful as they were, they felt like pressure, and she wouldn't be pressured into going back to Larry.

Minutes later as she drove home, her thoughts turned to Detective Jake Merridan. She couldn't

deny that there had been some sort of energy between her and Jake.

Had she not felt that tingling awareness, that
half-breathy kind of excitement with Jake, maybe
she would be more agreeable about seriously considering reconciling with Larry.

Even though she knew there would never be any
kind of a relationship with Jake Merridan, she wondered if she'd be satisfied with Larry without that
chemistry, that edge of sexual excitement, being
present.

Larry had always been safe. He'd never stirred
her to great passion, but that hadn't been as important to her at the time of their marriage as the fact
that he wanted her, scarred and wounded as she'd
been.

He'd represented safety, security at a time when
she was lonely and isolated and needy. She wasn't
any of those things anymore, and she'd rather remain alone than live in a marriage void of passion
and lacking trust.

All thoughts of men and relationships fell aside
as she pulled up to the curb next to where the bus
would stop and release a handful of children after
their day at school.

She shut off her car engine and leaned her head
back. At least the disturbing phone calls had
stopped. Her number had changed on Monday, but
the nights before the number change had been
silent.

She'd convinced herself that the two calls she'd

received had been silly pranks. Even though her new number was a private one, she'd already given it to slew of people—Chris at the radio station, Sarah at the office, Kayla, Larry, Charlie's school. Jessie sometimes wondered why she bothered having a private number when she gave it to so many other people.

She sat up straighter, her heart lifting at the sight of the big yellow school bus rumbling toward the corner. No matter how difficult her day, no matter how troubling her patients or her thoughts, all it took to soothe her spirit was her son.

The bus squealed to a halt and the door opened. Children tumbled out like colorful Easter eggs from a basket, all shapes and sizes and clad in the colors of spring.

Her heart expanded as she spied her son. Wearing a bright green T-shirt and jeans and with his SpongeBob pack riding his back, he raced toward her, a bright smile on his face.

"Hi, Mom," he said as he opened the car door and pulled off his backpack. He threw the pack into the backseat, then got in.

"Hi, Charlie. How was your day?" She waited until he was safely buckled in, then started the engine for the short drive home.

"Good. I got all my math problems right, and Jeremy brought in his pet turtle for us to see. It was cool. Could we get a turtle? It's not like having a dog or anything like that. You don't have to walk turtles or clean up after them." The words bubbled

out of him as if the restriction of the classroom set-
ting had forced his words to be held inside for too
long.

"I'll tell you what. You save enough money from
your allowance to buy all the things for a turtle,
and we'll go turtle shopping," she agreed.

"Cool!"

Jessie smiled to herself. She had a feeling getting
Charlie to do his chores wouldn't be a problem as
long as he wanted a turtle. She pulled into the
driveway and parked. She never parked in the
garage in the time between coming home from her
office and having to leave again for her show at the
radio station.

"What do you suppose Maria has fixed for dinner tonight?" she asked as they got out of the car. It
was part of the routine each afternoon, trying to
guess what was for dinner.

"I hope it's spaghetti, but it's probably meat
loaf." He made a face.

"I'm guessing chicken," Jessie said.

As they approached the door, it opened and
Maria greeted them. "Pork chops," she announced,
knowing the little game they played each afternoon.

"We both lost," Charlie said.

"And you know what that means—we both have
cleanup duty," Jessie said. "And now I'm going to
change into some comfortable clothes, and you,
young man, hit the homework."

Charlie headed to the kitchen table, where he did

his homework each afternoon, and Jessie went to her bedroom to change out of her office clothes and into something more casual.

It was a perfect afternoon and evening. Charlie finished his homework; then he and Jessie went out to the front yard and played catch before dinner.

The evening meal passed with Charlie discussing the imminent arrival of a turtle into the family. "I think I'll name him Tubby. Tubby the turtle," Charlie said.

"I think that sounds like a fine name," Jessie agreed.

"When I was a little girl I had a turtle," Maria said. "It was a box turtle my sister and I found by the side of the road. We kept it in our bedroom for two days, then my mother insisted we let it go."

"Were you sad?" Charlie asked.

"For a day or two, but I knew it was best that the turtle go his own way."

"Kind of like Dad went his own way," Charlie said matter-of-factly. Maria looked at Jessie, as if at a loss as to how to reply.

"Does that make you sad?" Jessie asked.

"Not really. I kind of like it better this way."

"You know your dad and I love you very much."

Charlie nodded. "I know. Gosh, Mom, most of the kids in my class have moms and dads who are divorced. It's not a big deal."

Later that night, after Charlie had been tucked into bed, Jessie and Maria sat at the kitchen table, having a cup of tea. "It's a sad state of the world when it's weird to come from a family where the mother and father are married and not divorced," Jessie said.

Maria smiled. "In some ways it's good that things have changed, that divorce doesn't hold any dreadful stigma anymore. If things had been different thirty years ago, I might have left Craig." She shrugged.

"Larry sent me flowers this morning," Jessie said.

Maria raised a dark brow. "Was it a special occasion of some kind?"

"He's making noises about a reconciliation, but I really don't know how serious he is. Apparently he and Tammi have parted ways, and I suspect I'm an easy convenience. Larry has never been a man who likes to be alone."

Jessie looked at the clock on the microwave and got up to carry her cup to the sink. "I'd better get ready to head out."

"I don't know how you do it," Maria said, also getting up from the table. "You're burning the candle at both ends."

"For now it works for me. As long as I have the weekends to catch up on sleep, I'm fine. Besides, it helps having you here." She smiled at Maria, then left the kitchen to change clothes once again and prepare to leave for her night job.

Even though as a radio personality she could have worn sweats or jeans to work, she always re-dressed in something business casual. She was a professional, and as such just couldn't convince herself to show up looking like anything but a professional.

In her bedroom she changed from her sweats to a pair of tailored black slacks and a cranberry-and-black blouse. She added a pair of black high heels, then walked over to the night-light that burned in the socket near her bed and pulled it out.

Every Wednesday night she changed the bulb in the night-light. It was as much a habit as taking her birth control pill first thing every morning.

She sat on the edge of the bed and opened the nightstand drawer that contained dozens of replacement bulbs and a flashlight. She changed the bulb in the night-light once a week to assure herself that she would never awaken in the middle of the night, in the dark, with a burned-out bulb. She changed the batteries in the flashlight every two weeks for the same reason.

It was an obsessive-compulsive need that would make any of her patients proud, but by changing the bulbs and batteries on a regular basis she felt as if she were in control of her fear.

As she plugged the night-light back in she gazed toward the window, where the last whisper of day had surrendered to the night. She looked forward to the dog days of summer, when each day lasted longer and the night hours of darkness were shorter.

She grabbed her purse from her bed, dug her keys out of the bottom, then paused at Charlie's bedroom door. He was asleep, and as she stood there staring at his still-baby features, she thought of the conversation they'd had at dinner.

There was such comfort knowing that Charlie was okay with the way things were, with the fact that his parents were divorced. Even though it had been Larry who had left the marriage, for weeks afterward Jessie had felt guilty because she'd done nothing to fight for her man, work for the marriage. But she'd never believed in one-sided affairs, and knew that if Larry's heart, his very soul, wasn't into her 100 percent, then he wasn't worth fighting for.

It hadn't taken her long to recognize that she was worth 100 percent, and if she couldn't have that she'd rather be alone.

Alone with Charlie. It was enough for her, she told herself as she left his doorway. If she never got the opportunity again to be the perfect wife, then she'd put all her effort, all her concentration into being the perfect mother, the best psychiatrist and the best friend that she could be.

"Maria, I'm leaving now." Maria sat on the sofa. When Jessie had changed her clothes, Maria had done the same and was now clad in her familiar blue terry bathrobe.

"I hope you have a good show. I'll be listening."

Jessie smiled. "You know, Maria, it isn't part of your job description to listen to my show every night."

"I know that. I like to listen." She got up to walk with Jessie to the door.

"I'll see you in a couple of hours," Jessie said, and opened the front door. She opened the screen door to step out, and gasped. She stumbled backward into Maria.

"Dr. Jessie, what's wrong?" Maria asked in alarm.

Jessie's heart hammered frantically as she stared at the funeral wreath hanging on a metal stand in the center of her front porch.

The cloying scent of carnations filled the night air, white carnations already in the beginning of decay, their edges brown and withered. A black ribbon was interwoven through the flowers with silver letters that read DEATH.

"Sweet Jesus," Maria exclaimed as Jessie slammed the door and locked it.

Breathe, Jessie, she told herself as she felt the familiar constriction in her chest, the insidious approach of panic clawing up her throat.

A funeral wreath. It belonged on a grave, not on her front porch. Where had it come from? Who had placed it there?

She dropped down to her haunches, the walls of the hallway spinning and pressing in around her. "The phone. Get me the phone," she managed to gasp to Maria.

As Maria hurried to do as she bid, Jessie dug in her purse for the card that Jake had given her the week before. He'd find out who had placed it there. He was a detective. That was his job.

DEATH. She'd escaped it once when by all rights

she shouldn't have. She felt it now, whispering down her back, tasted its stale, rancid breath in her mouth.

She had a vague impression of Maria's face as she handed her the phone, her skin pale and eyes huge. Maria was scared. Jessie was terrified.

With trembling fingers she punched in the number and prayed Jake answered.

Chapter 11

It had been his day off, and Jake had spent the day taking back his bedroom. The minute Jimmy had left for school that morning he'd gotten busy packing Colette's clothes and personal items in boxes.

When she'd left that night so long ago she'd taken almost nothing with her, nor had she contacted him in the last two years to request that he send her things to wherever she was living now.

He emptied her side of the closet, then upended dresser drawers and threw shoes into boxes that on another day would be picked up by some charitable organization.

As he worked he thought about the beautiful woman he'd married. Colette had been his high school sweetheart. They'd dated from their freshman year through graduation, then had gotten married. He'd thought it was forever.

When he'd finished in the bedroom he moved to the master bathroom and threw away old makeup and skin softeners, her toothbrush and anything else that had belonged to her.

When the last of his marriage and any trace of the woman he'd shared so many years with was contained in boxes in the garage, he'd returned to the bedroom and gazed around.

It still felt like her room. Colette had decided on the floral bedspread, the lamps on the nightstands, the very color scheme in the room.

He'd spent the afternoon at the mall, where he'd bought a new bedspread, new lamps and throw rugs for both the bedroom and the bathroom. The new colors were black and brown, boldly masculine, and when he finally had everything in place he felt as if he'd marked his territory.

It was funny. He'd thought he'd made peace with the fact that Colette was gone and never coming back. But it wasn't until all her things had been removed from the room that he felt a kind of cleansing relief, as if her ghost had ridden his back and he'd finally managed to shrug her off.

Jimmy had been pleased, and after dinner and cleanup the two of them had gone to the bedroom and turned on a ball game, a bowl of popcorn between them.

It was almost nine thirty and he'd already sent Jimmy to bed when his cell phone rang. He hoped it wasn't a call from the station letting him know another body had turned up. The killer leaving lilies at the scene had been blessedly quiet for the last week. Jake was hoping he'd be quiet for the rest of his life.

"Merridan," he said into the phone.

"Jake? It's Jessica. . . . Jessica Langford."

He knew in an instant that something was wrong. It was there in her voice, a tremble of barely suppressed emotion. "Yes, Jessica?"

"Can you come to my house right away? Please, I need you. . . . I need the police." She rattled off her address, and he made a mental note of it.

He didn't ask her any other questions. "I'm on my way," he said. He clicked off and called Mrs. Crawford to come over to stay with Jimmy.

It took the older woman only minutes to show up at the front door. She was accustomed to his odd hours, and no matter what time of the day or night was always available.

Minutes later as he drove toward Jessica Langford's home, he wondered what had happened. Why did she need a cop? He was ridiculously pleased that she'd called him and hadn't called 911.

It wasn't like he wanted any sort of a relationship with her. He'd decided in those months after Colette left that he wasn't interested in another long-term relationship with any woman. But he had to admit, he had wanted to see Jessica again.

Any pleasure he might have felt about her calling him dissipated as he pulled in behind her car and looked toward the porch. The light was on, illuminating what appeared to be a funeral wreath on a stand.

What the hell?

Somebody's idea of a very bad joke?

He got out of his car and approached the porch and the object that didn't belong there. His gut twisted in a cold, tight knot as he saw the ribbon that had DEATH written in glittery silver ink.

He touched nothing and had only been on the porch for a minute or so when the front door cracked open and he saw Jessie peering outside. When she saw him she opened the door all the way, a look of intense relief on her face. "Thank God you're here," she said through the screen.

"Lock the door. I'm going to take a look around the property," he told her. "I'll knock when I'm finished."

She nodded, closed the door, and he heard the audible click of a dead bolt being turned. He drew his gun even though he knew that whoever had left the ghastly bouquet was probably long gone from the area.

The left side of Jessica's place was connected to her neighbors', and the right side was a wooded lot that if cut through would lead to another road.

Had the person carried the wreath through the woods, left it on her porch, then cut back through the woods where he had his car waiting? Or had he parked on Jessica's street and simply walked through the shadows of the night to leave the present on her doorstep?

Was this somehow related to the phone calls she'd received? She'd refused to go into any detail when she'd come to the station to make a report. Now he wished he'd pressed her for details.

He walked the perimeter of her property and just as he'd suspected, saw nobody or any evidence of anyone having been there.

He returned to the front porch and once again stared at the wreath. If this was somebody's idea of a joke, then that person had a sick sense of humor. He knocked on the door, and Jessica opened it to allow him entry.

"Did you find anything?" she asked. A pulse beat at the base of her throat, letting him know that despite her outward composure she was frightened. He fought the impulse to wrap his arms around her, to somehow shelter her from her own fear.

"Nothing, but it's dark and difficult to see the area." He looked questioningly at the woman standing nearby, a dark-haired, plump woman clad in a light blue bathrobe.

"This is Maria Vernon, my housekeeper and nanny," Jessica said.

If Jessica looked frightened, Maria looked positively terrified. Her skin was a pasty white and her dark eyes were wide and shiny with a hint of tears. Jake nodded at her, then returned his attention to Jessica.

"Do you have any idea what time it was placed there?" he asked as he pulled a small notepad from his shirt pocket.

"I can't say for sure. It wasn't there at six. Charlie and I played catch until then, but it was there when I opened the door to leave for the radio station." With a gasp she looked at her watch. "I've got to call Chris at the station. My show is supposed to start in a few minutes."

She gestured for him to follow her through the foyer and into the living room. As she picked up the phone, Maria stood like a wraith nearby.

The living room décor appeared to be a reflection of his impression of Jessica; elegant yet with a warmth that subtly invited. The color scheme, rich green and deep burgundy, was neither masculine nor feminine, making it easy for anyone to feel at home.

The built-in entertainment system held not only a television and DVD player but also a PlayStation and an array of games that would make Jimmy happy to spend a little time here.

"Chris, it's me. You need to play a prerecorded program. I won't be in." She frowned and twisted the phone cord with her slender fingers. "I know, I know. It's important. It can't be helped."

She had her hair down this evening. Loose and flowing around her shoulders, it looked shiny and silky and his fingers itched with the desire to reach out and touch one of the dark strands.

What was it about this woman that made him want to touch her? Was it just a matter of the fact that he'd been so long without a woman? That his hormones were reminding him that he was a healthy thirty-eight-year-old male who had been without any physical release for almost two years?

"It isn't like I do this all the time. It's an emergency and you'll just have to understand." She replaced the phone in its cradle.

"Problems?" he asked.

She rubbed two fingers wearily across her forehead. "That was my producer. He's working to get the show syndicated, and he's upset that I won't be in tonight."

Jake worked to process this tidbit of information at the same time he tried to remember where they had been before she'd made the call. "So, you said the wreath wasn't there at six but was there a few minutes after nine."

She nodded and sank down on the sofa, looking nothing like the cool profession he'd seen speaking the week before. "Is it possible your producer might be trying to generate a little publicity?" he asked.

"Chris? He's ambitious, but he would never do anything like this," she said.

"Are you sure?"

She frowned thoughtfully. God, the woman even looked good when she frowned, he thought. He wondered if it was because he'd spent the day packing up his past relationship that he felt such an acute awareness of her not just as a victim, but as a woman.

"I certainly hate to think that Chris could be capable of something so awful as this just for a little publicity," she finally replied.

"Can you think of anyone else who might be responsible?" Jake asked. He'd expected her automatic no. If she had a clue who might be responsible she'd have already told him. What he didn't expect was that slight hesitation before she said no.

It was enough hesitation, coupled with her averting her gaze from him, that let him suspect this was a woman with secrets.

Was it possible this was nothing more than a publicity stunt? Or was it possible she suspected who might have left the gruesome gift on her porch but for some reason wasn't telling?

"I know who it is," Maria cried suddenly. "It's Craig. I just know it is. He's found me again and he's tormenting me." She wrung her hands as tears trekked down her plump cheeks.

It was obvious by the look on Jessica's face that she was stunned by Maria's outburst. "Dr. Jessie, I didn't want to tell you. I was afraid you'd make me leave. He called one night while you were at work."

"He identified himself?" Jessica asked, some of the darkness leaving her eyes.

"No, I mean, he didn't say who he was, but I knew. I knew it was him and he'd found me and I knew he was going to ruin everything." Deep, racking sobs gripped her and she stumbled to the sofa, where Jessica put an arm around her shoulders.

"Who exactly is Craig?" he asked.

"Maria's ex-husband." Jessie patted Maria's shoulders, almost ashamed by the relief that coursed through her.

She hadn't considered that the phone calls, the wreath might not be directed at her. And while she didn't like the idea of anyone terrorizing Maria, at least Maria's monster had a face and a name. Her monster from the past had neither.

"Craig Vernon? Either of you know where he might be right now? Where he lives or where he works?"

"I don't have a clue," Jessie replied.

Maria shook her head. "I don't know. I was hoping he was dead."

"When was the last time you spoke to him?" Jake asked.

"The night I left him and went to a shelter. That was just over two years ago," Maria explained.

As Jake asked Maria about where she'd lived with Craig and what kind of work he'd done in the past, Jessie found herself watching him, noting little things she hadn't noticed that night a week before in the Perkins restaurant.

She'd forgotten the rich darkness of his hair and how several errant strands fell forward on his forehead. He wasn't a pretty boy; his features were too rugged, the lines around his eyes etched too deep for that.

There was something solid about him, and it wasn't just in the width of his shoulders. He had a steady gaze that she found both comforting and incredibly sexy.

She'd been afraid when she called him that she'd have to expose herself and tell him about her past. She would have to disclose the damage done to her body, to her soul, and for some reason she found the idea of telling Jake, in particular, about that part of her especially difficult.

Was it Craig? Even though she liked to think of herself as relatively well-adjusted, was she so tied to her past as a victim that she'd jumped to conclusions? Had she been unable to look outside of herself to see what might have been happening around her?

"I'll see what I can do to find out the whereabouts of Craig," Jake said.

"And I want him arrested. I want him thrown into jail for the rest of his life," Maria exclaimed.

Jessie tightened her arm around the woman. "Don't worry, Detective Merridan will take care of this," she said.

Maria pulled away and stood. "Is it all right if I go to bed? I'm exhausted."

"Of course," Jessie replied. "And, Maria, he'll only ruin things if you let him, because as far as I'm concerned you're a part of this family for as long as you want to be."

Maria swiped her tears, nodded to Jake, then disappeared down the hallway to her bedroom.

"Would you like a cup of coffee?" she asked Jake. She wasn't ready for him to leave, was surprised to realize that the taste of fear still lingered in her mouth.

He smiled for the first time since he'd arrived, and heat swirled in Jessie's stomach. "A cup of coffee sounds great," he replied.

She led him into the kitchen and gestured him into a chair at the table while she prepared the coffee. "So, what happens now?" she asked as she waited for the brew to drip into the carafe. Jake Merridan looked good sitting at the oak table. Too good.

"I see if I can find Craig Vernon. If I find him, all I can do is give him an unofficial friendly warning to stay away from you and Maria. If it is him who's been calling and if he left that little surprise on your porch, I'd recommend Maria get a restraining order against him."

"Those never seem to work the way they are supposed to," she said.

"That's because people never act the way they're supposed to," he countered. "But as a psychiatrist, I guess I don't have to tell you that."

She smiled, feeling more relieved with each moment that passed. "No, you don't. Between my private practice and the radio show, I've pretty much seen and heard it all when it comes to human behavior."

His expression turned serious. "Is it possible this is the work of a patient or maybe some crazy fan from the radio show?"

"Surely a fan wouldn't send me a funeral wreath with a ribbon that says *death* on it. Maybe a critic, but I like to think my fans have better taste than that." She poured them each a cup of the coffee, then carried them to the table. "If I remember correctly, you take yours black," she said.

"You remember correctly."

She sat next to him, consciously trying to keep doubts and fears at bay. She didn't want to think about what it meant if it hadn't been Craig who had left the wreath, who had made those phone calls.

"Were you at work when I called?" she asked. She could smell his cologne, so different from the kind Larry wore. Larry smelled minty and familiar. Jake smelled like something spicy and slightly exotic.

"No, I was home."

"So my call pulled you away from your evening, from your son. I'm sorry. I should have called 911."

"Don't apologize," he said smoothly. "Besides, I'd already sent Jimmy to bed when you called. You didn't interrupt anything important."

She wrapped her fingers around her cup. "I just freaked out when I saw that thing on the porch, and my first instinct was to call you."

He reached out and touched her arm. It was a light, casual touch, but she felt it right down to her toes. "I'm glad you called." He pulled his hand back and cleared his throat. "I'm sorry you were frightened."

She laughed and heard the slight edge of fear in her voice. "I'm still frightened," she admitted. She took a sip of her coffee, then continued. "What bothers me is that somebody got close enough to the house to leave that on the porch. Somebody who obviously wanted to scare us knows where we live. And if you find out it wasn't Craig, then it's even more frightening."

"Let's take it one thing at a time. I should know by sometime tomorrow if this Craig is in the area and our best suspect. Until we exclude him, don't look any further—otherwise you'll make yourself crazy."

"At least if I make myself crazy I'm a psychiatrist and can heal myself," she said dryly.

She was rewarded with another one of his smiles, and again the gesture swept a flutter of inviting heat through her, a heat that had nothing to do with the warm cup in her hands.

"Tell me about your son. You said his name is Jimmy?" She wanted to keep the conversation going, was afraid that if a silence reigned between them for too long he'd decide it was time for him to leave. She wasn't ready to tell him good-bye yet.

"Yeah. He's twelve. He's a good kid, but we've been going through a rough patch lately," he said.

"Twelve is a tough age. He's not quite a teenager but not a baby anymore."

He took a sip of his coffee and leaned back in the chair. "He seems to know what buttons to push where I'm concerned."

She laughed. "Welcome to parenthood. Kids learn that pretty quickly. Charlie is only six but already knows a bunch of my buttons."

"Your ex-husband in the area?"

"Yes, Larry lives about fifteen minutes from here. We've managed to maintain a good relationship, and he gets Charlie every other weekend. What about you? Your ex-wife here in town?"

"No. She lives out of state." There was a flash of darkness in his eyes. "So, how long has Maria worked for you?"

It was an obvious attempt to change the subject. Was he still in love with his ex-wife? Not that she cared, not that she intended for anything to happen between herself and him.

For the next fifteen minutes or so she told him about how she'd met Maria, and Maria's tragic relationship with her husband.

"Craig Vernon was a vicious, horrible man who took pleasure in tormenting Maria. From what she's told me about the man, he's certainly capable of something like this," she said.

"Unfortunately there isn't a lot we can do at this point. It's going to be difficult to prove who made the phone calls, and unless there's a fingerprint on that bouquet outside, we probably won't be able to prove who put it there." He paused to drain his coffee cup. "The best thing you and Maria can do is document every phone call. Keep track of anything and everything that might happen."

Jessie felt a sense of panic as he stood, obviously preparing to leave. "Are you sure you don't want another cup of coffee?" she asked, hoping her desperation didn't show in her voice.

"No, thanks. I'd better get back home. What you

can do is get me a large garbage bag. I'll take the wreath and stand with me and see if I can pull off any fingerprints."

She got up from the table and went to the cabinet where she kept her box of garbage bags. She pulled one of the green bags from the box and handed it to him.

His gaze held hers for a long moment. "You going to be okay?"

She wanted to scream no, that she wouldn't be okay. She wanted to tell him that the only thing that would make her okay was if he wrapped his arms around her and held her so tight she could feel the steady, calming beat of his heart against her own. It was amazing how much she wanted to be in his arms.

"Of course," she replied. She followed him out of the kitchen and through the living room to the front door. When he reached the door he turned back to look at her. "I should know something tomorrow."

His eyes were dark and unreadable. He reached out and tucked a strand of her hair behind her ear, then quickly dropped his hand. "Have dinner with me tomorrow night?"

The invitation surprised her. She thought of all the reasons why she shouldn't have dinner with him. She didn't want to get involved with any man. She was far too attracted to Jake Merridan for comfort. It was stupid to begin something she had no intention of finishing.

"Okay." There was only one reason to say yes,

and that was because she couldn't think of anything that she'd rather do than have dinner with him.

His eyes flashed with an emotion slightly dangerous and provocative. "Why don't I pick you up here around six?"

She nodded, her breath catching in her chest in a way it had never done before. It felt scary and wonderful at the same time. "Thank you, Jake," she managed to say.

"Lock up behind me," he said, and with those words went out the door.

She closed the door and twisted the dead bolt, her heart beating an unnatural rhythm that had nothing to do with fear or anxiety.

"What are you doing, Jessie?" she murmured softly. She should have never agreed to dinner with him. The last thing she wanted was any kind of personal relationship, especially with a cop.

It's just dinner, she told herself. One meal. It certainly wasn't a commitment for anything else. As she turned off the lights in the living room and headed toward her bedroom she told herself two things.

The phone calls and the wreath had nothing to do with what had happened to her years ago, and she was capable of having dinner with Jake and not allowing anything to get out of control between them.

*   *   *

Tracy Unger was exhausted. She'd been working double shifts at the truck stop for the last two weeks, and tonight she felt every hour of those double shifts weighing heavily on her body.

Her feet hurt, her shoulders ached and her eyes burned with the need for sleep. The bus stop bench was hard under her ass, but it felt good to be off her feet. The sweet, scented night air was manna after the smoky warmth of the restaurant.

This time of the early morning there was no traffic on the streets. Even the restaurant had only a couple of customer cars parked out front.

She checked her wristwatch for the third time in the last fifteen minutes. It was just after three a.m. Where was Bob? She'd called him a half an hour ago to come pick her up.

If he fell back asleep there'd be hell to pay. Twice in the past two weeks he'd gotten her call, then rolled over and gone back to sleep.

Maybe she should go back inside and call him again. That's what she'd do in a minute or two. Right now she just wanted to sit. If she still had her cell phone she could have called him again without moving from the bench. But it had been turned off a month ago when she hadn't been able to keep up with the bills.

She just bet Bob had gone back to sleep. He was a terrific boyfriend, but he was terrible when it came to picking her up after work. They'd been dating for six months, and a month ago she'd moved in with him.

The last month of her life had been filled with more happiness than she'd ever known. Bob had asked her to marry him and she'd agreed. The extra work hours were a means to an end, money that she was putting into a special account for the wedding of her dreams.

She leaned her head back and closed her eyes, for a minute envisioning herself in the fairy tale ceremony. Her dress would be all lace and silk, with tiny buttons and at least a six-foot train. She'd seen a picture of the perfect dress in a *Bride's* magazine and had it taped to the mirror in their bedroom.

Bob would wear a black tuxedo, and her bridesmaids would be in pink. The church would be filled with flowers and friends. She smiled, eyes still closed, as her heart embraced the vivid image in her mind.

The vision burst apart as something hard crashed into the side of her head. Pain exploded, followed by a descending darkness that she struggled against and lost.

Consciousness came with shards of pain piercing through the veil of darkness. What had happened? Where was she? She tried to focus, but the ache in her head made it nearly impossible.

Dark. She was in the dark. Panic sliced through her as she realized something covered her mouth. She reached to try to remove it and found that her wrists were bound behind her. The panic that gripped her increased tenfold, and she struck out with her feet and tried to rise, only to bang her head on something metal.

It was then she heard the hum of an engine, felt the movement and realized she was in a car. She was in the trunk of a car.

What was happening? Jesus, what was going on? A sob broke in her chest.

She was in deep trouble, and she had a horrifying feeling that the fairy tale wedding she dreamed about, had been saving for, was never going to take place.

Chapter 12

"I am not going to move in with you, Larry," Jessie said into the phone. She should have never told him about the little surprise left on her porch the night before.

"Why not? I'd feel so much better if I knew you and Charlie were safely beneath my roof."

"We're safe right where we are," Jessie countered. "I have a detective working on it and everything should be fine."

Late-afternoon sunshine drifted through her office windows, and for the first time in as long as she could remember she was actually looking forward to the evening hours rather than dreading the coming of the night.

"I still don't like the idea of you being scared. You've had enough scare in your life for ten people."

Apparently Charlie wasn't the only man in her life who knew what buttons to push, she thought. Guilt stabbed through her as she remembered all the nights in their marriage when Larry had never complained about her ever present night-light or about the nightmares she sometimes suffered.

"I appreciate that, but I have good locks on the door and it's in the hands of the police now."

"What are they going to do? Leaving something on somebody's porch isn't even a crime. There's not a damn thing the cops can do in a case like this."

Jessie frowned. Was that true? When Jake had left last night she'd felt good knowing the police would somehow be on top of this, that he was going to take care of things. But if anyone knew the law it was Larry.

Maybe Jake had just told her he'd check for fingerprints and see if he could find the whereabouts of Craig so that he wouldn't have to deal with any hysterical women.

In any case, it didn't matter. She'd made her report to an official, and with the light of day flooding through the windows it was impossible to sustain the kind of fear that had gripped her the night before.

"It doesn't matter. Charlie and I aren't going to leave our home and move in with you," she said.

"Then have dinner with me. I miss talking to you, Jess, and if nothing else it sounds like you could use a friend right now."

"Okay," she agreed. "Tomorrow evening I'll meet you for dinner."

"How about Luciano's at six thirty?" The Italian

restaurant had been a favorite of theirs during their marriage.

"All right," she agreed, although she suspected his choice of restaurant was a subtle way of playing on her emotions. With the arrangements made, they hung up.

Jessie leaned back in her chair, an amused smile curving her lips. Feast or famine. It had been years since she'd had a date, and now in the space of two days she had two dates with two different men.

She'd been uncertain exactly what she wanted to do where Larry was concerned, and hoped that their dinner together would clear her mind.

She was perfectly clear on what she wanted from Jake—a little conversation, a nice meal and nothing more.

Even though she didn't want anything more from Jake, she couldn't ignore the flutter of excitement that coursed through her as she thought of seeing him again that evening.

Realizing it was time for her to leave the office for the day, she got up from her desk and grabbed her purse. "I'm out of here," she said to Sarah, who was typing on the computer at the reception desk.

"Okay, I'll see you in the morning." Sarah didn't look up from her work.

The afternoon sun was unusually warm and Jessie was grateful that it appeared that spring didn't intend to linger at all, but was rather being pushed away by summer weather. That was just fine with her.

Spring was always difficult, with its particular scents and sounds evoking distant memories that she tried to keep contained in the box on the shelf in her closet.

What were the odds that the serial killer who had nearly taken her life eighteen years ago was back? As far as anyone knew he'd never committed any other murders, at least not in the same fashion or with the same signature. She knew the general opinion was that he was either dead or in prison on other charges.

When she'd seen that funeral wreath the night before, her greatest fear had been that somehow the T&B killer was back, hunting the streets, hunting her. It had only been when Maria broke down and cried, certain that the culprit was Craig, that Jessie's terror had been tempered.

As she walked from her office building to her car in the parking lot, a sense of disquiet swept through her and the hairs on the nape of her neck rose. She glanced around, quickening her footsteps, as she had the distinct impression that she was not alone, that somebody was watching her.

She saw nobody. The building was filled with offices of professional people, doctors and lawyers and an insurance firm, but at this time of the afternoon there was little foot traffic in or out of the building.

Even though she tried to tell herself she was being silly, she couldn't shake the feeling that somebody was near, watching her every step, watching her every move. She breathed a sigh of relief as she slid behind the steering wheel in her car and punched the automatic door locks.

As she pulled out of the parking lot she checked her rearview mirror, and her heart jumped as she saw a dark blue sedan leave a parking space and follow behind her.

The car kept just enough distance from hers that she couldn't see who was behind the wheel. Was it just coincidence that it had pulled out at the same time she had?

There was no way she was driving home not knowing who was behind her or if they might be following her. She made a right turn, heading away from her house. Her heartbeat raced as a moment later she saw the car appear behind her once again.

She made a quick left turn in an effort to evade or at least make certain she was really being followed. The dark blue car followed suit, then veered into a gas station.

Jessie sighed in relief and unclenched her hands from the steering wheel. She was wound way too tight, her imagination working overtime. "Chill out," she muttered to herself.

One of the things Jessie had learned in her exploration of fear was that too much fear was like being in a room with too many people. The fear signals that were so important in determining danger got lost in the crowd.

She knew how important it was not to get caught up in manufacturing fear where none should exist, how important it was that she remain rational in decoding fear signals that were real and the ones that were bred in sheer emotion.

Despite what Larry had said about the police being able to do nothing about the "gift" left on her front porch, she had no doubt that Jake would do as he'd said he would and follow up on Craig Vernon.

If they discovered that Craig was responsible for the phone calls and for the wreath, then that information would go a long way in assuaging her fear that somehow the beast from her past was once again hunting her.

She pulled up to the curb and parked to wait for the school bus. Now that the fear that had gripped her when she'd thought she was being followed had passed, she was left with the fluttering, utterly feminine excitement of the evening to come.

At five forty-five that evening she stood in front of her dresser mirror, looking at her reflection one last time before Jake arrived.

Her bed was covered with outfits put on, then taken off as she tried to decide what she'd wanted to wear for dinner with Jake. Someplace in the back of her mind she knew she was taking far too much care, far too much time in choosing her clothes and fixing her makeup for what could be nothing more than a casual date.

She turned away from the mirror, satisfied with the three-piece silk coral-colored pantsuit she'd chosen to wear. Jake hadn't mentioned where they'd go to eat, so she wasn't exactly sure how dressy to get. The pantsuit with the jacket on was elegant enough for a fancy restaurant, but with the jacket off appeared more casual. She felt as if she were ready for anything.

"You look pretty, Mom," Charlie said, as she came into the living room where he was stretched out on the floor with a video game. He paused his game and sat up.

"Thanks, honey," she replied. "Now, you understand Mr. Merridan is just a friend," she said. She'd already explained that she was going out to dinner with somebody.

"It's okay to tell me you're going out on a date," Charlie said. "Billy's mom goes out on dates all the time. It's what divorced people do."

Sometimes Charlie amazed her. He still believed in Santa Claus but knew what divorced people did. Like so many children in today's world he was a curious blend of childhood innocence and worldliness.

"Well, I don't intend to make a habit of the dating stuff," Jessie said. "I'm pretty happy with the way things are." Except for the nerves that bounced around inside her, making her feel as if she was about to come out of her skin.

As Charlie returned to his video game, Jessie sat on the sofa and smoothed her hands over the cool silk material of her slacks.

She couldn't remember the last time she'd been so nervous. She thought about taking a Valium. She had a bottle in her bedroom in case of a particularly difficult panic attack, but she hadn't taken any in almost a year.

The Valium would take the edge off her nerves but it would also dull her senses, and she wasn't sure she wanted to be even slightly doped up during her time with Jake.

What you're feeling is normal, Jessie, she told herself. It was the nervous anticipation of being with somebody she liked, of wanting to make a good impression and being afraid she might not.

She was a bundle of contradictions, certain that she wanted nothing from Jake and yet afraid of making a bad impression. Most people thought psychiatrists were crazier than the people they treated, and if anyone could peer into Jessie's mind at this very moment she'd definitely confirm that belief.

It would be so much easier if she had no baggage, no scars. Even Larry, who had professed to love her, had been turned off by the raised welts and scar tissue that decorated her stomach. In all the years of their marriage Jessie had rarely allowed him to see her naked, nor had he ever touched her stomach unless by accident.

Maria came into the room from the kitchen. "You look real nice, Dr. Jessie," she said, and settled in on the opposite side of the sofa.

"Thanks." Jessie knew Maria was anxious to hear what Jake had learned about Craig's whereabouts. Hopefully he'd have something to tell them when he arrived.

"Depending on how late dinner runs, I may just have Jake drop me off at the station. I can always get a cab from there to bring me home," she said. Of course, there was always the possibility that after spending ten minutes with her he'd be eager to get her back home as soon as possible.

When the doorbell chimed she jumped up from the sofa as if she'd been goosed. She smoothed her jacket, drew a deep breath and went to answer the door.

The moment she saw the warm smile curving his lips, an unexpected tingle shot through her veins. A white dress shirt pulled across his shoulders and was tucked neatly into a pair of charcoal dress slacks.

"Hi," he said, taking in the length of her in one obvious, sweeping gaze. "You look great."

"Thanks. Come on in. You can meet Charlie." She opened the door wider to allow him to move past her and into the living room. As he did she caught his scent, a wonderful blend of clean and spicy cologne.

"Charlie, pause your game for a minute and come meet Detective Merridan," Jessie instructed. Her son stopped his game and stood.

Jessie's heart expanded with pride as her son approached Jake and held out his hand. "Nice to meet you, sir," he said soberly.

"It's nice to meet you, Charlie." Jake took the boy's hand. "And why don't you call me Jake?"

Charlie flashed a bright smile and dropped his hand. "Okay, cool."

"Is that *Highway Bandit*?" Jake asked, and pointed to the scene frozen on the television screen.

"Yeah. It's a good game," Charlie replied.

"I've got a twelve-year-old son named Jimmy. He likes that game. I think he's gotten to level twenty-two," Jake said.

A look of hero worship lit Charlie's eyes. "Wow, that's awesome. I can only get to the second level."

"Maybe sometime all of us can get together and Jimmy can show you the secrets to get to the other levels," Jake suggested.

Charlie looked at his mom, then back at Jake. "That would be great. Can we, Mom?"

Jessie laughed at her son's exuberance. "We'll see."

Jake nodded to Maria, who sat on the edge of the sofa, her features taut with expectation as she gazed at him. "Good evening, Maria."

"Detective Merridan," she returned, her voice holding a slight tremble.

"I'm afraid I have no information for you about the matter we discussed before. I'm hoping I'll have something by tomorrow." He smiled apologetically at Maria, who visibly sagged against the cushions.

"Then I'll take no news as good news," she replied.

Jake turned to Jessie. "Are you ready to go?"

"Just let me grab my purse." She hurried into the

kitchen, where her purse was on the table. As she grabbed it she drew a deep, steadying breath to try to halt the jig her nerves were dancing.

It was ridiculous that Jake Merridan made her feel like a teenage girl going out on her first date, ridiculous how much she liked the fact that he'd been good with Charlie.

Dinner and home, she reminded herself as she left the kitchen. Dinner, then home and nothing else. Those were Jessie's rules where Jake Merridan was concerned. She'd enjoy sharing a meal with him, some interesting conversation, and that was all.

Minutes later they were seated in Jake's car and backing out of the driveway. "I hope you like Italian," he said. "I made reservations at Tony's."

"I love Italian, although I've never heard of Tony's," she replied. Two men, two different nights and two Italian restaurants, one familiar and one new.

"The best-kept secret in Kansas City," he replied. "I found it about a year ago and it's become one of my favorite places to eat."

"Charlie and I don't eat out much. We go out for pizza occasionally, but Maria usually cooks and she's great at it."

"You're lucky. It's hard to get good child care. My son and I have a running argument about the fact that he thinks he doesn't need anybody taking care of him. But with my hours, I have a widowed neighbor lady who comes in whenever I have to leave."

Jessie flashed him a smile. "Sometimes I think it's safer to leave a three-year-old at home alone than a teenager."

"Isn't that the truth." They rode in silence for a few minutes. Jessie tried to ignore the scent of him that filled the car, a scent that seemed to whirl itself directly to her hormones. She also tried not to notice that his shirt was unbuttoned just enough to allow a tuft of dark chest hair to be visible.

Larry hadn't had a hair on his smooth, boyish chest, and she'd always wondered what it would be like to tangle her fingers in a patch of masculine chest hair.

"I'm sorry I don't have any information for you about Craig Vernon or the wreath," he said, breaking the silence. "I was in meetings for most of the day and when I finally got a chance to make some calls, the people I needed to talk to were either busy or out. Hopefully I'll hear something sometime tomorrow."

Jessie didn't want to talk about the funeral wreath; she didn't even want to think about it for the duration of her time with Jake. "That's all right. I don't want to dwell on anything negative tonight."

He flashed her another of those smiles that had the potential to curl her toes. "That makes two of us. So, tell me what Dr. Jessica Langford does when

she isn't talking on the radio or working with patients."

"Play with Charlie and sleep." She laughed with
a little bit of self-consciousness. "I know it sounds
boring, but that's pretty much the sum of my life at
the moment."

"Unfortunately it doesn't sound boring. It
sounds pretty familiar. I work, spend time with
Jimmy and sleep away whatever time is left." He
turned the wheel, and she noticed he had nice
hands. They looked strong and capable.

She eyed him curiously. "If you had all the free
time you wanted, what would you choose to do
with it?"

She was glad when he took a moment to think
about it rather than shooting something off the top
of his head. "I don't know, maybe take up a hobby
of some kind."

"Anything in particular?" Her curiosity about
him surprised her. It had been a very long time
since she'd been nosy when it came to a man who
wasn't a patient of hers.

"I used to be a pretty decent chess player, but I
haven't played in years. I also like tinkering with
cars and always thought it would be fun to get an
old classic and restore it."

So he was a man who liked mental challenges
and liked to fix things. She wasn't surprised by his
choice of hobbies. They fit with a man who would
choose to become a homicide detective.

"What about you?" he asked as he turned into a

parking lot in front of a low, flat building that had a small sign flashing TONY'S on the roof. He parked, shut off the engine, then unbuckled his seat belt and turned to look at her. "If you had a lot of spare time, what would you choose to do with it?"

She seriously considered his question even though she found it difficult to think when he gazed at her so intently. "I don't know. I sometimes think I'd like to grow a little garden or take a day each week to explore all the wonderful places here in town that I've never been."

"Like Tony's?"

She laughed. "Yes, like Tony's." She didn't wait for him to get out and come around to open her door, but instead got out of the car as he did. Together they walked toward the building where the mouthwatering scent of pungent garlic and sweet tomato sauce hung in the early night air.

It was instantly obvious that Jake wasn't a stranger in the small restaurant, as he was greeted by name by a couple of waiters and the hostess who seated them.

They were seated in a corner at an intimate table for two with a candle burning in the center. Before they'd even settled in a waiter arrived with a bottle of wine.

"I hope you don't mind," he said, as the waiter left after pouring them each a glass. "I took the liberty of ordering the wine ahead of time."

"I don't mind at all," she replied. "I must confess

I'm not much of a wine connoisseur. If it has a cork rather than a screw-off lid, I assume it's good."

He laughed and the lines at the corners of his eyes deepened, only adding to his attractiveness. Oh, Jessie girl, hang on to your good sense, she warned herself. This man with his sexy smile could definitely make a nice girl take leave of her senses.

"How did you ever find this place?" she asked.

"I've never been much of a cook, so after my divorce Jimmy and I decided to go on a hunt for good places to eat out. I don't think there's a burger joint, chicken place or pizza parlor we haven't tried. One night we were just cruising around and found Tony's. We've been fans ever since."

Jessie picked up the oversized menu and opened it. "So tell me what's good."

"Everything. Seriously, we've eaten here dozens of times and tried almost everything on the menu, and we have yet to get something we haven't liked. I have to confess, I'm pretty traditional when it comes to Italian food. I usually go for the lasagna."

She closed her menu and smiled. "Lasagna sounds perfect to me."

Any further conversation was halted as a waitress appeared at their table. She chatted for a moment with Jake and asked about Jimmy, then took their orders and departed.

As she left, Jessie picked up her wineglass and took a sip. For a moment she was terrified they would fall into an uncomfortable silence or that after ten minutes of conversation they'd realize they had nothing in common, nothing to talk about.

She needn't have worried. They fell into an easy conversation of discovery, talking about their parents and their early childhood life. That segued into what high schools they'd attended and memories of first dates, proms and other memorable events.

"I can't believe you didn't attend your senior prom," he exclaimed when she confessed that fact. "Either the boys in your school were idiots or you were a late bloomer."

"Maybe a little of both," she replied lightly. Of course, she wasn't willing to tell him the truth, that the senior prom had come at a time when she'd still been traumatized by the crimes that had ripped her life apart. Spinning, sparkling disco balls and sweet-smelling corsages had seemed absurd at that particular time in her life.

"What lucky girl did you take to your senior prom?" she asked, preferring the conversation be about him than about her.

He paused a moment and took a sip of his wine. "I took Colette Benson, the woman I eventually married," he said as he placed his glass back down on the table.

"You married your high school sweetheart?"

He nodded. "We got married right out of high school. What about you? Was your ex-husband a high school beau?"

"No, Larry and I met in college. We got married when he was in his last year of law school."

"He's a lawyer?"

She smiled. "A divorce lawyer. Thankfully our divorce was quite civil, because he has a reputation as being a barracuda."

"My divorce was as civil as they come. I got the papers in the mail, signed them and it was a done deal." His eyes appeared darker than normal. "Several months before, Colette went out one evening to a convenience store to buy bread and never came home."

Jessie looked at him in surprise. "Did you know there were problems?"

He picked up his wineglass once again and leaned back in his chair. "Looking back I see that there were problems, but at the time I wasn't aware of any."

"That must have been tough, especially on your son."

He frowned thoughtfully, the gesture cutting a deep line across his forehead. "It's funny. Jimmy seemed to pretty much take it all in stride. I think he was far more aware of Colette's unhappiness than I was."

He took another drink of his wine, set his glass down, then smiled, smoothing out the wrinkle that had creased his brow. "But I don't want to talk about the past. For the first time in two years I've finally started to look forward."

She sensed there was some emotional baggage left behind by his wife, but she also knew that most divorces resulted in some baggage of one kind or another.

Their meals arrived, and as they ate they continued the talk of two people getting to know one another. They spoke about movies they'd seen and books they'd read. They argued politics and laughed as they shared parenting stories and most embarrassing moments.

When they'd finished their meal Jake insisted they have dessert, and although she professed to be stuffed he talked her into sharing a huge piece of tiramisu.

Throughout the evening, even though Jessie tried to tell herself this was just a casual date, she couldn't help the fact that being with him made her acutely aware of herself as a woman. When he gazed at her with those dark, intense eyes she felt like a beautiful, desirable woman.

She wanted to blame the wine, that she was warm and tingly. But deep inside she knew it had nothing to do with the alcohol and everything to do with Jake Merridan.

He was not only charming and entertaining, but she found herself watching his lips as he talked, wondering how they'd taste, how they'd feel against her bare skin. His hands, so strong and masculine, evoked fantasies of them on her body, sliding up her rib cage to capture her breasts.

The whole time they were eating, and afterward as they lingered over coffee, his attention never wavered from her. He made her feel as if she were the only woman in the room, the only woman in the world. God, he was so dangerous, she thought.

Enjoy tonight, Jessie, she told herself. Because with every moment that passed she recognized this would have to be their one and only date. He made her want him, and she couldn't have that. She wouldn't have that.

After dinner they walked together back toward his car, and it seemed only natural that Jake reached for her hand. Her slender hand felt good in his.

He hadn't drunk enough wine to feel the way he did. He had a buzz on that had nothing to do with the alcohol consumed. She gave him a buzz. She reminded him that it had been too damn long since he'd kissed a woman, since he'd touched sweet-smelling, soft skin. It had been too damn long since he'd made love.

"You know, I was a little worried about having dinner with you," he said once they got into his car and he started the engine.

"Why?" She looked at him in surprise.

"I was afraid you'd spend the evening somehow analyzing me."

She laughed. He loved the sound of her laughter. It was deep and throaty and seemed to come from her very toes. "I don't mix business with pleasure, although I must confess a little analyzing comes with the territory."

"If you did do any where I'm concerned, I guess

you're okay with the conclusions you came to, because you didn't call a cab to take you home."

She smiled. "You seem pretty normal to me, Jake."

"My son would probably disagree with your opinion."

She laughed again. "Kids are supposed to think their parents are weird."

Jake had been on a slow simmer from the moment he'd arrived at her house. She looked gorgeous in the silky peach-colored outfit, with her dark hair loose and flowing around her shoulders.

Halfway through the meal she'd shrugged out of her jacket, leaving her in a sleeveless, scoop-necked little top that displayed just a hint of cleavage whenever she leaned forward, and creamy shoulders that begged to be stroked.

The scent of her, the look of her, everything about her had combined to keep him half aroused all night. As they drove home all he could think about was the moment when they'd reach her house and he'd tell her good night.

He intended to kiss her. He wanted, needed to taste those sweet, ripe-looking lips of hers, to pull her into his arms and feel her curves pressed against him body.

It was a given that physically she turned him on. What made it even more exciting was that he liked her. She stimulated him not only on a physical level but on an intellectual level as well.

He tried to tell himself to slow down, that even

though they had shared small talk and a few pieces of their past, he didn't really know her. But hell, that didn't mean he didn't want to sleep with her.

He also wasn't particularly interested in a long-term committed relationship. Been there, done that, and he apparently hadn't done it well at all. In fact, he'd done it so poorly that his wife had run away rather than try to work things out with him.

No, he had no desire for anything resembling permanent, but that didn't mean he didn't want Jessica Langford at least for a night or two.

When they pulled into her driveway a ridiculous burst of nerves balled in his stomach. Jesus, it had been years since he'd kissed a woman good night after a date. Suddenly his hands were damp with sweat and his heartbeat raced just a little bit faster.

Maybe she wouldn't want him to kiss her. He parked the car, irritated with his thoughts and his doubts. He felt like a schoolboy again and the feeling wasn't pleasant.

"It's a beautiful night," he said as they walked toward her front door. Stars filled the sky overhead and the night air was unusually warm.

"Yes, and it's been a lovely night." She stopped at the front door and looked up at him. There was a hint of anticipation in her blue-gray eyes, a whisper of longing that dictated his actions.

He reached out and ran his fingers through a strand of her dark hair. It was soft as silk, and she leaned her head just slightly toward his touch. It was all the encouragement he needed.

Without giving himself a chance to think, to doubt, he gathered her into his arms and pressed his lips to hers. He'd intended it to be just a chaste peck kind of kiss, but as she wrapped her arms around his neck, his best intentions went straight to hell.

He pulled her closer, so close he could feel the press of her breasts against his chest, so close he could smell the dizzying clean scent of her hair and the faint fragrance of her heady perfume. The kiss he'd intended to be light and simple became much more complicated as she opened her mouth beneath his.

Desire crashed through him, a desire so intense, so hot he nearly staggered beneath the unexpectedness of it. Their tongues danced together as he tangled his hands in her hair and she released just the slightest moan.

His hands left her hair, traveled down the slender length of her back, and he fought the impulse to grab her buttocks and pull her tight against his full arousal.

He wanted to lie her down in the sweet spring grass and strip her naked. He wanted to see her skin illuminated by the moonlight. Her mouth tasted of a hint of wine and tiramisu and a white-hot desire that electrified him.

His cell phone vibrated in his pocket. No, he thought and pulled her more tightly against him, so tight he could feel the heat of her body radiating through their clothing.

The phone vibrated again. There were only two reasons for the phone to ring. He was either needed at home or he was needed at work.

"Dammit," he muttered, and released her. She stumbled back from him, her eyes appearing glazed. "Sorry," he said, and yanked the phone from his pocket. "Merridan," he barked into the phone. He listened for a moment. "I'll be right there." He slapped the phone closed and looked at Jessie, wanting her back in his arms, wanting to taste her mouth yet again.

"Problem?" she asked, her voice slightly husky.

"Work. I've got to get down to the station."

She worried a hand through her hair, and he noticed it trembled slightly. It was good to realize she'd been as affected by the kiss as he had. "You'd better go, then."

"Yeah." He remained unmoving.

"Thank you, Jake. For a wonderful evening."

"I had a great time."

"You need to go."

"Yeah," he agreed reluctantly. He turned to leave, but turned back to her and pulled her against him for one last kiss. She went willingly back into his arms, but it was she who kept the kiss controlled and light; then she gently shoved against his chest and stepped back from him.

"Good night, Jake."

"Good night." He turned and headed back toward his car, wishing the phone hadn't rung, wondering what might have happened between them if he hadn't had to leave.

He got into his car and watched until she'd unlocked the front door and disappeared inside. He released a deep breath, needing to switch his thoughts from sex to death.

There had been another murder by the lily killer. As he drove away from Jessie's house he had two goals in mind. He needed to catch a killer, and he wanted to get Dr. Jessica Langford into his bed.

Chapter 13

"And I told him I can't run the vacuum because I have a horrible fear of being sucked up into the hose." Sandy Dessart smoothed a strand of her blond hair with a perfectly steady hand. "My husband just doesn't understand my fears."

Frankly, neither did Jessie. Sandy Dessart had been coming to see her for the past four weeks and on each visit she'd confessed a profound fear of anything that had to do with cleaning. The first visit had yielded a fear of furniture polish, the second a terror of glass cleaner. Last week she'd realized she was frightened of foam bathroom cleaner, and this week the vacuum.

Jessie's diagnosis was laziness and suspected these visits to see her were nothing more than a manipulation to get her husband to spring for a full-time housekeeper.

As Sandy droned on, Jessie tried to stay focused on the conversation but found her thoughts drifting back, back to that kiss.

Jake's kiss. In the single meeting of lips her knees had threatened to buckle, her heart had raced at a near-frightening speed and she'd been filled with a fierce longing the likes of which she'd never felt before.

She wanted to know him. She didn't just want to know what movies he liked and what his favorite food was; she wanted to know other, far more intimate things. Like how his chest hair felt beneath her fingertips, if he made love with the same kind of single-minded intensity that sometimes shone from his eyes.

Did he groan when he made love, or did he make no sound at all? Did he like to take a long time, or was he a fast, selfish lover?

Larry never made a sound and he'd been quick, most of the time too quick. Larry. She was meeting him for dinner tonight. Even though she told herself she was keeping an open mind where a possible reconciliation was concerned, deep inside she sensed that last night's date with Jake had determined that there was no way she'd go back to Larry.

Larry was safe, comfortable and familiar, but there had never been any real fireworks where he was concerned. At the time they'd dated and gotten married, Larry had been enough. But Jessie was a stronger, different kind of person now, and she wondered if after kissing Jake she would ever be satisfied with a life of kissing Larry.

"The smell of pine cleaners makes me dizzy. I get all breathless and scared."

Jessie forced her concentration back to Sandy. "There are a lot of cleansers now that have no scents," she said. "Perhaps you could try using some of them."

Sandy frowned resentfully. "You're not hearing me, Dr. Langford. It's the act of cleaning that makes me so scared. It doesn't matter what the cleanser smells like."

Jessie leaned back in her chair. "I'm afraid that I'm not going to be able to help you on this." She'd wasted enough of her time on this woman, whom she was certain was faking symptoms to hide the fact that she didn't want to clean her house.

There were people out there suffering real fears and phobias, ones that made living a normal, happy life impossible.

"I was afraid of that." Sandy feigned disappointment. "I told my husband that I suspected my fear was too deep for anyone to be able to help me." She picked up her purse from the floor and stood. "Then I guess I won't be seeing you again."

"I'm sorry I've been ineffectual in coming up with a game plan to treat your problems," Jessie said.

Sandy cast her a look of contrived misery. "I'll just have to work things out on my own. Thank you for trying."

When the woman left the office Jessie breathed a sigh of relief. She didn't suffer fools gladly, especially ones who tried to make a fool out of her. Sandy had talked of fear but had shown no physiological signs to back up her claims.

A knock fell on the door and Sarah popped her head in. "That's it for today. Mrs. Dessart didn't make another appointment."

Jessie nodded. "I know. I think I've done all I can for her." She got up and grabbed her purse from behind the desk. "And now I'm going home."

"Have a nice evening," Sarah said as together the two walked through the reception area.

At precisely six thirty that evening Jessie pulled into the parking lot of Luciano's. She didn't see Larry's familiar car in the parking lot, but wasn't surprised. Larry was rarely on time for anything.

It used to drive her crazy when they were dating, that he never arrived for a date on time. After they'd married his lack of punctuality hadn't changed. She'd come to realize that it was a passive-aggressive control thing for him.

She decided to wait in the car for him to arrive. The minutes ticked by, and as had happened all day long when she tried to keep her mind clear and empty, Jake jumped into her brain.

She told herself she didn't want to see him again, she certainly didn't want to go out with him again, but her mind and her heart, her lust, seemed to be working in opposite directions.

The last thing she wanted was to get close to him, fall in love with him, then watch his face radiate horror as she told him of her past, as she showed him her scars. She touched her stomach now, able to feel the faint ridge of scar tissue through the silk dress she wore.

She thought of the night-light she couldn't do without, the panic attacks that occasionally plagued her when she smelled spring flowers or overturned earth. She was and probably would be forever wounded by her past. Jake was the kind of man who deserved a whole woman without scars, without baggage.

She opened her car door and stepped out as she saw Larry's car wheel into a nearby parking space. He got out of his car and offered her a bright smile. "Sorry I'm late. I got hung up. Have you been waiting long?"

"Not too long." She'd learned a long time ago that admonishing him for his tardiness never did anything. He was dressed in one of his power suits; perfectly tailored, crisp white shirt and a muted tie in blues and grays.

Together they headed across the parking lot toward the upscale restaurant. Where Tony's had exploded with color and noise, Luciano's was decorated in subtle, understated tones of gold and beige. Everyone seemed to whisper, as if laughter or boisterous talk was forbidden.

A tuxedo-clad young man with a plastic smile and empty eyes led them to a table.

She couldn't help but compare her experience the night before to this dining experience. She'd been instantly relaxed in Tony's atmosphere, but something about Luciano's caused a small ball of tension to press against her chest. Or maybe it had nothing do with the surroundings and everything to do with the fact that she really didn't want to be here with Larry.

She had told herself that she had an open mind when it came to the idea of a reconciliation, but the moment Larry had stepped out of his car she realized there was no going back.

The meal was like so many she'd shared with Larry over the years. He talked and she pretended to listen. Larry was a man who liked the sound of his own voice, and for a long time it hadn't bothered Jessie that he monopolized the conversation. It relieved any pressure she felt to share thoughts or ideas.

Last night with Jake the conversation had held a natural give-and-take. He'd been genuinely interested in everything she'd had to say.

"Jessie!" Larry's tone held a sharp edge, and she directed her attention back to him, aware that at some point she'd zoned out.

"I'm sorry. What did you say?"

"I said it seems like old times, doesn't it?" He flashed her a smile, and she noticed he had almost no wrinkles around his eyes. Her brain flashed with an image of another set of eyes, dark with life lines crinkling at the corners.

She'd also noticed the flirtatious glint in Larry's eyes as he'd ordered from the pretty young waitress. Yes, it seemed like old times. She picked up her coffee cup and took a sip, as if the caffeine would fortify her for what she was about to do.

"How about we split a big piece of cheesecake for dessert?" he said, as she set her cup back down. He reached across the table and took her hand in his. "I know how much you love Luciano's cheesecake."

She withdrew her hand from his. She didn't like cheesecake. He did. "Larry, this isn't going to work."

"What?"

"This . . . us."

He frowned. "You don't want the cheesecake, we can order something else."

"That's not what I'm talking about," she replied, knowing he was being deliberately obtuse.

He sighed and raked a hand through his sandy hair. "Why not? It could be just like before, only better." He leaned forward, his blue eyes as earnest as she'd ever seen them. "You don't want to spend the rest of your life alone, Jessie."

"No, I don't," she agreed, and tried not to be offended that he assumed if she wasn't with him she'd be all alone. "But if that's the way it works out, so be it. I'm content right now. I like my life."

"You liked your life when we were together," he protested.

"But things have changed. I've changed." This time she reached across the table and took his hand. "There's a part of me that will always love you, Larry. And it's important that we always be friends for Charlie's sake, but I think it's best if we keep things the way they are now."

He squeezed her hand, regret shining from his eyes. "You know I was hoping for a different outcome this evening. But I guess I've got no other choice than to accept your decision." He let go of her hand.

"No hard feelings?"

"None," he replied without hesitation. "A lot of regret, maybe a little sadness, but no hard feelings. Never with you, Jessie."

For a brief, bittersweet moment she wondered if she'd just made the biggest mistake in her life. But as they parted ways and she was leaving the restaurant, she saw Larry talking to the cute little waitress and writing down what was probably her phone number. Larry might have good intentions, but he had lousy impulse control.

As she walked across the parking lot to her car she once again had the feeling of eyes watching her every movement, of somebody hiding in the shadows nearby.

She'd tried not to think about the funeral wreath, but it had niggled at the base of her brain since she'd seen it on her front porch.

She'd hoped to hear from Jake that day. She'd hoped for a phone call from him telling her that Craig Vernon had confessed to leaving the wreath in an effort to terrorize his ex-wife.

She'd hoped that the wreath had nothing whatsoever to do with her. But she'd heard nothing from

Jake, and the uncertainty of who had left the wreath and why had kept an edge of apprehension sifting through her.

She got into her car and hit the automatic locks, then started the engine and told herself she was just being paranoid. Easy to allow paranoia to become crippling fear and she wasn't about to let that happen.

Checking her rearview mirror, she backed out of the parking space. Another car engine roared to life as she drove toward the exit, and headlights followed her as she left the parking lot.

She pulled out of the lot and onto the street. The car pulled out right behind her. Luciano's was a busy restaurant; it wasn't unusual for several patrons to be arriving or leaving at the same time, she told herself.

She glanced in her rearview mirror and saw from the glow of the streetlights that the car behind her was a dark blue sedan. Just like the one she thought had followed her one time before.

In Kansas City there had to be hundreds of dark blue sedans, she reminded herself. Still a tiny wind of apprehension whispered through her.

At the next stoplight she made a left, even though the turn took her off route to the radio station. The car behind her also made a left turn.

There's no reason to panic. She swallowed hard against the lump that had jumped into her throat. What if the wreath hadn't come from Craig Vernon? What if the monster had come back?

She shook her head and tightened her grip on the steering wheel. Monsters didn't come back eighteen years later, did they? It didn't make sense that the T&B killer, who had attacked her so long ago, would suddenly reappear to finish the job he'd botched in the past.

Serial killers didn't just stop and take a vacation for years at a time. There had never been any news stories, any crime reports that would make her believe that the T&B killer was still at work.

He's dead or in prison, she told herself. He can't ever harm you again. If Craig Vernon wasn't responsible for the wreath, then hopefully what she had was a garden-variety nut who had crawled out of the woodwork from listening to her on the radio. Hopefully it was a harmless nut who only meant to frighten her.

She made a quick right turn. The car behind her turned as well. She could hear her heartbeat. *Bubup. Bubup. Bubup.* It beat too fast, aching in her chest. The first turn might have been a coincidence, but the odds of the car following her through the second turn were something more ominous.

She sped up and made another left turn. A gasp of relief escaped her as she peered in her rearview mirror and saw nobody. The relief was short-lived, as a moment later the car turned and fell in some distance behind her once again.

There would be people at the radio station. She needed to get there. Surely whoever was behind

Carla Cassidy

her wouldn't actually follow her into the lot and would be unable to follow her into the building.

She just needed to get someplace where there were other people, then she'd be able to breathe and the adrenaline surge inside her would dissipate.

It took only minutes for her to get to the radio station, and she sped through the lot, parked and left her car before the motor had stopped ticking. As she raced for the building she turned her head to look behind her and saw the dark sedan pulling into the lot.

"Daniel!" She yelled for the security guard as she ran. Panic squeezed her chest in a vise and she gasped for air. "Daniel!"

The uniformed guard stepped just outside the door and she nearly sobbed with relief. "Dr. Langford? Is everything all right?"

She pushed past him into the building and collapsed on the chair where he normally sat. "Following me . . . somebody was following me," she managed to gasp.

Daniel stared out the door, his broad shoulders rigid with tension. "I don't see anyone," he said.

"A blue car, dark blue sedan."

"It's leaving the lot now." Daniel turned and looked at her once again. His gaze seemed unusually intense. "You look frightened."

A hysterical bubble of laughter rose to her lips, but she swallowed against it. "I am. I was."

Was Daniel looking at her strangely or was she

seeing boogeymen in everyone? "I'll bet your heart is pounding right now."

What an odd thing to say, Jessica thought as she looked at the security guard. His words held no tone of sympathy and his gaze appeared more curious than concerned. Or maybe she was just being hypersensitive at the moment.

"Can I get you something? Maybe a glass of water?" he asked.

"A glass of water would be wonderful," she agreed, as Chris came hurrying down the hallway toward her.

"What's going on?" he asked as Daniel left to get her water.

"Nothing." The adrenaline ebbed away but the fear still lingered in the back of her throat. "Somebody was following me. With everything that's been going on, it frightened me."

"Everything that's been going on?" Chris frowned. "What are you talking about?"

Before she could answer Daniel reappeared with a bottle of water. She smiled gratefully and took it from him, hoping the cold liquid would help her swallow away the taste of fear.

Chris looked at his watch. "Come on, let's go into my office."

"Thank you, Daniel," she said as she stood from his chair. Her legs felt slightly wobbly.

"Just doing my job, Dr. Langford. Are you sure you're okay?"

"I'll be fine," she assured him, then together she

and Chris walked down the hallway and into Chris's office.

"Sit," he commanded, and pointed to the chair across from his desk. She cracked the lid on the bottle of water as she sat, then took a deep swallow of the water.

"Now, what's been going on? You called in the other night at the last minute and I didn't ask any questions, but now I'm asking."

Jessie recapped her bottle and gathered her thoughts before answering him. "I've had some strange phone calls, then the other night I was leaving the house to come here for work and there was a funeral wreath on my front porch."

"A funeral wreath?" Chris frowned and sank down at his desk. "What do you mean? Was it hanging on your door, or what?"

"It was on one of those metal stands, facing my door, and it had a black ribbon woven amid the flowers that said *death*." She fought back a shiver as she remembered the brown, dying flowers, the cloying scent that had filled the air and the way those silver letters had glittered in her porch light.

"Jesus, Jessie, why haven't you said anything?" Chris leaned forward, the concern on his boyish features sparking another dose of sick apprehension inside Jessie.

"There was nothing to say, nothing you can do," she replied.

"Then what are you doing about it? Do you think maybe it's a caller who's focused in on you?"

"I don't know, Chris. I don't know what to think. But I have a detective working on it to see what he can find out."

"Are you in danger?"

"I'm not sure how to answer that. I hope not. So far it's just been phone calls and the funeral wreath, and twice I thought a blue car was following me."

"That's what happened tonight? You thought you were being followed?"

"I didn't just think it; I know I was being followed," she replied. "I had dinner with Larry at Luciano's, and when I left there I noticed the car behind me. I made a dozen turns between the restaurant and here and the car stayed behind me the whole way."

"Is there anything I can do?" Chris asked.

"No. We have the name of somebody we think might be responsible and the detective is checking it out for me."

Chris looked at his watch again. Always the producer, keeping an eye on the bottom line. "You're set to go on in fifteen minutes. You okay to do this tonight?" Even though he asked it as a question, she knew he'd totally freak if she actually said no.

"Of course." She stood and drew several deep, steadying breaths. "I'm fine. Let's do it."

His look of relief was almost laughable. Minutes later Jessie was in the studio, earphones in place and ready to take her first call of the evening.

As she waited she once again told herself that none of what was happening now was related to her past. She'd seen a lot of patients who dealt with post-traumatic stress and knew the dangers of falling into the fear of the past.

She thought about calling Jake but decided against it. She was fine now and had no information that could help him find out who had been following her. He was in the middle of a difficult murder investigation and didn't need another hysterical call from her.

She needed to keep calm, keep rational, something difficult to do when the heart pounded at an unnatural rhythm, when the adrenaline surged to fight-or-flight proportions and when natural instincts were silenced by a full blowout of terror.

By the time she'd taken her third phone call of the night she was calm and back in control. Helping others with their fears had always worked as a panacea against her own. She was in her element when she was listening to people in emotional pain and trying to help them.

Focused on others, she had no time, no energy to look inside herself. The calls were the usual; fear of bugs, of heights and getting on an airplane.

People loved to talk about fear. It was a universal emotion. There were few people in the world who hadn't tasted the metallic tang of apprehension, felt the quiver of sharp panic inside their gut, experienced the cold sweat of exploding terror.

Most of the time what people feared was never fully realized. The person afraid of heights never fell or jumped from a high distance, the fear of flying rarely resulted in a plane crash, and the person afraid of bugs was never assaulted or harmed by one.

She'd read one time that if you were experiencing fear, then that which you feared wasn't happening at that moment. The fear of what if was what most people dealt with on a regular basis.

Eighteen years ago if somebody would have expressed to Jessie the fear of being a serial killer's victim, she would have dismissed the fear as irrational. But that was before she'd been standing at the bus stop, waiting for a friend to pick her up on a beautiful spring evening. That was before somebody had hit her from behind, slapped duct tape across her eyes and mouth and stuffed her into the trunk of a car.

Jessie didn't dismiss anyone's fear anymore, no matter how illogical or irrational the fear might be. For she knew that in the blink of an eye, on the faint breeze of a spring night, danger could ride into a life and change it forever.

Jake sat in the war room alone, too wound up to go home and go to bed yet too tired to do anything other than sit and think.

The rest of his team had called it a night a half an hour ago. He remained, seated at the table where the latest crime-scene photos were strewn across the wooden tabletop.

The kiss he'd shared with Jessica had been interrupted by the news that another victim had been found. The body of Tracy Unger had been discovered in a ditch on the grounds of a neighborhood park. A couple of teenagers had stumbled across the body when they'd gone to the park for a late-night rendezvous.

Just like the others, she'd been raped and stabbed and left with a plastic lily on her chest. The lily. He frowned. Was it left on the victims in an act of contrition? Or celebration? If he could figure out what the lily meant, then maybe he could figure out something about the killer.

They were still awaiting the results of the autopsy, but he didn't expect any surprises. The killer was remarkably organized, leaving behind no trace evidence that might lead to an arrest. He apparently wore a condom, as no semen was found, although the women displayed evidence of brutal violation.

No trace evidence. No DNA. The place each victim had been found was nothing but a dump site. They didn't have any idea where the women were being raped and stabbed, but those acts were accomplished somewhere other than where the bodies were dumped.

He sighed and raked a hand across his whisker-stubbled jaw. Staring at the map of Kansas City that was pinned to the bulletin board, he tried to figure out some pattern, something that would help them catch the person responsible.

Red pins in the map identified each of the four dump sites. Although they were all north of the

Missouri River in the Kansas City North area, there seemed to be no distinctive pattern.

There were no witnesses, nobody who saw anything suspicious on the night the bodies were dumped. The killer was either incredibly lucky or incredibly bright.

They had spent the day examining Tracy Unger's life in an effort to understand her death. Her boyfriend had been interviewed, and although his alibi was weak, he'd been asleep at the time of her death. At this time he was not on a suspect list.

They'd spoken to everyone at the truck stop where Tracy worked, tried to trace her footsteps for the week before she'd been killed, but all their efforts had yielded nothing.

He needed to go home. Get a good night's sleep and start fresh in the morning. As he placed the crime-scene photos back in the file where they belonged, he ran across the note he'd been given earlier in the evening.

He'd had no time to check into the Craig Vernon deal for Jessie, so he'd asked a buddy on the force to make some inquiries. He now knew it wasn't Vernon who'd left the wreath on Jessie's front porch. All he needed to do was break the news to Jessie.

He checked his watch. It was ten to midnight. She'd be at the radio station, finishing up her show. He'd meant to call her earlier, but with everything going on the time had gotten away from him.

She'd be waiting for the information. He dialed

her cell phone number and got her voice mail. "Jessie, it's me. I know you're in the middle of your show, but when you finish up could you give me a call on my cell? I have some information for you."

He clicked off and leaned back in his chair, his gaze captured by the crime-scene photos pinned to the bulletin board next to the city map.

Four dead women stared back at him.

Four in less than a month. They had no pattern to study, no way to know if the killer was on an accelerated path of decompression or if this was his natural rhythm of killing.

Jake hoped he was decompressing, disintegrating to the point where mistakes would be made, evidence would be left behind. They had come to the conclusion that the victims were chosen at random, picked for reasons known only by the killer. That made things more difficult.

He thought about getting up and getting another cup of coffee, but rejected the idea. He'd drunk enough coffee over the past twenty-four hours to keep him on a caffeine high for months.

Go home, a little voice whispered inside his head. Go home to your bed. Go home and put this all behind you for the rest of the night.

But it was getting more and more difficult to go to bed at night and forget the victims, forget that there was a killer who would strike again.

He was becoming obsessed, his thoughts filled with the killer and the victims, his dreams haunted by the same. He envied the cops who could turn it on and shut it off.

His partner, Monica, was like that. She'd often told him that when she left the station she left the crimes behind. The victims never came home with her, but they always did with Jake.

He jumped as his cell phone rang. Looking at the caller ID he recognized Jessie's cell number. "Hi, Jessie," he answered.

"I got your message. I just now finished up with the show."

"How did it go?" The sound of her voice sent the first wave of relaxation through him that he'd felt all day.

"The usual—nice people who just needed to talk to somebody. What are you still doing at the police station? Don't detectives get to sleep?"

"Only every other day or so."

He hated to tell her. He knew she was hoping that the person who had called her, the person who had left the wreath on her doorstep, had been Craig. The known was so much less frightening than the unknown.

"Jessie, I know you've been waiting to hear what I've been able to find out about Craig Vernon."

There was a long pause. "And what did you find out?" Her voice was low and steady, but the pause had spoken volumes.

"Craig Vernon went to prison six months ago for beating the hell out of his girlfriend. He's serving a two-year sentence."

"Oh." Again there was a heavy, thick silence. "I don't suppose he managed to escape for a day or two." She forced a laugh, but it sounded strained, almost painful.

"Afraid not. Jessie, are you all right?"

"No . . . yes. I'm fine."

She didn't sound fine. Her voice held the thick press of emotion that somehow stabbed at his heart. He told himself he didn't know this woman, couldn't know what she was feeling at the moment, but to him it felt like fear. He couldn't stand the thought of Jessie afraid.

"Has something else happened?" he asked. "Is there something you aren't telling me?"

"No." The word was drawn out so that it was almost two syllables.

Something was on her mind. "Jessie, we need to talk. Why don't I meet you at your house in fifteen minutes or so?"

"It's late, Jake." Although it was a protest, it was a weak one.

"I know, and I promise I won't stay long."

"All right. Don't knock—it might wake up Charlie and Maria. I'll just watch for you and let you in when you get there."

Ten minutes later Jake was in his car and headed toward Jessie's place. It was crazy. He hardly knew her, had only shared one dinner, one kiss with her, but he thought he'd heard some kind of need in her voice. And he wanted to be there for her.

Chapter 14

It wasn't Craig Vernon. It wasn't Craig Vernon. The words played and replayed in Jessie's head as she drove home from the station.

Thankfully no cars followed her as she made her way home. She kept an eye on the rearview mirror but saw nothing that caused her any apprehension.

Not that she didn't have apprehension. At the moment it screamed through her body. Craig Vernon was in prison. He hadn't made the phone calls to her house. He hadn't left the wreath on her porch.

So who was responsible? If it wasn't about Maria and Craig, then it must be about Jessie and who? Who would do such a thing and why?

Her apprehension didn't ebb as she pulled into her garage. She'd been half afraid that Jake would tell her exactly what he had, but she hadn't allowed herself to think about it.

She hadn't wanted Jake to come over, and she'd desperately wanted him to come. For the first time in a very long time she felt the need to talk to somebody. Not Larry, not Maria, but Jake.

She knew instinctively that he would be the voice of sanity in the chaos that reigned in her head at the moment. He would be able to cut through the fear with calm, rational thinking and assure her that nothing bad was going to happen.

The house was quiet when she entered the kitchen. Sometimes Maria waited up for her and sometimes she went on to bed.

Jessie was glad that tonight Maria was in bed, that she didn't have to explain why Jake was coming over at this time of night. She couldn't explain. She wasn't sure she could explain her need to see him.

The first thing she did was make a pot of coffee. As it dripped into the glass carafe she tried to decide if she would tell Jake about her past tonight.

The only way she'd get her fear out of her head was to tell him everything, let him tell her that the past was gone and could no longer harm her. But if she told him, then he would see her without the sheen of her professional aura. He'd see her as a victim.

"Only if you let him see you that way," she muttered aloud. She wasn't a victim; she was a survivor, and she refused to become a victim to her own fear.

Before the coffee was finished being made she left the kitchen and went to the front door to watch for him to arrive. She and Jake didn't have enough of a relationship for her to know what kind of a man he was, to know how he might react to her tale of rape and attempted murder.

"Play it by ear," she whispered as she saw his headlights fill the driveway.

The sight of his broad shoulders, his confident gait as he approached the door filled her with a calm that hadn't been present since he'd told her the news about Craig.

She opened the door and forced a smile. "Hi."

"Hi, yourself." He stepped through the doorway and just past her. She closed the door, locked it behind him, then led him into the kitchen, where she gestured him to one of the chairs at the table.

He ignored the gesture and instead stepped close to her, so close their bodies nearly touched and she could see the silver flecks that sparked in his dark eyes. "You sounded weird on the phone. . . . Scared."

She wanted to step back. She wanted to break his intense eye contact, but she couldn't. "I am." The words whispered from her, not the words she'd intended to say at all. To her horror her vision blurred as tears filled her eyes.

"Hey, it's okay." He pulled her into his arms, and she went willingly. She hadn't realized how tightly she'd been wound until this moment. She hadn't realized how badly she'd needed to be held until his arms wrapped around her and held her tight.

She leaned her head into the front of his shirt, unable to stop the flood of tears that had begun to flow. "Shh, it's all right," his low voice soothed as his hands rubbed up and down her back.

Jessie had never been much for crying and the tears lasted only a moment, but she lingered in his arms, her face still buried in the shirt that smelled of fabric softener and his cologne.

It smelled good. Too good. She stepped back from him, embarrassed by her tears, embarrassed by the show of weakness. "I'm sorry, I don't know what's wrong with me." She laughed self-consciously. "Please sit down and let me get you a cup of coffee."

He hesitated, his gaze still so intense she felt as if he could see into her heart, see into her soul. She breathed a sigh of relief as he finally moved toward the table and sank into one of the chairs.

She busied herself pouring them each a cup of coffee, then set the mugs on the table and joined him there. "I feel so foolish. You should be home in bed, not sitting here at my table."

"At the moment I'm exactly where I want to be," he replied. He leaned forward, ignoring the mug in front of him. "Jessie, I know the appearance of that wreath on your doorstep freaked you out, but the odds are good that it's probably just a stunt intended to frighten you and nothing more will come from it."

"Logically I know that." She wrapped her fingers around the warmth of the coffee mug. He looked tired. The lines around his eyes were deeper than they'd been the night before, and she felt guilty about keeping him from his bed.

"So tell me about your illogical thoughts," he said.

She thought he might be teasing her, but could tell by his expression that he was dead serious. She sighed and chewed thoughtfully on her bottom lip, trying to decide what and how much to tell him.

"I specialize in fear. I've studied it for years, tried to find ways to help ease it in other people, but for the last week or so I can't seem to get a handle on my own."

"Because of the wreath?"

"It started with the phone calls and peaked with the wreath." She laced her fingers together on the top of the table, aware that they trembled slightly. "Whenever a patient who is suffering from some kind of fear comes to see me, I have them answer some questions."

"Like what?"

"Like, What is the danger? Is it from the present or the past? Is it real fear or imagined? Things like that. When you get messages of fear, like suspicion, apprehension and hunches, they need to be decoded, so to speak." She felt herself relaxing somewhat as she spoke about the work she did. "It's my job to help the patient decode their feelings and identify the root cause of their fear, but I seem to be sadly lacking when it comes to doing the same for myself."

"Okay, then let me help you gain some objectivity." His voice was soft, supportive, and he reached across the table and covered her interlocked fingers with his big, warm hand. "We can't know for sure that the phone calls were connected to the wreath.

Those calls might have just been the work of bored teenagers."

She nodded, understanding that he was approaching the situation with the logic and rational thought of a cop.

"The wreath was obviously meant to frighten you, and because of what you do it's very possible it's somebody who called your show or has seen you for therapy and didn't like what you told them." He offered her a half-smile. "You know, frighten the fear expert. What a power trip."

"I think somebody has been following me too."

His dark brows raised and the half-smile fell from his lips. "What do you mean?"

She told him about the two times she'd thought the dark blue car had followed her. "Why didn't you call me?" he asked. "You should be making incident reports of these kinds of things so we have it all on record."

"I didn't think about it."

"But the car didn't try to force you off the road or drive aggressively toward you in any way?"

"No." She shook her head. "It just stayed behind me."

"And you didn't get the license plate number?"

Damn. Why hadn't she thought of that? With the plate number Jake could have probably solved the entire mess. "I just freaked. I wasn't thinking rationally."

He squeezed her hands. "The next time you

think somebody is following you, get the plate number and I'll get to the bottom of it."

It was amazing how much better she felt just talking to him. She was certain he was right, that somehow she'd managed to piss off a caller at the station or one of her patients in her private practice, and now they were trying to frighten her.

This made so much more sense than believing the man who'd nearly killed her eighteen years ago had suddenly reappeared to finish the job. She'd allowed her past to color the present and instill in her irrational fears.

Jake leaned back once again, his hand leaving hers. "You know, these kinds of things often happen to people who are in the public eye. It's part of the price you pay for being famous and having a successful radio show."

"I'm not famous enough for this kind of thing," she protested with a weak laugh.

"Anything happens that unsettles you, anything that happens that makes you feel at risk, you call me. Or you go down to the station and demand to make a report. Hopefully whoever is responsible is just your ordinary garden-variety nut and they'll grow tired of the game or find another target to harass."

"I hope you're right." Once again she noticed the deep lines that cut out from his eyes, the strain that showed around his mouth. "I heard another body was found late last night."

"Yeah." He grimaced, his lips a thin slash. "This one has us all chasing our tails."

"Go home, Jake. You look exhausted."

He offered a tired smile and swiped his hand through his unruly hair. "I am pretty beat." He pushed back from the table. "Are you sure you're okay? I don't want you to go to bed scared."

It would be so easy to allow this man into my heart, she thought. Despite the fact that he was dealing with a murderer running amok in the city, in spite of his obvious exhaustion, he'd run to her when she'd needed somebody.

"I'm fine," she assured him. "It helped to just talk." She stood as he did and together they walked toward her front door.

He stopped at the front door and turned back to face her. "Look, just because I don't think you really have anything to worry about doesn't mean I don't want you to remain vigilant. You probably know the drill—keep an eye on your surroundings, listen to your instinct and if you feel threatened get someplace safe."

"I will. Thank you, Jake."

He smiled. "For what? All I did was show up for a few minutes."

"I guess that's all that was necessary."

"Look, if I can see my way clear by then, why don't we get the kids together for a barbecue or something on Saturday afternoon? I haven't forgotten I promised Charlie that Jimmy could show him some tricks on that video game."

Say no. Stop it all right now, an inner voice whispered to her. Shut up, she mentally commanded. "Why don't you and Jimmy come here? I'll take care of the meal. You have enough on your mind."

"Are you sure? I don't mind throwing together something for the grill."

"I'm positive. Why don't we say around four, and if you see you can't make it just call me."

His eyes glinted with a look that had nothing to do with tiredness, nothing to do with stress. "Trust me, I'll do everything in my power to be here." Before she could guess his intent, he leaned forward and kissed her.

Even though it was a soft, gentle kiss it shimmered with the promise of something deeper, something richer, and she was both grateful yet disappointed when he broke the kiss and stepped back from her. "Good night, Jessie."

"'Night, Jake."

She locked up after him, then peered through the small window in the door until his headlights had disappeared down the street.

It wasn't until she returned to the kitchen to clean up that she realized neither of them had touched their coffee.

And she hadn't told him about her past.

Chapter 15

Charlie was beside himself with excitement. He nearly danced out of his seat belt as Jessie drove him to the nearest pet store. For Charlie, today wasn't just turtle-buying day, it was also the day to meet a new friend and find out the secrets of the *Highway Bandit* video game.

Jessie tried not to be excited about the barbecue and spending more time with Jake. She told herself that this afternoon was about Charlie and Jimmy. A simple afternoon for the kids, not for the grown-ups.

At least with Charlie and Jimmy there she didn't have to worry about her relationship with Jake deepening. She didn't have to fear him touching her, kissing her and forcing her to call a halt to love-making she'd like nothing more than to experience.

"Mom, when I go to Dad's on the weekends, you've got to promise me that you'll feed Tommy."

The turtle's name had changed at least a hundred times in the past week, but as of this morning

Charlie had announced that it would be Tommy the turtle. "Of course I'll feed Tommy," she assured him.

"And you got to love him," Charlie exclaimed. "He's gonna be a new member of our family."

How hard could it be to love a turtle, Jessie thought. At least a turtle wouldn't pee on her carpet or chew on her slippers. "I'm sure I'll love Tommy."

Charlie settled back in his seat, satisfied for the moment. Jessie figured she'd better enjoy the turtle, for she had a feeling a peeing, chewing, barking kind of pet was next in line on Charlie's wish list. He'd already mentioned a couple of times that it was too bad turtles couldn't play fetch and give sloppy kisses.

"There it is! There's Pete's Pets." Charlie pointed to the strip mall on the right. His entire body wiggled as she pulled into a parking space in front of the store.

"Now, remember, we're here for a turtle," she reminded him as she shut off the car engine. "We can look at everything in the store, but we're not taking home anything but a turtle."

"Deal," he agreed. He was out of the car and waiting impatiently on the sidewalk before Jessie could grab her purse off the seat.

As she got out of her car she smiled at him, and the smile he returned to her filled her heart with love. He's enough, she told herself. I don't need a man in my life. Watching Charlie grow and become the kind of man she wanted could be enough if it had to be.

Together mother and son entered the exotic world of Pete's Pets, a world of dogs and cats, lizards and snakes, bunnies and gerbils. And turtles.

Jessie followed her son from display to display, loving the enraptured look on his face as he watched the fish swimming, the hamsters racing around their cages and the dogs crying for attention.

She wasn't sure how long they'd been in the store when she glanced out the large picture window and saw a man standing just outside the shop. He faced away from the store, but there was something familiar about his size and shape.

It could be anyone. . . . A man waiting for his wife who was in the dress shop next door, a walker who had chosen that particular place to stop and catch his breath. Yes, it could be anyone standing there for any number of innocent reasons, but a tiny alarm went off in her head.

"Mom, come over and look at the snakes again." Charlie grabbed her hand and tugged.

"You go ahead. I'll be over there in just a second," she replied, not taking her gaze off the man. Turn around, she mentally commanded. Turn around and let me see who you are.

As Charlie ran off toward the snake display, the man outside glanced toward the shop and Jessie's breath caught in her throat. Mark Smith. He jerked his head back around and took off walking away from the store.

Was it he who had been following her? Did he drive a dark blue sedan? Mark Smith. She'd thought some of his questions to her had been intrusive, far too personal for the doctor-patient relationship.

He disappeared from her sight and she hurried toward the snake display to find Charlie, her thoughts whirling with a dizzying speed.

Somehow the idea that Mark Smith was her stalker, the caller in the middle of the night, the blue sedan following her around the city, soothed her deepest, darkest fears. Putting a face on the fear went a long way toward alleviating it.

She'd sensed a simmering anger in Smith, along with some obvious issues concerning the death of his brother. It was possible he'd turned his grief and maybe some guilt outward and she had become a target for those unresolved issues.

If he came back to the office they could work on those issues together. It had been obvious by the way Mark had reacted when he'd seen her looking at him that he hadn't wanted her to notice him. Suspicious behavior that sent a ridiculous wave of relief through her.

For the first time in two weeks she felt as if a load had been lifted from her shoulders. She could deal with Mark Smith. What she couldn't deal with was a terror from her past coming back to haunt her.

"What do you say we pick out Tommy and head

home?" she said to Charlie. "We've got new friends coming this afternoon, and I still need to make the potato salad."

Thirty minutes later they were back in the car, this time with Charlie as the proud owner of a turtle no bigger than his finger and enough food to keep the turtle alive for the next year. He balanced the glass bowl that contained the turtle carefully in his lap, occassionally looking at Jessie to offer her a happy smile.

Happy. That's what she felt at the moment. Happiness without the taint of any other negative emotion. It had been weeks since she'd felt this way and she embraced it, knowing how fleeting sheer happiness could be.

Early afternoon came and went with a flurry of activity. Jessie made potato salad while Maria made her famous baked bean casserole. They pressed out hamburger patties, cut up tomatoes and onions and arranged pickles in a cut-glass dish that had once belonged to Jessie's mom.

At three thirty Jessie raced into her bedroom to take a quick shower and dress for the barbecue. She wondered how Jimmy and Charlie would get along. The age difference between an almost-seven-year-old and a twelve-year-old could be enormous.

If they don't get along, it doesn't matter, she told herself as she stepped beneath the hot spray of the shower. It's just one barbecue, one afternoon, not a lifetime commitment.

The day was once again unusually warm. She

stood in her underpants and bra and stared into her closet. As she tried to decide what to wear, her hand absently rubbed the scars that over the years had become as much a part of her as her eye color.

She decided on a casual light blue sundress. It took her only minutes to step into a pair of white sandals and add small white hoop earrings. She'd just spritzed herself with perfume when the doorbell rang.

Jake looked wonderful in a short-sleeved white sports shirt tucked into the waist of a pair of worn jeans. He looked far more rested than he had the last time she'd seen him, and she couldn't help the way her heart leapt at the sight of him.

Jimmy was a miniature of his father, dark-haired, dark-eyed and with the same features. He was a good-looking kid who would grow up to be a handsome man. He was clad in normal kid attire, a pair of jeans and a T-shirt advertising a brand of athletic wear.

"Jessie, this is my son, Jimmy," Jake said, making the introductions. "Jimmy, this is Dr. Langford."

Jessie held up a hand. "Please, call me Jessie." She smiled at the boy, who returned her smile with a shy one of his own. At that moment Charlie joined them and Jessie introduced the two boys to each other.

As the boys disappeared down the hallway toward Charlie's bedroom Jessie and Jake headed for the kitchen. The moment they entered the room,

Jake twirled her into his arms and planted a kiss on her lips.

"Jake," she protested in a whisper, although the brief kiss caused her blood to heat in her veins.

He laughed and released her. "You look gorgeous, and I couldn't help myself."

A blush warmed her cheeks and she slapped him playfully on the chest. "Well, try to contain yourself. There are minors around."

"I'll try, but it's going to be difficult. If you don't want to drive a man wild, then you should never wear blue." He smiled at her, a flirting, gorgeous smile.

"Come on." She grabbed him by the arm and led him toward the back door. "With all that pent-up energy you should be great at flipping hamburgers on the grill."

"Lead me to the fire. I'm already feeling the heat." He winked at her and she laughed. This was a side of him she hadn't seen much of before, a fun-loving side that was intensely appealing.

Just go with it, Jessie, she told herself. For once in your life don't think too much, don't analyze. Just enjoy the day with this man.

The kid was a baby. Charlie had already shown Jimmy his DVDs, mostly Disney movies, and a leaf collection and his dumb turtle that didn't do anything but sleep on a rock in a glass bowl.

The kid was lame. Jimmy hadn't wanted to come, but he knew it was important to his dad. For the first time in a long time his dad had been humming while he got dressed and he'd splashed on cologne not once, but twice before they left the house.

Charlie's mom seemed all right. When she smiled her eyes smiled too. Jimmy's mom's eyes had never smiled. Sometimes he felt bad because he didn't really miss his mom. And sometimes he got mad at her for leaving because it had messed up so many things.

Right after his mom had left, Jimmy stopped hanging out with his friends. They all thought it was totally weird that she'd left and hadn't taken Jimmy with her. He'd also stopped having friends come to the house because he was embarrassed that his dad slept on the sofa and he had an old-woman babysitter to watch over him.

"You got a night-light in your room. What's the matter, you scared of the dark?" Jimmy asked.

"Nah, but my mom likes it to be on so she can look in my room in the night and see that I'm okay."

A swift burst of envy kicked Jimmy in the gut. Must be nice, he thought. To have a mom who wants to check on you in the middle of the night. Jimmy's mom would put him to bed and tell him not to bother her the rest of the night.

"You wanna play catch or go outside?" Charlie asked eagerly. "Or we could play some video games. Your dad said that you're real good at *Highway Bandit*."

The kid might be lame, but he was trying real hard to be friends. He was kinda cute, with his freckled face and blue eyes. Jimmy had always wondered what it would be like to have a little brother, somebody to watch over and teach the ways of life.

Maybe just for today he could pretend Charlie was his little brother. It would make his dad happy if Jimmy was nice to the kid. Jimmy wanted to see his dad happy. There was nobody on the face of the earth he loved more than his dad, even though he sometimes got so mad at him he wanted to spit in his face.

"My dad told me you're having trouble with the game," Jimmy said.

"I can't get past the second level."

"Come on, kid." Jimmy threw an arm around Charlie's slender shoulders. "I'll show you how to play the game."

Charlie smiled with excitement. "Thanks, Jimmy. I think you're cool."

Yeah, the kid was definitely lame and needed some lessons in cool himself. At least for today that was Jimmy's job.

Jessie checked on the kids, who were planted in front of the television with game controls in hand, then returned to the back porch where Jake was cooking burgers.

He smiled and picked up his beer bottle as she stepped back outside. "Almost done," he said.

She sat at the glass-topped table and took a sip of her wine cooler. "I haven't had a chance to tell you, but I think I've solved the mystery of who might be stalking me."

"Really?" His dark brows danced upward as he set down the tongs. "Who?"

"A patient of mine. I can't tell you his name because of the doctor-client relationship." She told him about seeing her patient outside the pet store and how that had gotten her thinking that he was a strong possibility for who was giving her trouble.

"Is he dangerous?" The light shining in Jake's eyes had darkened.

Jessie hesitated a moment before replying, thinking of what little she knew about Mark Smith. "I can't be positive, but I don't think so. I'm just going on gut instinct. I haven't seen him enough times to be certain."

Jake was silent for a long moment. He took a drink of his beer, his gaze not leaving her. "You know you have a responsibility to report any patient who you think might be a danger to anyone else," he said as he lowered his bottle.

"I know," she replied easily. "And if I was certain this man was a danger, then I'd speak up. As it stands now, he's just a potential suspect."

He grinned at her. "You're starting to sound like a cop."

"That's what I get for hanging around one," she said with a laugh, then sobered. "Seriously, Jake, I feel a little better knowing that it might be this patient, and if I think he's becoming dangerous, I won't hesitate to tell you."

He looped an arm around her shoulders. "Make sure you do. I can't have anything happening to my girl." He picked up the spatula once again and returned to the grill to check on the burgers.

"My girl." His words resonated in her for the remainder of the afternoon. It was easy to entertain the fantasy that she was his girl as they all shared the meal, laughing with and teasing each other.

Jimmy seemed like a nice kid, and it was obvious Charlie had developed a severe case of hero worship. Charlie, who never ate pickles, ate three because that's how many Jimmy ate.

Although Jake had said he and his son were experiencing some tension, there was none evident as they all finished eating, then played a game of gin rummy at the kitchen table.

This is what it could be like, she thought as the kids returned to the video game and Jake helped her clean up the last of the dishes. They had sent Maria in to sit with the kids, telling her they'd take care of the last of the mess.

The warmth and laughter of family—it was what she missed most since her divorce. Well, maybe not most. As she and Jake stood side by side at the sink, she tried to ignore the heavenly feel of his body warmth radiating toward her, the evocative way he gazed at her, the scent of his masculine cologne that wrapped around her and made her want to seek the source.

When he'd dried the last casserole dish and she'd placed it in the cabinet where it belonged, she started for the living room, but gasped as he grabbed her arm and whirled her around to face him. He pulled her into his arms with a low growl.

"Jake." She laughed and attempted to get free, but he held tight. "The kids . . ."

"Are in the middle of a video game, and nothing short of a nuclear blast will make them move from their current positions."

He was right. She knew he was right and she relaxed, enjoying the moment of being in his arms. "I need to kiss you, Jessie," he said softly. "I've needed to kiss you all afternoon."

"Talk, talk, talk. Can't a girl get a little action around here?"

She gasped as his lips crashed down on hers, lips filled with fire and intent. She opened her mouth beneath his, for a moment wanting to go wherever he wanted to take her.

Jake didn't just kiss with his lips; he kissed with his tongue and with the arms that pulled her closer and closer, so close she could feel his arousal. His hands moved down her back, to her waist, then cupped her buttocks.

It would be so easy to allow her desire for this man to sweep her away, to silence the doubts, the fears that she had of any new relationship.

But as his hands moved from her buttocks, back to her waist, his fingers threatened to splay across her lower abdomen.

She broke the kiss and jerked back from him, afraid that he might feel the ridge of her scars beneath the lightweight sundress. And afraid that if she remained another minute in his arms she'd never want to leave them.

His eyes were glazed as he stared at her. "You know I want you, Jessie." His voice was low, husky with obvious desire.

She wanted him too. But it wasn't going to happen. "Jake." She said his name, but nothing else followed.

He jammed his hands into his jeans pockets. "I'm rushing you. I'm sorry. It's just that it's been a hell of a long time since I've felt this way about anyone. But I know now isn't the time or the place to talk about it." Once again he placed an arm around her shoulder. "Come on, let's see how the munchkins are doing."

It was almost ten that night when Jake and Jimmy left and Jessie tucked Charlie into bed. By the night-light burning in the socket next to his bed she saw that her son's face shone with tired happiness.

"Jimmy said maybe sometime we could go over to his house and he'd show me how to throw a curve ball," Charlie said. "And he's got a book about animals in Africa and he said I could have it cause he's already read it."

"So you liked Jimmy," she said, stating the obvious.

"Yeah, he's cool." Charlie frowned. "He doesn't have a mom. His mom ran away from home."

"That must make him sad."

"He said it didn't matter that much, that she wasn't that good of a mom anyway." Charlie gazed up at his mother with half-closed, sleepy eyes. "You'd never run away, would you?"

She leaned down and kissed his sweet cheek. "No, honey. I would never, ever in a million years run away. You're stuck with me."

"That's what I told Jimmy." Charlie yawned, the wide, openmouthed yawn of a child. "And I told him you were a good enough mom I could share you with him."

Jessie's heart expanded with love for the son who was willing to share his mom with a new friend. "'Night, Charlie," she said softly, as his eyelids drifted closed. There was no reply, and she knew he had fallen asleep.

"It was a nice day," Maria said, as Jessie joined her in the living room.

"It was," she agreed.

"Detective Jake and his son are good people." Maria had been intensely relieved to discover that the man who had terrorized her for so many years was now in prison. "What kind of a mother leaves her son?"

Jessie flopped down on the sofa next to Maria. "Charlie told you about Jimmy's mother?"

"I overheard the two boys talking." Maria's frown deepened. "That Jimmy, he loves his daddy, but he needs a mama in his life. I saw the way he watched you whenever you touched Charlie in any way. That boy had a hunger in his eyes." She slid a sly glance at Jessie. "And I won't even talk about the hunger I saw in his daddy's eyes whenever he looked at you."

A blush warmed Jessie's cheeks. "Good, let's not talk about that."

But an hour later as Jessie lay in her bed, she thought about it. She tried to tell herself that her attraction to Jake was nothing more than a physical one, but she knew she was fooling herself.

She loved the way his eyes glinted when he was teasing. She liked the dark intensity that possessed them when he was serious. She liked the way he thought and the fact that she trusted him with her thoughts.

He wasn't just good with his own son; he'd been good with hers, showing no impatience when Charlie had rambled on about his turtle at the dinner table.

It would have been easier if he'd been crappy with Charlie. She would never allow herself to get close to any man who wasn't good with kids. But it had been obvious that Jake loved his son and that his heart was open to caring about another little boy.

She punched her pillow with her hand and rolled over on her back to stare at the shadows dancing on her ceiling. Jake hadn't had to remind her of her duty as a professional to contact the authorities if she thought a patient was a danger to himself or others.

She believed Mark Smith was the person who had made the calls to her, who had left the wreath on her doorstep and who had followed her in his car, but her gut instinct still told her the man wasn't violent.

If he'd wanted to harm her he could have on either of the two appointments he'd made in her office. He could have waited for her to leave the security of the office and accosted her in the parking lot.

She hoped he came back into the office. She wanted to see if she could get him to talk about what might have happened to make her a target for him. She wanted to get a better handle on what forces were driving him. First thing Monday morning she'd try to do a little detective work of her own and see what she could find out about Mark Smith.

Now, if she could just figure out what she was going to do about Jake.

Chapter 16

Jessie was seated at the kitchen table, drinking her morning cup of coffee when a soft knock sounded at her front door. Maria had already left for early services at the church she attended, and Charlie was still in bed.

As she went to answer the door she pulled the belt of her robe more tightly around her. Peering out the tiny door window she saw the top of a familiar blond head. Kayla.

She opened the door and smiled at her neighbor. "You must not have had a good time last night, since you're up so early this morning."

"Ugh, don't remind me about last night," Kayla said as she walked past Jessie and into the kitchen. She plopped the folded morning paper on the table and sat while Jessie poured her a cup of coffee.

"Picture this," Kayla said once they were both seated. "I'm looking hot in a new little leather miniskirt and a blouse that makes my boobs look young again. This young man comes up and asks me to dance, so we hit the dance floor together. The kid was so sexy, by the time we finished the dance I was burning with lust. Then he dropped the bombshell that destroyed my evening. He wanted to set me up with his newly divorced father. His father, for Christ's sake!"

Jessie laughed as Kayla scowled. "I hope the police aren't looking for you for a homicide."

"No, I showed an enormous amount of restraint and told him that I wasn't interested in his father, but if he had a younger brother I'd be more than happy to meet him. But apparently I'm not the one at this table having an exciting life."

"What are you talking about?" Jessie asked, although she assumed Kayla might have seen Jake and Jimmy in the backyard the day before.

"I guess you haven't had a chance to glance through the paper this morning."

"Not yet. Why?" Now she had Jessie confused.

Kayla moved her coffee cup aside and opened the morning paper. "You made page two."

"What?" Jessie got up and moved to stand just behind where Kayla sat so she could see the paper over Kayla's shoulder. Kayla pointed a perfectly manicured fingernail at the headline: LOCAL RADIO PERSONALITY STALKED.

"Oh, my God." Jessie grabbed the paper from in front of Kayla to read the article.

Dr. Jessica Langford, local psychiatrist and host of the late night radio show *Are You Afraid of the*

Dark?, is being stalked by an unknown assailant. Sources close to the psychiatrist indicate that the doctor has not only been receiving disturbing phone calls, but most recently found a funeral wreath on her front porch.

The article went on to say that Jessie specialized in fears and phobias and that she encouraged the person responsible for the incidents to call her radio show so she could talk to them about their issues.

"What the hell?" Jessie threw the paper across the room, both angry and appalled.

"Why didn't you tell me you had a stalker?" Kayla asked.

"Because that's not something you advertise," Jessie replied.

"Gee, why can't I get a stalker? Maybe mine would be the man of my dreams."

"That's not funny, Kayla." Jessie sat in her chair, a knot in her chest that was a mixture of anger and concern.

"Well, somebody advertised it for you," Kayla observed.

"Yes, and I intend to find out who is responsible for that. Nobody even called me to see if the story was true."

"I guess it was enough for the reporter to talk to 'sources close to the psychiatrist.'"

Jessie had no idea what kind of ramifications the story might hold, except she could guess that every

nut in the Kansas City area would be calling her
show in the next couple of days.

The phone rang and Jessie jumped up to answer
it, noting on the caller ID box that it was Jake.

"You want to tell me what's going on?" he said
without so much as a hello. "I mean, was this all
just some sort of publicity stunt to get your show
picked up for syndication?"

He was pissed. She'd never heard his voice so
harsh, so cold. "Jake," she began, but he cut her off.

"If I find out you've wasted my time, that you
were involved in leaving the wreath on your own
door just to get a dose of publicity, I'll bring you up
on charges so fast your head will spin."

"Now, just a damn minute." Jessie's anger exploded. "How dare you even accuse me of such a
thing? I would like to think that you know me better than that, but I guess not."

As she paused to catch her breath there was a
long, tension-filled silence. "We need to talk," he finally said. "Not over the phone, but in person. I'm
down at the station. Can you meet me here?"

Her first reaction was to hell with him. How dare
he think she could have anything to do with this
mess? "I can't come there for another hour or so,"
she heard herself explaining. "Maria has gone to
church, and I can't leave Charlie here by himself."

"I can hang around until Maria gets home,"
Kayla said, hearing only Jessie's side of the conversation.

Jessie frowned, a pounding headache stretching

across the width of her forehead. "All right," she said into the phone receiver. "I can be there in about thirty minutes." She slammed down the receiver, unsure what made her angrier—the appearance of the story in the paper or Jake's response to it.

"That was the detective who's kind of been working with me," Jessie explained. "He was wondering if I planted the story in the newspaper to get a little free publicity." The headache pounded harder as Jessie's blood threatened to boil over.

Kayla shrugged. "I suppose that would be a natural reaction from a cop."

Not this cop, Jessie thought as she left the kitchen to get dressed. Jake should have known better than to even entertain such a thought. He should have known her well enough to realize that she would never be a party to such nonsense.

"Are you sure you're okay with this?" she asked Kayla a few minutes later when she was dressed and ready to leave. "I can wait for Maria."

Kayla waved a hand to dismiss her. "Go, take care of whatever you need to do. I'm just going to sit here, drink coffee and nurse my grudge against a certain young man who destroyed my self-image."

"If Charlie wakes up and when Maria gets home, tell them I'll be back as soon as I can."

A few minutes later Jessie was in her car headed for the police station. As had become her habit over the past week, she checked her rearview mirror, looking to see if anyone seemed to be following her. She saw nobody suspicious, but she didn't relax.

She was livid with Jake. She wasn't sure why he wanted to talk to her, but she intended to give him a piece of her mind.

It just went to show that a couple of dates didn't mean they knew each other. And maybe this was just the prod she needed to recognize it was time to stop pretending that they could be anything of importance to each other.

The North Patrol station where Jake worked was quiet as she walked through the front door. Maybe all the criminals in the city went to church, or believed in taking off one day a week.

She walked up to the counter and asked to see Detective Merridan, then sat in one of the yellow plastic chairs nearby to wait.

As she waited she realized it wasn't just anger that coursed through her. It was disappointment, a disappointment that Jake could question her character.

"Jessie."

She looked up to see him standing at the counter. "Come on back," he said.

She followed him down a long hallway and into a small private room that she assumed was used for interrogations. Once they were inside he closed the door and turned to face her.

"I owe you an apology."

"Yes, you do," she replied, not cutting him any

slack. She set her purse on the table, then crossed her arms and glared at him.

"I apologize." He raked a hand through his hair, which was more unruly than she'd ever seen it. "I can only plead exhaustion and frustration over the current case I'm working on. I let that frustration spill over on you this morning."

It would be so easy to remain angry with him if he didn't look so contrite, if he didn't look so utterly exhausted. "Has something else happened on your case?" she asked. "Another murder?"

"No, right now the count is still three." He motioned her into a chair at the table, then sat next to her. "But the press has linked up the cases, and the mayor is on our ass to solve this thing as soon as possible. As if that hasn't been what we've been trying to do." Once again his hand skated through his hair.

"Jake, I had nothing to do with that story in the paper this morning."

He released a deep sigh. "I know that. I knew it before I called you, but I just blew up when I saw it, especially the part where you encouraged whoever was doing these things to you to call in to the radio station."

"If you think that upset you, imagine what it did to me. I'm so angry I could spit."

"You know who planted the story?"

"No. I noticed the byline. A reporter I've never even heard of wrote it. Nobody called me. Nobody checked any facts with me. I should sue the damn paper."

"You can't sue. The story was true." Jake leaned back, his brow wrinkled in obvious thought. "So, who in your life knew what was going on?"

"Maria, of course, and Larry. My producer, Chris, and the security guard down at the station. I suppose it's possible any one of those people might have mentioned it to somebody else."

"Your ex-husband, he isn't fighting with you for custody or anything like that?"

"No."

"So he'd have no reason to leak the story?"

"I can't imagine what reason he'd have." Jessie's thoughts whirled in a dizzying fashion. Would Larry do something like this in an effort to somehow get her to come back to him? No, that just didn't make any sense, and she knew Larry wasn't that kind of man.

"If you had to lay odds on who broke the story, where would you put them?"

She rubbed her forehead with two fingers in an attempt to alleviate the throb that lingered there. "I'd like to think that none of them are responsible, but if I were a betting woman, I'd bet on my producer." Jessie's heart grew cold as she thought of Chris.

"And his full name is?" Jake pulled a small notepad from his pocket.

"Chris Mathison. But he can't get in any trouble

for this. If he did leak the story it isn't against the law."

"True, but I want to know who's responsible. I want to make sure it wasn't leaked by the perp in a bid for instant fame."

"Jake, you have enough on your plate without this. Let me talk to Chris. If he's responsible I'll know, then I can let you know."

"Are you sure?"

She nodded. "Positive." She wanted to be the one who confronted Chris.

"What concerns me is that sometimes the stalker types thrive on publicity. I'd hate to think that this story escalates anything," he said, more to himself than to her.

"Are you trying to make me feel better or worse?" she asked dryly.

He reached out and took her hand in his. "I just want you to be aware. I don't want anything to happen to you." His fingers squeezed hers.

"Then we both want the same thing," she replied. Any lingering anger she might have felt toward him was gone, replaced by the sweet rush of knowing somebody cared and that somebody was Jake.

"Jimmy had a great time yesterday," he said, not releasing his grip on her hand. "So did I."

"Charlie thinks Jimmy can walk on water."

He smiled, a modicum of relaxation sweeping over his features for the first time since she'd arrived. "We need to get them together again. We need to get together again."

Jessie pulled her hand from his, her heart aching with all the what-ifs she'd ever entertained in her life. She knew it was time to slow things down. Being with Jake was kind of like being in an avalanche, and if she wasn't careful the momentum would carry her straight into heartbreak hell.

"Jake, you're in the middle of a difficult case, and I have my own personal drama going on. Why don't we just play things by ear for the next week or two?"

She saw the stab of disappointment that darkened his eyes, but she refused to allow it to sway her decision. Better cool things now than later, when her heart was irrevocably tied up with him.

"I scared you yesterday," he said. "By telling you that I want you. I should have kept my mouth shut."

She wanted to protest his words, but figured it was better if he thought what he did, so she said nothing. Instead of saying anything she stood. "I'll talk to Chris and give you a call, okay?"

He nodded, once again the weariness back on his features. She started to walk out of the room but paused and turned back to him as he called her name. "On your terms, I want to keep seeing you."

"One day at a time, Jake. I think that's what we both need right now." She didn't wait to hear his reply, but turned and left the interrogation room.

It would be nice if relationships didn't come

with issues and baggage. It would be wonderful if she could trust a man to see her flaws and love her in spite of them.

She'd thought she'd had that in Larry, but Larry had left her for a woman who didn't have scars on her belly, who didn't need a night-light and who probably couldn't summon a panic attack unless it involved shopping and discovering she'd left her credit card at home.

Shoving aside thoughts of Jake, she focused on the newspaper article, her ire rising once again. She'd intended to go right home, but instead found herself taking the route that would lead her to Chris's apartment building.

She'd only been there once, for a surprise birthday party for him two months ago. She figured that on a Sunday morning he'd probably be home, recuperating after a late Saturday night.

She didn't want to wait until she'd cooled down to confront Chris. If he was responsible for the story, then she was going to give him more than a piece of her mind. He had no right to invade her privacy.

Chris's familiar Mustang was parked in front of the complex where his apartment was located. Good, he was home. She knew he had a live-in girlfriend, but the young woman's name escaped her at the moment.

She parked next to the Mustang and got out of the car. With each footstep her anger grew. How dare anyone talk about her personal life? She'd been so careful to keep personal and professional separate.

When she'd told Chris what had been happening to her she never dreamed that he'd call up a reporter and spill his guts, spill her life.

Nobody could know what that article might do to the perpetrator. As Jake had suggested, it was possible the publicity might incite him to new heights. She didn't have just herself to think about; she also worried about Charlie's safety and Maria's.

Her knuckles communicated her anger on Chris's apartment door. Sharp. Staccato. Loud. She waited only a moment before knocking once again.

"All right, all right. Hold your horses." Chris's voice drifted through the door. He jerked the door open and his sleepy blue eyes widened at the sight of her. "Jessie. Uh . . . come in."

His hair stood at odd angles and he hurriedly zipped up the jeans he must have pulled on to get the door. She could tell by the pillow creases on his face that she'd awakened him.

She swept past him and into the living room, which looked as if a night of wild partying had preceded her visit. Beer bottles and pizza boxes littered every surface available, and in the center of the coffee table was a bowl full of pot.

"What brings you here? Sorry the place is such a mess. We had a little party last night." As Chris spoke he picked up a couple of the pizza boxes along with the bowl and quickly carried them into the kitchen.

He returned to the living room and shifted from one foot to the other, obviously uncomfortable. "Jessie, what's going on?"

"Chris?" A blonde, obviously naked save for the multicolored sheet wrapped around her, appeared in the hallway. "What's going on?"

"Go back to bed, Stacy. It's just a problem with work. I'll take care of it." The blonde disappeared back into the bedroom, and Chris motioned Jessie to the sofa.

"I assume you haven't had a chance to read the paper this morning," Jessie said as she sat gingerly on the very edge of the sofa.

He scratched the center of his pale, bare chest. "I haven't had time to do anything this morning. Why?" His eyes were guarded as he gazed at her.

"There was an interesting article in it this morning. All about me and my stalker."

"No shit?" His gaze darted away from her, then back again. He blinked. Once. Twice. Three times in rapid succession.

Evasive. Like a man preparing to lie. She didn't intend to give him an opportunity. She leaned forward and held his gaze. "Chris, I know you're ambitious and I know the syndication deal is your dream come true. But if you ever pull any crap like this again, I'll walk out."

She stood and glared at him. "Do you understand me? This is my life we're talking about, and

you had no right to run to the paper with the details of my personal life. Do we understand each
other?"

He frowned, then sighed. "Jessie, I'm sorry. I
didn't mean any harm."

She held up a hand to stop whatever else he
might want to say. "You're a good producer, but
you made a major error in judgement with this.
Don't ever talk about my life to anyone—not your
mother, not your father and not your naked girlfriend in the other room." She headed for the door,
her piece spoken.

"Jessie, wait." He jumped up off the sofa and ran
after her. "Seriously, I'm so sorry. It just seemed like
a good idea at the time, you know?"

God, he was so young. There was no doubt in her
mind that he'd meant no harm. He was just young
and eager and stupid as only youth could be.

"Do you forgive me?"

Like a child who had made his mommy angry,
she saw Chris's need to know that everything was
all right between them, that she wouldn't stay
angry at him forever. And she couldn't stay angry
with him.

"Just don't ever do anything like this again,
okay?"

"Okay. Promise. So we're all right?"

She smiled. "I always give second chances,
Chris. Just don't push your luck."

"I'll bet our listening audience doubles on Monday

night. But don't worry, I'll never do anything like that again."

Minutes later as Jessie drove home, a wave of exhaustion struck her. She'd only been awake for a couple of hours but she would love nothing more than to crawl back into her bed and pull the covers over her head.

It wasn't even noon and already she'd cooled things with Jake and identified the source of the newspaper article. Now, if she could just confirm that Mark Smith was a harmless stalker, her life would be back to normal.

At the moment normal sounded blissfully wonderful.

He sat at his kitchen table, sipping coffee and reading the article on Dr. Langford over and over again. He finished reading the article for the third time, then set the paper aside and leaned back in his chair.

The scent of spring flowers drifted into his open window. Lilacs were in full bloom, as were the azaleas and honeysuckle that choked his backyard.

He never smelled spring and didn't feel the hunger, the sweet rush of need to possess, kill, then bury. He'd thought about his compulsion often over the years. He had no idea where it had come from and couldn't remember a childhood trauma that might have bred the perversion.

On some level he knew his needs weren't normal, but he didn't care. All that was important to him was satisfying those needs and not getting caught. He was good at doing both.

He had to be careful, for the hunger seemed to be appearing too quickly after satiation. He left one woman's body and before he got into his car to drive away from her dump site, he was already looking forward to the next young woman.

He knew the hunger was fed by the fact that *she* was still out there, waiting for him to put her in her final resting place.

He pulled the newspaper back over in front of him and read the article once again. Interesting that she'd decided to go public. Even more interesting that the article mentioned the wreath, the phone calls and the fact that she'd been pursued by somebody while in her car.

He'd made the calls and he'd left the wreath, but if somebody was following her in her car it wasn't him. He didn't need to follow her. He knew where to find her and at what time.

Closing his eyes, he breathed deeply of the spring breeze that rustled the curtains at the kitchen window. This little farmhouse was so perfect for him. He'd bought it for a song because, as the Realtor had said, it needed updating and plenty of TLC.

He had a feeling the Realtor would be astonished at the updating he'd done. Very little had gone into the house, but the root cellar had been transformed from a place to hang vegetables and store canned goods to his own personal playroom.

His latest toy was down there now, awaiting him. He'd grabbed her early this morning as she'd waited at a bus stop. Amazing how many women were out alone between the hours of three and four in the morning. She worked at a convenience store that closed at three. He'd watched and waited, and now she was his.

He never killed where he dumped; knew that too often forensic clues were left behind at a kill site. It was so much easier to have his fun with them in the root cellar, then wipe them down, roll them in plastic and find the perfect place for them to rest in peace.

His latest conquest, Maggie Brown, awaited him. But before he joined her in the cellar he was going to make himself a big breakfast. Bacon and eggs and wheat toast with jelly. It was amazing to him the appetite that a little anticipation could produce.

He neatly folded the paper and got up from the table. Maggie Brown would be the last of his appetizers. It was time to get to the main course. Dr. Jessica Langford might be the doctor of fear, but he was the doctor of death.

Chapter 17

By two o'clock on Monday, Jessie had accomplished several things. She'd seen half a dozen patients, she'd called Jake to let him know that Chris was responsible for the news story and she'd determined that the personal information Mark Smith had written on his initial paperwork was false.

She'd put off calling him Sunday about the information on Chris and had been grateful that when she had called him that morning he hadn't answered his phone, and she'd simply left a message on his voice mail. She'd been half afraid if she talked to him, if she heard his voice and he encouraged her to meet him, she would succumb.

His desire for her was intoxicating, and she couldn't allow herself to lose her head, to become drunk on the taste of his lips and the fever in his eyes.

After she'd made the call to Jake she'd dialed the number Mark Smith had listed as his home phone number. The number had been a nonworking one. At noon she'd driven by the address he'd written on his personal information form and had discovered the address belonged to a tattoo parlor.

She had no idea when he might come in again for another session, but somehow knew she'd see him again in her office. Sooner or later he'd tell her his issues and why he'd developed some sort of obsession with her.

Her day was done, but before leaving she picked up the phone once again, this time to call Larry. He was in court, so she left a message for him to return the call later that evening.

As she left the office she automatically looked around, seeking the blue sedan or any sign of Mark Smith. She saw neither.

For the first time in weeks she was relaxed as she drove home, and she continued to be relaxed for the next week. Since she'd changed her phone number there had been no more calls. Mark Smith seemed to have faded away, and she could live with the possibility of never knowing the reason why he'd been following her.

Jake called several times, each time sounding more weary than the last. There had been another murder victim found, a young woman named Maggie Brown, and Jessie knew he had his hands full with the investigation.

Saturday morning, Larry arrived to get Charlie for his weekend at his house. As Charlie got his things to load in the car, she and Larry sat at the table and had a cup of coffee.

"I can't help but think it might be good if Charlie stays with me for a while," Larry said.

Jessie looked at him in alarm. "Why?"

"This stalker stuff just has me a little worried."

"Larry, you know I'd never put Charlie at risk. If I thought I was in any real danger, I'd be the first to pack Charlie's bags."

"Then you don't think there's any danger?"

Jessie paused before answering and took a sip of her coffee. "You know what I think? I think maybe that article in the newspaper was the best thing that could have happened, even though at the time I wanted to wring Chris's neck."

"Why do you think the article was a good thing?"

"Because I think it might have scared my stalker. Things have been wonderfully quiet ever since the article appeared in the paper."

Larry smiled. "Except the two nights I listened to your show this week, it seems like you've gotten more nuts than usual."

She laughed. "That's true. Did you hear the caller who confessed being my stalker because I reminded him of the pet poodle he'd had when he was a child?"

"No, but I heard the woman who said she'd been following you because Amos, the God of Mars, had directed her to."

Jessie shook her head ruefully. "Most of those

people who call my show don't really suffer from anything except intense loneliness. They call to touch base with somebody, to hear a human voice in the darkness of the night."

"Speaking of the darkness of night, isn't it awful about all those murders?"

"Terrible. The detective who was working with me is the lead investigator on that case."

"Jake, right?"

She looked at him in surprise. "Right. How did you know?"

"Charlie mentioned that you'd had a date with a guy named Jake who was a cop and that his son had showed Charlie how to get past some level or another on some video game or another." Larry's smile held a touch of censure. "Why didn't you tell me you were seeing somebody?"

"I wasn't. I'm not." She cursed the blush that warmed her cheeks. "What I mean is that it was just a casual kind of thing—no big deal."

He held her gaze for a long moment. "You know, Jess, it's okay if you get on with your life, find somebody to share it with. I'd hoped you and I could, you know, work things out. But if you aren't with me, then I want you to be with somebody who will love you and care for you."

A thick rush of emotion rose up in her chest at his words. He was a nice man; weak but nice. And she knew him probably as well as he knew himself.

She picked up her coffee cup and eyed him over the rim. "What's her name?"

"Who?" The flush of red that crept up his neck gave him away.

"Whatever woman you're sleeping with." She laughed as his blush deepened. "Oh, come on, Larry. If you don't tell me, Charlie will."

He grinned and nodded. "Her name is Trisha."

"Is she old enough to drink?"

"Ha ha. I'll have you know she's thirty-five. She's a fellow attorney. Our paths crossed a couple of days ago at a luncheon."

"Dad." Charlie flew into the kitchen, his face a study of frustration. "How long does it take you to have a cup of coffee? I've been waiting in the car forever."

"I'm done. I'm ready." He stood from the table, as did Jessie.

Charlie shot back out the front door as Larry and Jessie followed. "Larry, the same goes for me, you know," she said as they stepped outside.

"What?"

"I want you to find somebody to love you, to care for you, and this time I want you to be smart enough not to screw it up."

"Point taken," he said. He smiled at her, then pulled her into his arms for a tight hug. She allowed herself to relax against him for a moment and breathe in the familiar scent of him.

They had come a long way, she and Larry. It was nice to know that they could lead separate lives but still love and care for each other as special friends.

It was a gift for themselves but also one for their son.

Minutes later Jessie stood at the curb and waved as Larry's car disappeared down the street. She turned to go back into the house, thinking of everything she had planned for the weekend without Charlie.

A long, soaking bubble bath was at the top of the list. She might rent a couple movies at the local Blockbuster and order in Chinese for dinner.

The one thing she didn't intend to do was give herself any time to think about Jake. There was no point in thinking about what might have been.

When she returned to the kitchen she took a few minutes to read the morning paper. The headline story was about the murders that had taken place over the past couple of weeks. Four young women raped, stabbed, then left in shallow ditches around the Northland Kansas City area.

She normally didn't read or listen to reports concerning these kinds of crimes. They ripped her up inside and brought back horrid memories of her own brush with death.

The article ended with a quote from Detective Jake Merridan, indicating that the murderer would be caught, that it was just a matter of time. A picture of Jake accompanied the article, and she brushed a finger across the grainy photo as wistful regret filled her.

Folding the paper, she could imagine the frustration of the cops working on the case. She reached for her coffee cup and took a swallow, her thoughts drifting back in time.

The detective who had pulled her from her grave had been Adam Cappa, a tall, broad-shouldered man who on that night when he'd dug her out had looked like God.

For the next year Adam Cappa and Jessie had shared a strange relationship. Adam was obsessed with solving the case, and in some ways he was obsessed with her. He called her almost every day, wanting to know how she was doing, if she'd remembered anything else that might help them in their investigation of the T&B killer.

He helped her find a counselor; he drove her to places she needed to go. He was both friend and support at a time when she'd desperately needed both.

They'd lost touch when Jessie had gone away to college. She'd consciously put her past and Adam Cappa behind her in an effort to go forward with her life.

As much as she appreciated everything Adam Cappa had done for her, she was also aware on some level that as long as he remained in her life, asking questions and tugging her back again and again to her night of horror, she'd never really heal.

There had been a darkness in the detective, a passion, a drive that she now knew had probably been unhealthy. He'd been possessed by the need to solve the crime, a crime that had never been solved.

She'd often wondered what happened to the detective and could only assume he'd probably retired by now and was fishing in Florida or sunning in Arizona. She hoped he'd managed to put the T&B killer behind him better than she had done.

The afternoon flew by. She spent a couple of hours packing away her winter wardrobe and hanging up her summer clothing. She had an emergency call from a patient and successfully talked the woman through a panic attack.

By eight o'clock that evening she was in the tub, scented bubbles surrounding her as soft music played from the radio. It was only then that she allowed her thoughts to drift to Jake.

There had been moments during the past week when a fierce longing had struck her, a longing to be in his arms and to taste the fire in his lips. There had also been moments of loneliness, something she hadn't experienced between the time of her divorce and her meeting Jake.

It was funny that when she'd been completely alone with no male company at all she hadn't been lonely, but after only a handful of dates with Jake, a deep loneliness now filled her.

It was a matter of habit and mind-set, she told herself as she pulled a soapy sponge across her shoulders. In a couple of short weeks Jake had become a habit she needed to break, and she needed to go back to thinking of spending her life alone.

It was just after nine when she got into bed with the latest novel she'd been reading. She expected a call from Charlie at any time and wouldn't go to sleep until she'd told her son good night.

Ten minutes later the phone rang and she picked up the receiver. "Hi, Charlie," she said.

"How did you know it was me?" he asked.

She laughed. "Because you're the only guy who calls me around nine on a Saturday night. How are things going?"

"Good. Me and Dad and his new girlfriend went out to dinner. We went to Charlie's Crab Shack. I got shrimp."

"How do you like Trisha?"

"She's okay. I mean, she wasn't mean to me or anything like that. She's got a dog named Snickers and she said maybe sometime I could meet him."

"That would be fun."

"Yeah, it would be funner if I could get my own dog." There was a pause, as if Charlie was holding his breath, waiting for her answer.

"We'll see how well you take care of Tommy the turtle before we talk about a dog," she replied.

"Okay. At least you didn't say 'No way.'"

"I didn't say yes either," she reminded him, to keep the record straight.

"I know. I just called to tell you good night and I love you."

"I love you more," she replied.

She hung up, the world right because her son was happy, healthy and loved her. She'd figure out the dog issue later. For the next hour she read, and by ten o'clock she turned out her bedside lamp and waited for sleep to claim her.

The shadows from the night-light danced across the ceiling in hypnotic fashion, and within minutes she was asleep. The dream came almost immediately, and on some level she recognized that it was a dream.

There was no color. The entire dreamscape was in black-and-white. She was deep in the bottom of an open grave, hands and feet bound with duct tape, and her mouth taped shut so she couldn't scream.

Jake and Adam Cappa stood near the grave, their voices drifting down to where she struggled against her bindings to get free.

"We'll never find her," Cappa said, and in the weirdness of dreams Jessie saw what he saw: hundreds of open graves that stretched as far as the eyes could see.

"Jimmy doesn't want a babysitter anymore," Jake said. "He wants a mom, but if I can't find Jessie he'll just have to deal with the babysitter."

"I'm here!" she screamed against the tape that held her mouth closed. "Just look down! Look down and help me." In horror she watched the two men walk away.

Silence. She was alone in the silence, in the darkness of the grave. There was nobody to find her, nobody to help her.

Tears of despair seeped from her eyes as she

stared up at the distant stars that lit the blanket of night sky. She would die here, in this grave.

Hope buoyed inside her as she heard the approach of footsteps. Help! She screamed in her mind. The footsteps drew closer. . . . Closer. Then she heard the sound of a shovel hitting dirt. "It's time, Jessica," a voice whispered from above.

Hope crashed away as terror swept through her. No. God, no, please. Dirt flew over the side of the open pit and hit her in the middle of her chest. Once again she heard the sound of a shovel moving against earth.

This time the dirt that flew over the lip of the grave hit her in the face. Again and again damp, cold earth hit her. She twisted her head from side to side in an effort to keep breathing. But she knew it was hopeless.

She awoke with a gasp and twisted so violently she fell to the floor next to the bed. Her head crashed into the nightstand as her heart hammered so hard in her chest it felt as if it might explode.

"Shit! Shit!" The expletive burst from her as she rubbed her head, then sat up on the floor next to the bed. In the faint illumination from the night-light she touched her head, then looked at her fingertips, happy to see there was no blood.

She needed light. More light to banish the nightmare. She crawled on her hands and knees to the wall with the light switch, then stood and flipped it on. The room burst into the light of several 150-watt bulbs.

Leaning weakly against the wall, she drew deep, steadying breaths. Whew. It had been one hell of a dream. After several minutes she felt stable enough to leave the support of the wall.

She headed for the kitchen, turning on each light switch that she passed. It was ridiculous even to contemplate going right back to bed. There was no way she'd go back to sleep until the last of the horror of the dream had left her.

Putting on a kettle of water for tea, she wondered what on earth had prompted the dream. Maybe it had been her thoughts earlier in the day of Detective Adam Cappa. As she sat at the table, waiting for the water to boil, she glanced at the clock on the oven door.

It seemed as if the dream had lasted forever, but it was only just a few minutes after ten thirty. She rubbed her head where it had connected with the edge of the nightstand. No lump, but it was tender to the touch. "You'll live," she muttered aloud.

The cup of tea helped relax her, and by the time she'd finished drinking it she thought she could go back to sleep. Thank goodness for chamomile tea. Even though it tasted like crap, it definitely soothed the savage beast.

By eleven o'clock she was back in bed, hoping for a night of sweet dreams, or better yet no dreams. She'd just about drifted off when her phone rang.

The shrill ring pierced the silence and jarred her back to full consciousness. She turned on her lamp next to her bed and eyed the offending instrument with trepidation.

As it rang a second time she grabbed the receiver. "Hello?"

Silence. Then the sound of a faint breath.

She squeezed her eyes tightly closed. "Hello? Who is this?"

"You know who it is." The voice, so deep, so smooth, raised the hair on the back of her neck and sent her heart crashing against her rib cage once again.

She couldn't speak, could only listen in frozen horror as he began to whistle the melody to "Amazing Grace."

Just like that night. That night eighteen years ago. He'd whistled then as he'd attempted to bury her. "Amazing Grace."

He was back. The monster from her past. With a deep, gut-wrenching sob she crashed the receiver back on the cradle, but instantly picked it up again. Her fingers flew over the keypad and it was only when she heard his voice on the other end of the line that she realized she'd called Jake.

Chapter 18

Jake had been getting ready to go to bed when he got the call. It took him a moment to identify the voice. Jessie. A very upset Jessie.

"Please come to my house. I need you," she'd sobbed.

He told her he'd be right there, had called the neighbor to come over and jumped into his car. He had no idea what had happened, and knew with certainty that it was a bad thing when a woman called crying and said she needed you.

He'd had a bitch of a week. The press, the mayor and all the powers that be were on the task force to get some answers, as if that wasn't what the officers working the murder cases had been trying to do.

Things hadn't gotten better by the fact that Jessie had distanced herself from him, and he knew he was to blame. He'd come on too hard, too fast, and it had scared her away.

He had no idea why she'd called him, but it had been obvious she was in some sort of crisis. Had something happened with her stalker? Was there another "present" on her front porch? He tromped on the gas pedal, a new urgency whipping through him.

When he pulled up in front of Jessie's place the first thing that struck him was that it looked as if every light in the house was on. There was nothing on the porch to give him any alarm. But when she answered the door, he knew something dreadful had happened or was about to happen.

Her eyes were wide with alarm and red-rimmed from tears. She wore nothing but a dark blue night-shirt, the bottom just skimming her upper thighs.

"Jessie, what's wrong?" he asked. He fought the impulse to sweep her into his arms, hold her tight until the look of fear disappeared from her eyes. Instead he took her by the arm and led her to the sofa, where they both sat.

"I got a phone call. Just a few minutes ago." She didn't just close her eyes, but rather squeezed them shut as if the sight of him or some inner vision pained her.

He waited a moment, then took her hand in his. She held tightly. "Jessie, talk to me. Tell me what's going on."

She opened her eyes and stared at him for a long moment, then released his hand and stood, poised as if to run away. Her eyes held a wildness that frightened him.

"What do you know about the T and B killer?"

He sat back, surprised by the question that she

seemed to have pulled out of thin air. "The T and B killer?" Anyone who was on the Kansas City police force knew about the ones that had gotten away, but that particular case had occurred way before Jake's time. "I know the T and B killer terrorized the city about fifteen or twenty years ago and that it's a cold case—the killer was never arrested. Why?"

She was as still as a statue. "Because the T and B killer just called me." Tears filled her eyes.

Jake felt as if he'd entered the audience of a play at intermission and now grappled to make sense of the second act when he'd missed the first. "Jessie, what are you talking about?" Once again he grabbed her hand and gently forced her to sit.

She pulled her hand from his and hunched her shoulders, as if she could make herself small enough to disappear. "Eighteen years ago I was sixteen years old." Her voice was soft but steady as she continued. "On a pretty spring evening I walked to a corner where there was a bus stop, to meet a girlfriend who was going to pick me up. We were going to study together for a history final we had to take the next day."

Jake felt a sickness begin in the pit of his stomach as he waited for her to go on. "I sat on the bench at the bus stop. I never heard whoever sneaked up behind me. I never had a hint, a clue, a flutter of intuition that danger was near."

She stopped speaking for a minute and drew a deep breath. Her gaze remained directed at some point on the distant wall. "Something hit me in the back of my head and I blacked out for I don't know how long. When I came to I was in the trunk of a car. My hands and feet were bound with duct tape, as were my eyes and my mouth."

Jesus, he didn't want her to say anymore. He didn't want to hear anymore. He couldn't stand the thought of a young Jessie, so frightened, so alone. He ached for her.

"I didn't know it at the time, but I had just become the sixth victim of the T and B killer." She straightened her shoulders, and when her gaze met his he saw a surprising strength shining there. "That night I was raped and sliced and diced by a madman. After he finished with me he wrapped me in plastic and took me to the Hillside Cemetery, where he threw me into an empty grave and proceeded to bury me alive."

Jake's mouth had gone dry as a bone and the sickness that had begun in the pit of his stomach spread outward. "Jesus, Jessie." They weren't the words of a cop, but rather the words of a man who cared too deeply.

"If a handful of teenagers hadn't picked that night, at that time, to have an impromptu party in the local cemetery, I wouldn't be here telling you this. I would have been the very dead sixth victim."

Jake struggled to focus, to wrap his mind around what she'd just told him. Eighteen years ago. A lifetime ago, and yet it was obvious she thought her past had returned with a vengeance.

He started to speak but had to swallow around the lump in his throat. "So, what makes you think you got a call from the killer tonight? Did you recognize his voice?"

She hesitated a long moment. "That night he only spoke to me once. When he threw me into that grave, he said, 'Bye-bye, Jessica.' I thought at the time that I'd remember his voice forever. For months afterward I thought I heard that voice everywhere. The boy who dipped me ice cream at the Dairy Queen had his voice. The man who pumped my gas sounded just like him. Even my father sounded like him when he spoke to me. I realized I couldn't trust my memory."

"So, tell me about the phone call," Jake said softly.

She broke eye contact with him and instead once again stared at the wall opposite where they sat. Her fingers clenched together in her lap. "That night as he shoveled dirt on top of me, he whistled 'Amazing Grace.' A little while ago when I answered the phone somebody whistled 'Amazing Grace.'"

Once again Jake worked to make sense of everything she'd thrown at him. "Are you sure? I mean, you weren't asleep? You weren't dreaming?"

"No. I was wide awake. The caller ID shows the call came in, but it showed as an unknown number."

"Probably a cell phone," he said absently. She'd been raped, beaten and God knew what else. It was difficult for him to think of anything else but her suffering. She'd been nothing more than a child at the time. "But why would he come back after all these years?"

She stared at him, her beautiful blue-gray eyes hollow. "To finish what he began."

Jake ripped a hand through his hair and wished he knew more about the crimes that had happened almost two decades before. "I don't know, Jessie. It's hard to believe that this guy went dormant for eighteen years, then finds you just to terrorize you. That's not the way serial killers usually work."

For the first time since he'd arrived at her door she seemed to relax just a little bit. "I'm open to any and all alternatives you might come up with," she said.

He frowned. "Maybe it's somebody just trying to screw with your head. Somebody who would know the details about what happened to you. Who knew those details?"

It was her turn to frown. "At the time my parents, some of their friends, the investigating officers. Later my therapist and, of course, Larry. But why would any of those people want to screw with my head?" She looked at him, seeking answers, and he hated the fact that he had none.

"I don't know, but I'm going to see what I can find out. I need to read the files about the T and B murders." He held out his hands, implying helplessness. "I don't know enough, Jess."

She was a rape victim. No wonder she'd pushed

him away when he'd come on too strong. If he'd known her history he might have taken things slower. "Why didn't you tell me all this sooner?"

"Because for the most part I'm not that victim." She looked down at her hands clasped so tightly in her lap that her knuckles were white. "Because I didn't want you to see me as a victim."

"Jessie." He put a finger under her chin and lifted her head so she was looking at him once again. "When I look at you I don't see a victim. I see a beautiful, vital woman filled with strength and heart."

Jessie wanted to weep. Telling him her story had been the most difficult thing she'd ever done. Her past was a part of her she'd held close for so long, but the phone call had stripped away all of her defenses.

Jake reached out to her and she leaned forward into his arms and closed her eyes as he enfolded her. Fear still shivered through her, the fear of knowing she'd cheated death once and wouldn't be so lucky the next time. Fear that the monster who had nearly destroyed her was back to finish the job.

Jake stroked her hair, and neither of them spoke for several moments. The strength of his arms surrounding her helped, but couldn't banish the taste of terror that still lingered in her mouth. Nor was she willing now to bare her physical scars to him.

He'd accepted the facts of her past with appropriate emotion, displaying pain at her ordeal, matching her memory of horror with a new horror of his own. But hearing the story and seeing the ugly results on her flesh were two different things.

"I want to see what I can dig up on the original crime," he murmured as his hand continued to stroke the length of her hair. "I also want to check out those people you mentioned who knew about the crime."

She rose up to look at him. "So you don't think he's come back for me?"

She was grateful he didn't answer immediately. She didn't want empty platitudes or a sense of false security. "It just doesn't make sense to me. It's not the way these guys work. Besides, why wait eighteen years? Why didn't he come back for you a year later? Two years?" He shook his head. "No, I think something else is going on now, and I promise you I won't rest until I get to the bottom of it."

"As if you don't have enough on your plate right now," she said. Once again she leaned forward and rested her head against his broad chest.

She wanted to believe him, that it wasn't the T&B killer who had called, but rather somebody less dangerous, somebody less threatening. But she was afraid to believe. The stakes were too high to make a mistake.

"Thank you for coming right over," she murmured. "I don't know what I would have done if you hadn't."

"You want me to stay the rest of the night? I could bunk here on the sofa if it would make you feel better."

Once again she raised her head and looked at him. "I can't ask you to do that." Although the last thing she wanted was to spend the rest of the hours of the dark all alone in the house.

"Why not?" His gaze was so soft, so tender on her it made her want to cry again. "Jessie, I can't think of anything I'd rather do than be here for you if you need me to be."

"I need you tonight." She moved away from him, even though she would have gladly remained in his arms forever. "I need you with me, in my bed, holding me." She frowned, knowing what she asked was unfair to him, unfair because of the desire he'd already voiced for her. "But nothing more, Jake. I just need to be held."

He stood and held out his hand to her. "Come on. Let's go to bed. You don't have to worry, Jessie."

As they walked toward her bedroom she wondered what on earth she had done in her life that had brought a man like Jake into it. He pointed to the bed. "You get settled in. I'm going to check the doors and windows and make sure they're all locked up tight. I'll be right back."

He left the room and Jessie got into the bed, her mind still working through everything that had happened. One thing was certain: in the morning she was going to ask Larry about keeping Charlie for the next couple of weeks, and she'd call Maria and tell her to make arrangements to stay with her sister until this was resolved.

She'd rather err on the side of caution. She didn't

want to put the people she loved most at risk. Until they knew exactly what was going on, she didn't want Charlie or Maria here.

The lights went out in the hallway and Jake returned to the bedroom. "All locked up safe and sound." He shut off the bedroom light; then using the illumination from the night-light, he moved to the opposite side of the bed.

She watched as he placed his gun and his cell phone on the nightstand, then pulled his T-shirt over his head and laid it on the nearby chair. Under any other circumstances she would have been weak at the sight of his bronzed, muscular chest and the thought of sleeping next to him.

But she couldn't allow herself to go there. There was still a piece of herself she kept guarded and wasn't willing to share, and that was the physical scars that were her legacy of survival. He kicked off his shoes, removed his socks, then got into bed, still wearing his jeans.

"Do you always go to bed wearing your jeans?" she asked.

He rose on one elbow and gazed down at her, his dark eyes glowing in the faint light. "I like to think I'm a good man, Jessie. But I'm not a saint."

A flutter of heat swept through her, a heat that momentarily banished the fear. He moved next to her and pulled her into his arms. She went willingly, needing to feel his heartbeat against her own, his body warmth surrounding her to take away the chill that had taken up residence inside her.

"Talk to me, Jake," she whispered against his bare chest.

"What do you want me to talk about?" His chest rumbled as he spoke.

"Anything, everything. Just talk to me so your voice erases the voice in my head."

And he did. He talked about summer plans and picnics in the park. He spoke of movie nights with popcorn and beer. He talked of ordinary pleasures, and his voice was the last thing she heard before she drifted off to sleep.

Chapter 19

Jake awoke before dawn, an arm trapped beneath Jessie and completely numb. He turned his head to gaze at her but didn't move anything else, not wanting to disturb her sleep.

She looked beautiful. Her hair was sleep tousled, her mouth was open slightly and her cheek held the faint crease of a pillow. Still she looked beautiful.

He turned his head and stared up at the ceiling, a crush of emotions weighing heavily in his chest. Thinking about what Jessie had suffered at the hands of the T&B killer was almost too much to bear.

He wished he could go back in time and rescue her. He wished he had a magic pill to erase all the bad memories that must surely be stored in her head.

Her inner strength awed him. He'd seen too many victims of violent crimes who never recovered, who turned to drink or drugs to ease the pain.

He'd seen too many people who never managed to get past the trauma to lead productive, happy lives.

Jessie had not only survived, she'd also triumphed, and he knew it took a very strong, special woman to do that. He needed to find out who was torturing her now. He just couldn't believe that the killer had waited eighteen years to come after her once again. That simply didn't make sense.

But somebody close to her was tormenting her. Somebody close to her was using intimate information to scare the hell out of her. He was going to find out who and why and then he was going to bust them up.

Careful not to awaken her, he eased his arm from beneath her. It had been a difficult night for him, lying next to her, feeling the warmth of her curves so close, the scent of her filling his head and not acting on the sharp desire that stabbed him.

What he needed was a very cold shower to banish the tension that begged to be relieved. But instead of showering here he grabbed his gun and cell phone, wrote her a brief note and left it in the kitchen, then headed for the police station.

When he got to the station he went into the locker room, showered and shaved and changed into the spare set of clothes he kept in his locker. Then, armed with a cup of strong coffee, he went in search of the records of the T&B case in storage.

"What—you don't have enough to do, you got to look at ancient cases?" the officer in charge of records said when Jake had made his request.

"What can I tell you? I'm an overachiever," he replied.

"It's going to take me a while to locate these files. You want me to give you a call when I've got them for you?"

"Yeah, I'll be around, waiting to hear from you." Jake left the records area and headed for the war room, where his other headache resided.

There was nobody else in the room. He hadn't expected anyone here at the crack of dawn on a Sunday morning. He sat in the silence of the room, sipping his coffee and thinking about the woman he'd just left in bed.

It didn't matter that he hadn't known her for very long. He knew what was in his heart. He was in love with her. He hadn't been looking to fall in love. Hell, after Colette he'd sworn off women altogether. But fate had brought him Jessie Langford.

He stared at the bulletin board, at the victims of the lily killer. The thought of Jessie's picture on a similar board ripped at his guts.

It was two hours later that he got the call from the records department that he could pick up the files he'd requested.

The files were in two large boxes, and he loaded each of them into the trunk of his car and headed home. He didn't want to go through them at the station. He wanted the privacy of his home. He was afraid of seeing what they might contain and yet was driven to probe the crime that had molded the kind of woman Jessie had become.

Jimmy had just rolled out of bed when Jake walked into the house, carrying one of the file boxes. The scent of cinnamon filled the air and a pang of hunger stirred in the pit of Jake's stomach.

"Hey, kid. What's cooking?"

"Mrs. Crawford made a cinnamon coffee cake." Jimmy made a face of disgust. They had tasted Mrs. Crawford's cinnamon cake before. It had not been a pleasant experience. "What's that?" Jimmy gestured toward the box.

"Work. There's another box in the trunk. You want to grab it for me?"

"Sure." Jimmy disappeared out the door, and Jake went into the kitchen to find his elderly neighbor washing dishes at the sink.

"Something smells like heaven," he said as he set the box on the floor next to the table.

"Smells like coffee cake to me," she replied, and flashed him a smile, then turned back to her dish washing.

At that moment Jimmy came into the kitchen, lugging the other box of files. "Just put it there on the floor," Jake instructed.

"Looks like plenty of work," Mrs. Crawford said as she dried her hands on the dish towel.

"Is that stuff about the murders that have been happening?" Jimmy asked.

"No, this is a cold case."

Jimmy sat at the table. "I know all about cold cases. I watch that show on TV. Mostly because I think the woman detective is a hot babe."

Jake leaned over and pretended to punch his son in the arm. "I keep telling you that you're way too young to notice hot babes."

Mrs. Crawford laughed. "I think that's my cue to head home. The coffee cake should be done in about ten minutes, and you just call me when you need me here again."

"Thanks, Mrs. Crawford. We appreciate you," Jake said.

"So, what kind of case is it?" Jimmy asked when Mrs. Crawford had left.

"An old serial killer case." Jake eased into a chair across from his son.

"Cool. Can I see some of it?"

"Nope. It's private police business and not meant for anyone else to see." He waited to see if Jimmy was going to give him a hard time.

Jimmy frowned thoughtfully. "Serial killers, they're the worst, aren't they, Dad?"

"There are a lot of sick, bad people in the world," Jake replied. And one of them had for hours raped and tortured Jessie.

"When I get older, I want to be a cop just like you."

Jimmy's words caused a lump of emotion to rise in Jake's throat. The fact that his son wanted to emulate him in any way warmed him with pleasure.

"When are we going to see Dr. Jessie and Charlie again?" Jimmy asked.

"Did you like Dr. Jessie?"

"Yeah, she was all right. But it's that kid who needs help."

Jake raised an eyebrow. "Charlie? Why does he need help?"

"'Cause he doesn't know anything about being cool. He needs somebody like me to, you know, teach him stuff. He's totally lame."

Jake smiled inwardly. So Jimmy had a cause. Certainly there were worse things his son could focus on than helping a six-year-old achieve coolness.

Jake suddenly remembered the coffee cake and hurriedly removed it from the oven. Jimmy drifted back to his bedroom and Jake opened the first box of files.

When he looked at the clock some time later he realized it was almost noon. And he hadn't even gotten to the files relating to Jessica in particular.

He broke for lunch with Jimmy, then Jimmy disappeared back into his room, where he was in the process of cleaning out his closet and boxing up old toys.

Jake returned to studying the case of the T&B killer. Jessica Clinton; that had been her name when she'd been sixteen years old. There were photos in her file, but he set those aside, facedown, not ready to look at them until he'd read the initial reports of the case.

She'd been right when she'd told him that if not for a group of partying teenagers, she'd be dead. Apparently the arrival of the teenagers that night at the cemetery had scared off the murderer before he could finish burying Jessie alive, as he'd done to the five victims before her. Unfortunately the kids hadn't seen, with any detail, the man responsible. They'd only heard the sound of running feet in the darkness.

Just like the current lily killer, the T&B killer had left very little evidence behind. Bits of plastic consistent with a garbage bag had been found on one victim. The knife wounds had been made by what the coroner had identified as probably an ordinary paring knife.

The notes, made by the investigative officer, Adam Cappa, had rung with the man's frustration. After Jessica had been found alive, the city had held its breath, waiting for the next victim to surface, but there had been none.

There were notes made to indicate that over the years the T&B case had been revisited by other officers in an attempt to close the cold case. With the advent of computer systems as recently as a year ago, the MO of the T&B killer had been fed into a data system to see if any other crimes with the same characteristics had occurred anywhere else in the United States.

Nothing. Nada. It was as if the killer had dropped off the face of the earth. The general consensus was that he'd either been arrested and was in prison on unrelated crimes or he'd died.

But dead men didn't make phone calls. Dead men didn't leave wreaths on porches.

He eyed the photos on the table next to him. He dreaded seeing them, knowing they would be depictions of Jessie at the worst time in her life.

Drawing a deep breath to steady himself, he flipped over the first picture. It was a head shot of a young Jessica. He would have recognized her anywhere, with her dark hair and beautiful eyes. However, there was no innocent youth clinging to her features. She looked strained and as if she'd seen the flames of hell and might never recover from the experience.

The next couple of photos showed the grave where she'd been found, with a headstone reading CAMERON JACKSON. He closed his eyes for a moment, imagining her terror when she'd been thrown down inside that pit, imagining her horror as dirt began to fall down on her.

God, just thinking about it made him need to cough, as if to clear dirt from his throat.

The next photo sent him nearly reeling out of his chair. A moan escaped him, a deep moan of agony as he stared at the picture of Jessie. It was a photo of her stomach, ripped with the point of a knife in a pattern of slashes and gashes. According to the medical personnel on the scene, the wounds were deep enough to warrant stitches, but not so deep as to be lethal.

Jake hadn't cried since the night that Jimmy had been born, and on that night his tears had been ones of joy. He hadn't cried when Colette left him. He hadn't wept when the divorce papers came, but tears pressed perilously close to the surface as he stared at the knife wounds that Jessie had endured.

He understood now why she'd not wanted to make love to him. She hadn't wanted him to see those scars, perhaps had been afraid of his reaction to them. The wounds were ugly and time might have healed the worst of them, but he knew she'd wear the scars of that night for the rest of her life.

His need to see her at that moment was overwhelming. He wanted to tell her he was sorry that she'd suffered so much, that he was amazed by her indomitable spirit. He needed to hold her in his arms and tell her he didn't give a damn about any scars her body might have, that they were a part of her that only made his love for her deeper, stronger.

It took him fifteen minutes to get his neighbor back to his house and explain to Jimmy that he had to go out and didn't know when he'd be back.

"I promise you, son, that when I catch this killer, we're going to spend some quality time together," Jake said. "Maybe we'll head up to Colorado again. Remember that summer we spent two weeks at Lake Vallecito?"

"Mom hated it," Jimmy said.

Jake grimaced. Yes, Colette had hated it. She'd hated any kind of family trip they'd ever taken. "Well, she won't be there this time. We'll fish and do some horseback riding and anything else you'd like to do."

"That would be cool. Catch the killer fast, okay?"

Jake smiled. "I'm doing the best I can."

Minutes later as he was in his car and headed back to Jessie's, he thought of the woman who'd been his wife. Colette had been a terrific girlfriend when he'd been young, but she had been a horrible wife, and according to his son, a not-so-terrific mom.

Unfortunately Jake had been working so much of the time he hadn't seen firsthand the interaction between Colette and his son. Even when he was home he'd hadn't been aware of the dynamics between mother and son.

Colette had been a poor mother, but Jake had to accept a certain amount of responsibility in being an emotionally absent father.

Colette had never cared much about emotional intimacy of any kind. Only now, with his feelings for Jessie so raw and new, could he objectively look back and see all that had been missing from his marriage, all the things he wanted to share with Jessie.

When he pulled out of his driveway, his mind exploded with a vision of her stomach, cut and bleeding. And her eyes. Those lovely eyes so filled with residual terror that no young teenager should ever know.

It was just after three when he pulled into her driveway. He turned off his engine and sat for a moment, pulling himself together, trying to erase the vision that crushed his heart as no other he'd ever seen.

She answered on the second knock, and the gaze

that warmed her eyes when she smiled at him threatened to undo him. "Jake." She opened the door to allow him in, and he noted that she immediately locked the door after him.

"You didn't have to come back over here today. You did more than enough last night."

"I went straight to the station this morning and got the files on the T and B killer."

A hollow wind of painful memories blew through Jessie at his words. She'd hoped he'd never know what had happened to her so long ago, but the phone call she'd received last night had changed everything.

She searched his face, looking for a hint of repulsion, a whisper of aversion in his eyes. There was none. Rather there was only a dark intensity, a look of emotion that captured and held her breath in her chest.

"And what did you discover?" she finally managed to ask.

"What I knew all along. That you are an amazing woman." He pulled her into his arms, and she went hesitantly at first, then slowly relaxed in the warmth.

Words couldn't speak of her gratitude toward this man, a man who had held her all night long, a man who had wrapped himself around her without threatening her in any way.

She'd fallen asleep the night before not just with the deep, low melody of his voice, but also to the sure and steady beat of his heart against her own.

She'd felt bereft when she'd awakened alone in her bed that morning.

"I am utterly amazed by you," he murmured against her hair. His lips moved from the top of her head to the sensitive skin just behind her ear. A shiver of unexpected delight raced through her.

She fought against it, afraid of letting go. He might know the cold, dry facts of the case, but he didn't know the cost she'd paid in blood.

"Jessie, look at me."

There was something in his tone, a husky need that made her both afraid to look at him and unable not to do as he bid. His gaze held the fires of desire, fires so hot they threatened to burn her from the inside out.

He bent his head and took her lips with his. Greedy, hungry, his mouth demanded response. And she was helpless to do anything but to return the kiss as greedily, as hungrily as his own.

She raised her arms and wound them around his neck as the kiss continued, building inside her a desire that made her breathless and weak.

His hands worked their way down her back in slow, sensual circles until they came to rest just on the top of her buttocks.

Her heartbeat raced and every nerve ending in her body was electrified. Someplace in the very back of her mind she knew she should step away, end the kiss and gain some distance. Her body reacted too intensely to his, her want of him had flared too quickly for her to feel any kind of control.

His hands moved farther down to cup her buttocks, then he pulled her against him. It was only when she felt the hard length of his arousal that she surfaced from her momentary lapse of judgement.

"Jake." She tore her mouth from his to protest.

Instantly he dropped his hands and took several steps back from her, his eyes still filled with a hunger but also with something else. "I want to make love to you, Jessie."

His words both thrilled her and sent a crashing pain through her. Never had she wanted anything as desperately as to make love with Jake. But fear kept her from reaching for what she wanted.

"Jake, I . . ."

"I saw the pictures, Jessie." His voice was low and filled with emotion.

She looked at him in surprise. "What? What pictures?" Dread filled her.

"Photos the officers took, photos that were taken at the hospital. I saw what he did to you. I saw the cuts he left on you."

Tears sprang to her eyes and she crossed her hands over her stomach, as if to shield the sight from him. "It's ugly. It's disgusting." She was aware that this excruciating moment was yet another violation by the man who had nearly killed her years before. "If you saw them you'd be sickened."

He took a small step toward her. "I saw the pictures of the wounds right after you were rescued.

They aren't ugly or disgusting. They don't repulse me. They make me want to weep for you."

It wasn't so much his words that threatened to unravel her but the look in his eyes, the expression on his face. It was an expression of simmering desire and aching tenderness.

The next step he took brought him so close to her she could feel the warmth of his breath on her face. "Jessie, how could I be repulsed by anything that was a part of you? What happened to you back then is what made you the person you have become, a person I'm falling in love with."

Tears ran down her cheeks faster than she could have ever wiped them away. Did she dare hope that this man could love not only her, but all the scars that marred her body?

Deep in her heart she'd always harbored the belief that the reason Larry had cheated on her was because he'd secretly found her repugnant.

But in Jake's eyes she saw no hint of anything remotely resembling disgust or repugnance. She saw only the fires of a man who wanted her, and the deeper emotion of a caring that sought out every lonely piece of her soul and soothed it.

"Let me love you, Jessie," he whispered, his voice husky with his own need.

Speech was impossible for her at the moment. Myriad emotions tumbled inside her. Hope. Fear. Desire. They tangled around one another, making it impossible for her to know exactly what she felt at the moment. Except desire. That emotion shone brighter than any other. Burned hotter.

She nodded. A quick shake of her head broke the inertia that had held him apart from her. He reached for her hand, gripping tightly as he led her down the hallway toward her bedroom.

Her limbs felt unaccountably heavy as she walked into her room. Heavy with a need she hadn't known she'd possessed. Heavy with the desire to fall into his arms, to touch him intimately, to encourage him to touch her as intimately.

When he dropped her hand she started toward the windows. "What are you doing?" he asked.

She turned to look back at him. "I'm closing the blinds and pulling the drapes."

"You don't want to see who is making love to you?"

The warmth of a blush swept over her face. "It's not that," she protested. She and Larry had always had sex beneath the cover of darkness.

"Leave the blinds alone and come here." There was a quiet command in his voice, and she found herself moving toward him. When she reached him he reached for the top button on her blouse.

She shivered as his fingers brushed the bare skin of her collarbone. She felt the slight tremble in his fingers, a tremble that spoke of his barely contained control.

When he'd unfastened the first two buttons, he dipped his head and kissed the skin he'd bared. Jessie grabbed the back of his head, needing to hold on as her knees weakened at the exquisite sensation of his lips against her bare flesh.

He kissed her only briefly; then his fingers worked the next two buttons, completing the task of unbuttoning the blouse. It fell apart, exposing the wispy white lace bra she wore beneath.

For the first time since they'd come into the bedroom, his gaze left hers and instead drank in the sight of her half-naked breasts. She felt the gaze as intimately as a touch. Her nipples hardened against the thin lace material as her heart beat frantically.

He didn't shove the blouse from her shoulders, but rather stepped back from her and pulled his T-shirt over his head. His chest gleamed in the afternoon sunshine coming in through the windows.

Her mouth went completely dry and her breath caught almost painfully in her throat as he kicked off his shoes and placed his cell phone and gun on the dresser with slow deliberation.

His hands moved to the fastening of his jeans, and the sound of the zipper ripped through her like the sizzle of lightning in the middle of a storm. As he removed his jeans, leaving him clad only in a pair of briefs, his arousal was boldly evident.

Magnificent. He took her breath away with his physical beauty. Despite her fervor for him, she didn't want him to look at her. A man like him deserved perfection in his mate. Even though he wouldn't allow her the darkness of the room, she needed the cover of the sheets on the bed.

"Jessie." He spoke her name as if he knew her

inner thoughts, understood her deepest, darkest fears.

"Please. Let me do this my way." She turned her back to him and undressed, shrugging off the unbuttoned blouse, removing her bra, then pulled off her slacks. With her back still toward him, and clad only in a pair of white bikini panties, she pulled down the sheets and slid beneath them, one hand splayed across the scars on her stomach.

He got into the other side of the bed and scooted as close to her as he could physically get. He placed his hand against hers. The one on her stomach. The one that covered her scars.

"Don't be afraid." He leaned forward and kissed her forehead, her eyelids, her cheeks, and in the softness of his lips, the sheen in his eyes, she knew as only her heart could know that she could trust him.

Staring into his eyes and drawing a deep, shuddering breath, she eased her hand from beneath his. His warm hand remained firmly against the scar tissue that had been her shame for so long. The loving gaze in his eyes didn't waver.

Some piece of herself, a piece that had been imprisoned and filled with tormenting pain for years, fell away. A sob rose in her throat but disappeared as his mouth covered hers in a kiss that filled all the emptiness in her heart, her soul.

With that kiss it was as if the dam broke loose for both of them. They became nothing but hunger, drawing sustenance from each other as they continued to share deep, hot kisses.

The entire time they kissed, Jake's hand never stopped touching the skin that had not been touched since a killer's knife had been there. She sensed no hesitancy in him, no pulling back as he smoothed his hand across the ridged skin in slow, languid caresses.

The hunger that built inside her wanted more, but before she could indicate to him in any way that she was ready for more, he took it. His hands moved to cover her breasts, his thumbs rubbing erotically over the hardened tips.

She moaned with pleasure and felt as if she might go out of her mind as his mouth found one of those tips and he licked and sucked.

He didn't just breathe; he panted, the sound of his short, shallow breaths raising her desire to new heights. Without warning he flung the sheet from them, exposing them to the full light of the sun shining into the room.

She flinched like a vampire afraid of deathly exposure. Her hand sought the edge of the sheet so she could cover them once again. His fingers clasped around her wrist and held tight. He raised his head and looked at her. "Now let me do this my way," he said.

She relaxed, but only briefly as his mouth trailed down the center of her chest and found the scars. He kissed each and every one, and in that moment he held her heart as nobody had ever done before. As nobody would again.

Raising her hips, she helped him as he shimmied her panties down and off her legs. She was ready for him. Wet and wanting. Needing him not just touching her, not just kissing her, but inside her.

In the space of a breath he was out of his briefs and poised above her, his dark eyes holding her as captive as his body.

He eased into her with a deep groan, and when he was buried inside her he froze. Tension sharpened his features as he remained still. She fought the need to move against him, knowing that he was struggling for control.

He shuddered and closed his eyes, then with a breath that expanded the width of his chest, he moved his hips. She gasped in exquisite pleasure as waves of sensation swept through her.

He stroked into her slow and steady, and when he opened his eyes to gaze down at her she saw he was lost in a haze of sweet ecstasy.

As he quickened the rhythm of his hips, all thoughts fled from her mind. She couldn't think, as she was nothing more than nerve endings and sensations building to a crescendo she thought might be her death.

Nothing had prepared her for this, his mastery. And nothing before had prepared her for the intensity of the climax that crashed through her in wave after wave of blinding rapture.

As she came, he groaned her name and stiffened

against her, shuddering violently as he found his own release. He collapsed on top of her, then rolled slightly to her side so his weight wasn't completely on top of her.

She closed her eyes, savoring the moment, storing the memory of this first time with him as her body cooled and her heartbeat returned to a more normal pace. She smiled as his lips touched her temple. She opened her eyes to see him watching her.

She felt the need to speak, but didn't know what to say to the man who had given her back a piece of her self-respect, a chunk of her soul that had been missing for a very long time.

He smiled then, the smile that lit his eyes and warmed his features. "Give me your hand."

She frowned with curiosity but placed her hand in his. He pulled her hand toward his lower body, and she laughed. "Don't tell me you're ready again so soon."

His smile widened. "I'm good, but I'm not that good."

He placed her hand on his upper thigh, and beneath her fingertips she felt the rippled ridge of a scar. "There are a couple more on my back."

She propped herself up on one elbow, facing him. "What happened?"

"My father was partial to a belt with an oversized buckle."

"He abused you?"

"According to him, he disciplined me." The

smile that had lifted the corners of his mouth fell away. "I was fifteen years old the last time he tried to discipline me. I surprised him. I got the belt away from him and told him if he ever hurt my mother or me again I'd kill him. I guess he believed me, because the next morning he packed his bags and left. We never saw him again."

"I'm sorry." And she was. He was such a good man, a loving and kind man. She didn't want to think about a childhood of fear and abuse for him.

"I didn't tell you to get your sympathy. I told you so you'd understand we all have scars of one sort or another."

"Larry never wanted to talk about it. He never wanted to see them or touch me."

"Then Larry is an ass."

She laughed, and he pulled her closer to him, so they cuddled in the waning light of day. "Yes, Larry is an ass," she agreed easily.

"Is that why you divorced him?"

"Not entirely. He cheated on me. Often."

"Then he's a stupid ass."

She leaned her head back to gaze at him. "What about you and Colette? What happened between the two of you that caused the split?"

He frowned and absently ran his fingers lightly over her forehead. "For a long time after she left I thought maybe it was me, that she saw something awful in me, maybe something of my father that I wasn't even aware of. I thought that was why she left me the way she did, without warning, without any discussion."

"Jake. I don't know your father, but I know you. There's nothing awful inside you, no darkness that chased her away in fear."

He smiled again. "I know that now." He rolled over on his back and stared up at the ceiling. "It's funny, but it was something Jimmy said a couple of weeks ago that made me think about things objectively for the first time."

"What did he say?" Her hand moved to his chest, to stroke the dark hair she found so appealing.

"He said he thought his mother had liked the flowers she planted in the backyard better than she liked him. It made me start to think, really think, about the woman I'd married. When we were young and dating I knew she could be selfish and shallow and cold, but she was also exciting and beautiful."

The frown returned to his forehead. "The first couple of years of our marriage were okay, mostly because while I worked she had lunch with friends, shopped and had no real responsibilities. Then she had Jimmy."

"You know, there are some women who just aren't cut out to be mothers," Jessie said softly.

He nodded. "All the things that irritated me about Colette when we were young, her selfishness and cold nature, I thought for sure would change as she gained some maturity. When she left and finally contacted me through a letter, she told me she didn't like being my wife and didn't want to be a mother."

"Then she's a stupid ass," she said.

He laughed. "What time are Charlie and Maria coming home? I don't want them to walk in and find us naked in here."

"They're not coming home. Charlie is staying with Larry for a while and Maria is staying with her sister." Jessie's heart constricted as she thought of her life without the everyday presence of her son. "Until we know what's going on, I didn't want them here. I'd never risk their safety."

As quickly as that, reality came crashing down on her. She dropped her hand from his chest, then sat up. As wonderful as it was making love with Jake, it didn't change anything else that was going on in her life.

Chapter 20

"I'm going to take a quick shower," she said. "I'll be out in just a few minutes." She got up from the bed and went into the master bath.

She'd only been beneath the hot shower spray for a moment when the glass door opened and Jake stepped in beside her. "I thought you might need somebody to scrub your back." He took the soapy sponge from her, then pulled her against his body and beneath the spray.

Her intention for a quick shower disappeared as Jake kissed her, then soaped her body inch by inch. Slick with soap, humming with a new need that his touch had evoked in her, she welcomed him as he took her once again.

By the time he was finished with her, she leaned weakly against the glass enclosure, her knees threatening to buckle beneath her.

Thirty minutes later they were both dressed and seated at the table, eating ham sandwiches and chips. "I still find it hard to believe that the T and B killer has resurfaced after all this time to come after you," he said.

"I know the police never released the information about the killer whistling 'Amazing Grace' as he buried me. But whoever made that call to me was whistling the same song."

Jake thought of the lilies that were being left at the current murder scenes. The police had managed to hang on to that fact without the public learning of it, but it didn't mean that eighteen years from now the information would still be a secret.

"That information might have been leaked at some time or another over the last eighteen years," he said. "I think you have to consider the possibility that whoever it is, they're close to you. They obviously know your history."

He paused a moment to pop a chip into his mouth. After he'd finished chewing, he continued. "What about that producer of yours? Chris? We both know now he's capable of doing stupid things to generate a little publicity. Does he know about what happened to you?"

She shook her head, and he could smell the fruity shampoo of her still-damp hair. "I never told Chris about the T and B thing, but I guess that doesn't mean he doesn't know."

Jake tried to keep focused on the conversation at hand, but it was difficult with her looking so beautiful. It was difficult with the thought of how she'd tasted, how she'd felt as they'd made love. It had been better than in his wildest imagination.

Her scars were bad. They weren't pretty. But they'd done nothing to temper his desire for her. In truth, those badges of survival had only made him want her more.

"I just don't understand the motivation for all this. I mean, what's the point?"

Her words tore his thoughts from making love to the problem at hand. "The point may be nothing more than your fear. You should know from your work that there are people out there who get off on making other people afraid. Imagine what a coup it would be to make the fear expert afraid."

"It still bothers me that whoever is doing this knows the intimate details of the crime," she said.

Jake shoved his empty plate aside and leaned back in his chair. "I only did a cursory read of some of the files. I'll go through them more carefully and see if anything or anyone catches my interest. What I'd like you to do is make a list of everyone who knows your history. Friends, lovers, neighbors—anyone."

"The lover list will be pretty short," she said dryly.

He smiled. "And am I glad I'm on it." Her cheeks flushed with color and a new wave of tenderness swept through him. His smile faded. "Jessie, do you want me to stay here until we figure this all out?"

"Absolutely not. While I appreciate the offer, you have a son who needs you, and a murder case to solve. Besides, I have good locks on my windows and doors, and I won't answer the phone again without looking at the caller ID."

"You know I'd stay if you wanted me to."

"I know." She tucked a strand of hair behind her ear. "I won't lie to you. I'm scared. But I'd be more scared if the car that has been following me had tried to force me off the road, or if instead of leaving a wreath on my doorstep somebody had tried to break into the house. But so far nothing that's happened has been up close and in my face."

"Which leads me to believe somebody is trying to frighten you, not necessarily hurt you."

She stared at someplace over his shoulder, her eyes more stormy gray than blue. "What makes me so angry is that all of this is taking me back to a place I never wanted to go again." Her gaze sought his and she smiled ruefully. "You've seen my physical scars. I might as well confess to all my emotional ones."

He remained silent as she got up from her chair and paced the space between the table and the sink. "You might have noticed I have a night-light in my room. That's because Dr. Jessica Langford, expert in fear issues, is afraid of the dark. Not only that, but these phone calls have brought back panic attacks. I feel like I'm in that grave again. I can't breathe and my heart races. All I smell is the scent of dirt and spring flowers, and I'm certain I'm going to die."

He couldn't just sit there and listen to her, see the torment in her eyes. He had a feeling she was telling him these things to show that she was a bad bet, a woman too wounded for any man to love.

He got up and went to her, wrapped her in his arms and pulled her tight. "And your point is?"

She raised her face and her eyes glistened with the burden of unshed tears. "My point is what are you doing with me?"

"Funny, at this point I can't imagine what I'd do without you," he replied.

She buried her face into the front of his shirt and held tight to him for a long moment; then she drew a deep breath and stepped out of his arms. "You need to get out of here."

"Are you kicking me out?"

"Absolutely. You need to go home and spend time with your son. Do whatever it is detectives do when they have a minute of free time. Please, Jake. I'll be fine."

He wanted to protest, to tell her that he'd stay as long as she needed him, as long as she'd let him. But he knew she was right. He had a son who'd seen far too little of him in the past couple of weeks, and things that had to be done that couldn't be done here in her house.

"I'm going to arrange for extra patrols to drive by here," he said. "And I'll call you later for that list of names you're going to make for me. Of course, I want you to call me anytime, day or night, if you need me." He grinned. "Or if you just want me."

She laughed, the sound a parting gift to him. Together they walked to the door and shared a long, lingering kiss good-bye.

He was suddenly eager to get back home, to delve more deeply into the files chronicling the T&B killer. He was anxious to find out who was responsible for tormenting the woman he intended to spend the rest of his life with.

Mark Smith sat behind the steering wheel of his wife's SUV. He watched as Detective Jake Merridan left Dr. Langford's house. He recognized the man from a grainy photo that had been in one of the papers. He was the investigator in charge of the latest string of murders. He was also the man Jessica was seeing on a personal basis.

He now recognized everyone who was anyone in Dr. Jessica Langford's life. He'd watched her long enough to be able to identify the ex-husband, the neighbor, the housekeeper. At the station he had learned the other people in her life—the producer, the various security guards and the production assistants.

Mark wasn't worried about the detective or Dr. Jessie recognizing his car now. Cindy's SUV was a far cry from his own dark blue Taurus.

The article in the newspaper about Dr. Jessie had freaked him out. He'd thought he'd been so careful in following her, spying on her. The fact that she'd seen him hanging out in front of the pet store last weekend had nearly undone him.

For the last couple of days he'd kept a low profile, going to and from work and spending all of his free time at home with Cindy.

The anniversary of the event that had changed lives was quickly approaching, the anniversary of the night that Jessica Clinton had been found alive in that grave.

It had been a Thursday night, just before the Memorial weekend would begin. That night had marked the beginning of the end of life as he knew it. Nothing had been the same for him and his family after that night.

He wondered if she knew now that his name wasn't really Mark Smith, that the information he'd given her about where he lived and worked was bogus.

He rubbed his forehead wearily, then started the engine on the SUV. It was hell knowing that you were losing your mind, unraveling in ways that were terrifying, doing things that made no sense.

Like following her wherever she went. Like wanting to know everything about her and her life. As if that could fix things. As if that could change the past.

He pulled away from the curb and headed home, home to Cindy, who was losing patience with him, home to battle the demons of grief, the darkness of despair.

Chapter 21

"What do you know about the T and B killer?" Jake asked Monica the next morning as they drove to work together.

"When I was a rookie, I studied that case." She laughed. "I thought I'd make my mark in the department by solving the case nobody else had been able to solve. Why? Surely you don't think those murders and the ones we're working on now are related. The signatures are different."

"No, it's nothing like that. There's another reason I'm interested in the T and B case."

"Does this have something to do with your hot new girlfriend, the sexy psychiatrist?"

Sexy psychiatrist, yes, she was that, but so much more, he thought. "Jessie was the last known victim of the T and B killer."

Monica shot him a look of surprise. "No shit?"

"Yeah. She was the young woman found alive in that grave in Hillside Cemetery."

"Wow, talk about baggage."

"She's amazingly well-adjusted considering what she went through," Jake replied. "But there are some things going on in her life that have me disturbed." He told her everything that had been happening to Jessie.

"So somebody's having fun bringing back all those memories to her," Monica said when he was finished. "But surely you don't think the T and B killer has returned after all these years."

"No, I don't. And I told her as much. But I want to find out who is responsible for this crap, and I realize with the current case going on, I can't do all the legwork for Jessie without help."

He felt Monica's gaze on him. "You and the doc, you're getting close?"

"I'm in love with her." It was the first time he'd spoken aloud the emotion that had been in his heart. He liked the way the words felt as they left his mouth.

"It's about damn time you hooked up," Monica said. "I was beginning to think that when Colette left she didn't just take your heart, but she also took your balls."

A surprised laugh burst from Jake. "I'm happy to inform you that all my body parts are intact."

"So what do you need from me? You know I'll do whatever I can to help."

"I've got Jessie making a list of everyone in her life who knows what happened to her. Personally I think it's somebody close to her or somebody who was involved in investigating the original crime, screwing with her head."

"Why? I mean, what would be their motivation?"

Jake cast her a sideways glance as he pulled into a parking space in the police station lot. "If I knew why, I'd probably know who."

"So basically you want to check out the people close to her." They got out of the car and headed toward the building.

"Yeah, along with solving this damn lily case."

"You know, I'm sure there's still some people on the force who worked on the T and B case. Maybe you should talk to some of them and see if they have any clues as to who might be bothering Dr. Jessie."

"Good idea," Jake replied. "Maybe I'll start with the captain. I'm sure he'll remember the case."

"It was the worst time in the history of Kansas City," Captain Broadbent said an hour later as the two men sat in his office. "Five victims dead, five families ripped apart, and we couldn't get a break. The press was all over our asses to find the son of a bitch, and we had nothing to go on." Broadbent eyed him curiously. "Why are you asking me about this? Don't tell me you think we've got another unsolvable one with these recent murders."

"Hell, no. I'm not about to cry uncle when it comes to the lily murders," Jake replied. "Although you know we're struggling with lack of evidence."

"So why the questions about the T and B case?"

Jake told the captain what he'd related to Monica only an hour before, about everything that had happened to Jessie in the last couple of weeks, culminating in the phone call where somebody had whistled "Amazing Grace."

Broadbent frowned. "We never released the information about the perp whistling that song as he buried Jessica Clinton. As far as I know that information has never been made public."

Jake nodded thoughtfully. "Then whoever is terrorizing Dr. Langford is either somebody who she told about the details of the crime, or somebody who had access to the information from either first-hand experience or reading the files."

Captain Broadbent leaned forward, his eyes holding the hint of a challenge. "The officers that worked that case were the best on the force. Good men with honor. None of my men would be capable of something like this."

"I didn't recognize the names of the men who worked the case," Jake said.

Broadbent shrugged. "It's been eighteen years. Cops retire, move, burn out and quit. I don't think you'll find your answer in the files. I would imagine the answer lies with Jessica Langford."

Minutes later as Jake returned to the war room, he realized there wasn't much he could do for Jessie until she got him that list. All he could do was hope and pray that whomever was tormenting her wouldn't escalate actions into any kind of violence.

Monday evening Jessie sat at her kitchen table and stared down at the list she had made to give Jake. She wasn't sure what disturbed her more, the idea that the T&B killer had returned for her or that somebody close to her, somebody she cared about, was capable of using her past to scare the hell out of her.

The list before her wasn't long. Even right after that night she'd been reticent to discuss the details of her time with the killer.

She certainly hadn't shared all the details with her parents. Their eyes had been haunted enough without knowing each and every excruciating, minute fact.

She hadn't told them everything about the sexual assault. They'd known she'd been raped, and that's all they needed to know. Nor had she told them about the man whistling "Amazing Grace" while he'd shoveled dirt down on her in an effort to bury her alive.

But her therapist had known all the details. Larry had known. Her roommate at college had also been privy to most of the details. She'd lost touch with the college roommate years ago but still saw her former therapist on occasion at professional functions. Then there was Larry.

With a sigh of frustration she shoved the list aside and left the table, restless in a way she experienced once a year in the days leading up to the official anniversary of the crime.

Four days from today it would be exactly eighteen years. And this anniversary was worse than any other, because somebody was intent on bringing it all back to her.

She grabbed a can of orange-scented Pledge and a rag from beneath the sink cabinet. Maybe she'd dust a little, work off some of the excess energy she felt.

Funny that this anniversary was both the worst and the best. The best because of Jake. Whoever was responsible for the phone calls that had initially sent her to the police station had been responsible for bringing her Jake.

Jake. She couldn't begin to catalogue all that he'd brought to her life. At a time when she'd been certain she would live the rest of her life alone, he'd stormed in beneath her defenses and had captured her heart.

She loved just looking at him. She loved talking with him about anything and everything. And she loved making love with him. The passion between them was undeniable, overwhelming and explosive. She might have worried about it being so bright it would burn itself out if not for the tenderness, compassion and caring that accompanied it.

Dammit, she wanted a normal life. Was that too much to ask? Was it too much to ask for a life without fear? And damn the person who had brought such fear back to her.

She finished dusting the living room, then checked her watch. Jake should be arriving anytime to pick up the list she'd prepared.

He'd invited her to his house for dinner with him and Jimmy, but she'd declined. She'd had a full day at the office and the show later that night. She was in love and being terrorized, but life went on and there were responsibilities to be taken care of.

The doorbell rang and she dropped her dusting items on the floor and hurried to the door. Her heart jumped at the sight of Jake.

He stepped through the door and kissed her on the forehead. "How are you doing?" he asked.

"All right. I survived a Sunday night without Charlie or Maria in the house."

"I told you to call me if you got scared," he said.

"I was fine. I'm stronger than you might think."

"Oh, sweetheart, trust me, I know that."

"I've got the list on the kitchen table." She gestured for him to follow her through the living room.

"Wait," he said, and grabbed her hand to halt her forward motion. When she turned to face him he smiled and pulled her into his arms. "That little peck on the forehead didn't begin to satisfy me."

She smiled up at him. "Me neither." He slanted his mouth over hers, and as always it was magic. The restlessness ebbed as she stood in the shelter of his arms. When the kiss ended she leaned against him, reluctant to break the embrace. "Do you think we could lead a normal, healthy life if we never moved from this position?"

"I can think of another position I would seriously never consider moving from," he replied.

She laughed and stepped back from him. "We might have trouble explaining that to our children."

"Ah, always the realist." He drew a deep sigh. "Okay, let's go take a look at this list."

Moments later they sat at the kitchen table, her list of potential suspects in front of Jake.

"Jessie, it's important that you don't hold anything back," he said. "If you have a gut instinct, any intuition about any of these people, you tell me, no matter how crazy it might sound."

She nodded, a knot of tension forming in the center of her chest. She sat so close to Jake she could smell the dizzying scent of his cologne, see the individual dark lashes that framed his beautiful eyes. He looked so safe, so solid, but his nearness couldn't dispel the sudden coldness in her veins.

"It's just so hard to imagine that somebody I trust might be responsible," she said. "Whoever is doing these things has to know that they're hurting me."

"I know." His eyes were so warm, so filled with compassion. "But, Jessie, it's got to be somebody you know, and you need to think about not only who might be responsible, but why." He directed his gaze to the first name. "Larry."

"Larry." She repeated his name aloud thoughtfully.

"Just talk to me," Jake urged her. "Just tell me anything and everything that pops into your head."

"He wanted to reconcile." She looked at Jake, saw the surprise in his eyes.

"When? Recently?"

"Just about the same time I got the first phone call. But I can't imagine Larry having anything to do with any of this."

"How serious was his attempt to reconcile with you?" Jake asked, obviously ignoring her faint protest of Larry's innocence.

"I don't know. Serious enough for Larry. But why would he be doing any of this now?"

"To scare you back to him? Maybe he decided to pad the odds in his favor. It's a motive. A perverted one, but a motive nevertheless."

"It's crazy," she scoffed. But was it? She knew Larry had a ruthless streak in him, a ruthlessness that made him so successful as a divorce lawyer. "I hate this."

"What?"

"I hate that I'm going to have to rethink every relationship with every person in my life. I hate that I have to dissect all my friendships and acquaintances to see which one of them might be a nut."

"I'm sorry for you," he said softly. "I'll tell you one thing—I intend to spend the night here with you on Thursday. I don't want you to be alone."

Thursday night. Anniversary night. The knot in her chest squeezed tighter. "I want to tell you that it's not necessary." She managed to speak around the lump in her throat. "I want to tell you that you should be in your own bed resting peacefully, but I can't." She offered him what she knew was a wobbly smile. "I've never spent an anniversary night alone. I always had Larry, and after Larry I had Charlie and Maria."

Jake took one of her hands in his. "If I have my way, you'll never, for the rest of your life, spend an anniversary all alone." He squeezed her hand slightly. "Jessie, even though I've read the files and seen the pictures, I can't begin to imagine what you went through that night. But I can promise you I'd like to spend the rest of my life making you happy."

Despite her desire to never revisit that night in her thoughts, she found herself going back in time. She pulled her hand from Jake's and leaned back in the chair, needing to distance herself from him as memories burst forth in her head. She stared up at the ceiling and let the words fall from her.

"You know, it's funny. Before that night I always assumed that the worst thing that could happen to a woman was rape. To be violated against your will seemed like a fate worse than death."

She sensed Jake stirring in his chair as if to console or stop her from speaking. She continued hurriedly, not wanting to be stopped. "That night he kept my eyes taped shut. I could see nothing, and when he ripped my clothes off I remember thinking, Okay, he's going to rape me. But I can live through that."

She looked at him then, saw the glisten of tears in his eyes. On some level she understood she was burdening him with her pain, and on another level she wanted him to know all of it.

Larry had never wanted to know. He hadn't been strong enough to carry the pain. But she knew Jake was. She wanted no secrets between them. If they were going to have any kind of lasting future together, then she wanted him to know everything.

"One of the coping mechanisms I teach to patients is that when they find themselves facing a fearful situation, they need to think about worst-case scenarios. So my worst-case scenario was that I was going to be raped. I figured it was a good thing that I couldn't see him, couldn't identify him, because that meant he'd probably let me go when he was finished."

"But he didn't let you go." Jake's eyes were hot pools of emotion. They held not only pain, but also a rising rage.

"Then I felt the first knife prick on my belly. Even though it hurt like hell, I knew it wasn't meant to kill me. Suddenly the rape seemed unimportant, and my worst-case scenario was that he was going to cut me badly. With each cut that wasn't lethal, I knew I could survive and still had the hope that he'd have his fun, then let me go. If I got someplace for medical treatment quickly enough, I wouldn't bleed to death and eventually I'd be fine."

A muscle ticked in his jaw, throbbing with an intensity she might have found frightening if she didn't understand it. She wanted to place her fingers against it, soothe him, but fought the impulse.

"And what happened next?" The words escaped him on a low growl, as if his throat had tightened and he was strangling.

"I was half mad with the pain, but so relieved when he wrapped me in plastic, picked me up and I was put in the trunk of a vehicle. All I could think of was that finally it was over. He'd dump me on the side of the road and leave me. I knew I was badly hurt and there was a possibility he'd dump me someplace remote. But I was young and resourceful. I figured I could staunch the bleeding on my stomach and somehow, someway make my way to safety."

There was a quiet fury in Jake. She could see it in his eyes, smell it wafting from him like hell's fire. "I'd kill him for you," he said between clenched teeth. "If I knew who he was, if I knew where to find him, I'd kill him for what he did to you."

This time she gave in to the impulse to touch him. She reached out and stroked down his jaw to where the muscle twitched in taut rhythm. His skin was warm beneath her touch and heated the coldness that her memories had wrought.

"Finish it," he said, both with an edge of dread and with the resignation of a man who knew she had to tell the rest of it.

She dropped her hand from his face and instead

clenched it into a fist on her lap. "When the car stopped and he picked me up out of the trunk, I was sure it was over. I was elated up until the time he rolled me over and I fell into what seemed like thin air. I hit the ground with enough force to lose my breath. I didn't know where I was, but by kicking my legs and twisting my body I knew I was in some sort of a pit."

She jerked up out of her chair, her throat closing in, her heart pounding with a force to leap right out of her chest. She closed her eyes against the panic attack that was about to erupt.

Damp earth.

Spring flowers.

The haunting whistle of "Amazing Grace."

She was falling. . . . Falling into the darkness of the night, into the world of a madman. Help me. Please, somebody help me. The voice that cried inside her head was that of a sixteen-year-old who had never dreamed such evil existed in the world.

"Jessie. It's all right." The deep male voice sliced through her memory as she found herself in Jake's arms. Safe. Secure.

His hands were on either side of her face and he used his thumbs to swipe at the tears that cascaded down her cheeks. As she gazed into his eyes she felt a momentary stab of guilt, knowing that she'd put the anguish there.

"I swear to you, I'll do anything in my power to make sure you never have to suffer like that again."

His voice vibrated with emotion and any threat of a panic attack faded away.

She was safe here, with this man. She leaned her head against his shoulder. "I'm sorry I put you through that."

"I wanted to go through it. I want every piece of you, Jessica. Both the good and the bad. Don't you get it? I'm in love with you."

She looked up at him once again. "And I'm in love with you."

He expelled his breath, as if he'd been holding it for a very long time. "Good." He nodded. "That's very good. So, when is the wedding?"

She laughed and stepped out of his embrace. "Not anytime soon." Disappointment flashed across his features. "We need some time to meld the families together, time for Jimmy and Charlie to adjust." She wrapped her arms around herself in an effort to keep from reaching for him again. "Besides, when we marry I don't want any dark clouds hanging over our heads."

"You realize you've just given me one hell of a motivation for solving your issue."

She smiled. "I like a man with purpose." She cleared her throat, afraid that if they lingered for another minute they'd be in bed. "And now it's time for you to get home."

He moved back to the table with reluctant, dragging footsteps and grabbed the list she'd prepared. "Will you be okay? "

"You might not believe me, but I feel surprisingly strong and good. I feel cleansed." It was true. Sharing the darkness had produced light.

She walked with him to the front door, wanting him more than anything else in the world and loving him enough to send him home, where he belonged. . . . At least for now.

"Why don't you call me tonight when you get home from the station?" he said.

"Absolutely not," she replied. "I know the hours you've been keeping these last few weeks because of the murders. The last thing you need is an after-midnight phone call to disturb what sleep you're able to get."

He reached out and stroked his fingers down the side of her face in a touch so loving it seemed to caress the surface of her heart. "First thing in the morning, then. You call me."

"I will." As she watched him walk down the sidewalk to his car in her driveway, she knew with a certainty that Jake was the man she'd been waiting for, the man who was strong enough to share the torment of her past and soft enough to comfort her.

As she locked the door the phone rang. She checked her watch and smiled. That would be Charlie calling to tell her good night.

Chapter 22

If his dad wasn't getting laid, then he was planning on it, Jimmy thought on Tuesday when his dad explained to him that Mrs. Crawford would be spending the night on Thursday and Jake would be gone.

It wasn't unusual for his dad to be gone overnight. Killers didn't wait until daylight hours to do their dirty work, and the people who got killed were sometimes found in the middle of the night.

But always before his dad got a phone call, then rushed out. This time the night away from home was planned, and Jimmy figured it had to be Dr. Jessie.

He didn't really like to think about his dad having sex. It was kind of gross, but Dr. Jessie had made his dad smile again and that made Jimmy happier than he'd been in a long time.

"Jimmy? Are you about ready? We don't want to be late."

"I'm just putting on my shoes, Dad," Jimmy yelled back. The two of them were meeting Dr. Jessie and Charlie at one of those lame pizza places where they had puppets dancing on stage and singing dopey songs. The only good things about it were Jimmy was starving and the place also had a decent collection of arcade games.

"Ready?" Jake stuck his head into Jimmy's room as he finished tying his second sneaker.

"Ready." Jimmy followed his dad out of the house. He couldn't help but notice that his dad smelled like the counters in the department stores where they sold cologne. "Jeez, Dad, what did you do, bathe in that stuff?"

Jake shot him a worried glance. "Too much?"

"Nah, Dr. Jessie will probably like it." Even grown-ups got dopey about the love stuff, he thought as he got into the passenger's seat and fastened his belt.

"You like Dr. Jessie, don't you, Jimmy?"

"I guess. I don't know her very well."

"She's very nice. And Charlie thinks the world of you. He thinks you're smarter than anyone else on the face of the earth."

Jimmy eyed his father suspiciously. He was talking faster than usual and he seemed sort of nervous. "Dad, what are you trying to say?"

"Nothing. I mean, I just thought maybe it would be nice if we spent more time with Charlie and Dr. Jessie."

"You like her."

His dad flashed a bright smile. "A lot."

"Are you guys gonna get married?"

"I hope so, but only if it's okay with you."

Jimmy thought about it. Dr. Jessie would become his stepmom, and Charlie would be his little stepbrother. Lots of his friends had stepmoms and -brothers and -sisters, and they were like real families. A real family. He'd never really had that.

"Would I have to share my bedroom with the squirt?"

"I think we could arrange for each of you boys to have your own bedrooms."

"Even if we had to share, I guess it wouldn't be too bad as long as he doesn't snore or mess with my stuff." He paused thoughtfully, then looked at his dad once again. "Does Dr. Jessie know you like her a lot?"

"Yes, she knows."

"And does she like you a lot?"

His dad smiled. A big smile. "Yes, yes, she does. Why?"

"I was just wondering. I wouldn't want it to be like mom. Where we like her and she doesn't really like us."

The smile on his dad's face fell away. "It's not like that, son. I'll make sure it's never like that again."

By that time they'd arrived at the pizza place. They got out of their car and were approaching the front door when Dr. Jessie arrived. They stood just outside the door and waited for the other two to join them.

"Hi, Jimmy." Charlie came racing toward Jimmy, that goofy grin of happiness on his face. The kid definitely didn't know cool, but something about his eager face warmed Jimmy's heart.

Dr. Jessie approached, a smile on her face. She greeted Jimmy and Jake, then quickly finger combed Charlie's hair. She turned to Jimmy, and to his surprise, she ran her fingers through his hair, smoothing it down with a gentle touch.

"There, now you two young men look ready to face the singing puppets," she said.

Jimmy had the craziest impulse to cry. His mom had never touched him like that, so gently, so casually. Jimmy could get used to that. As they all entered the pizza place together, he decided this new family stuff might just work out fine.

"How was your day?" Jessie asked Jake when the boys left the table to turn dollars into tokens and play some arcade games. It was the first chance the two of them had to talk alone.

"Tough. Frustrating. Exhausting." He smiled. "The only thing that got me through it was knowing I'd see you tonight. What about you? How did your day go?"

"It was okay. I saw patients, had lunch with Kayla, my next-door neighbor, then saw a few more patients. And speaking of patients, I've got some-

thing to tell you that might or might not be important."

"What?"

She'd battled with herself about whether to
share the mystery of Mark Smith with him. On the
one hand, she was reluctant to break doctor-patient
confidentiality, but on the other hand, she told herself, Mark Smith had broken her trust by not giving
her his real name or address.

"You know that patient I mentioned before, the
one I thought might be my stalker?"

"What about him?" He became completely still,
his gaze intent on her.

"I've only seen him a couple of times as a patient, but I discovered all the personal information
he gave me is false. I'm not sure if he used his real
name or not, but his address and phone number are
bogus."

"How did he pay for his visits?"

"Cash. He told my receptionist he had no insurance."

"More than a little bit suspicious. What's his
name? I'll see if I can check him out."

Jessie hesitated and took a sip of her soda. When
she was finished she toyed with her napkin. "If you
check him out, please be discreet. It's quite possible
the man isn't guilty of anything, and I feel terrible
about breaking the confidentiality rule." She drew
a deep breath. "Mark Smith. He told me his name
was Mark Smith."

"I don't suppose you have a driver's license or

social security number." Jake said, and she shook her head. "Smith. There's probably dozens of Mark Smiths just in the greater Kansas City area alone."

"I know. I just thought I should mention him to you."

"What about your own therapist? Dr. Mary Franklin?"

"What about her?"

Jake glanced over to where the two boys were at an arcade machine with two steering wheels, then looked back at her. "I'm assuming she knew pretty much everything that had happened that night. Is it possible she's jealous of your success in the field? You know, the student has surpassed the teacher."

"No. I can't imagine her doing anything like what's been going on. For one thing, she's over sixty now and talking about retiring."

He shrugged. "It was just a thought."

She smiled. "And I appreciate all your thoughts. How's your other case coming?"

"About as frustrating as yours. No leads, no clues, no evidence. This killer is either the smartest we've ever hunted or the luckiest."

"That's what they thought about the T and B killer."

"Don't let my captain hear you mention the two cases in the same breath. The last thing he wants to be reminded of is the failure of the department in the T and B case." Once again his gaze sought out the two boys, who had moved from the driving game to throw basketballs at a hoop.

Jessie followed his gaze, her heart warming at the sight of the two laughing together. "I don't know what issues you and Jimmy were having, but he's a great kid."

Jake smiled, causing endearing sunbursts of fine lines to deepen at the corners of his eyes. "I think we resolved our issue. When Colette left I started sleeping on the sofa. At first it just didn't feel right to be alone in the bedroom, then the sofa became a habit, a habit that Jimmy had a problem with. He told me it wasn't normal and he wanted things back to normal. So, I moved back into the bedroom, Jimmy is happier and things are fine between us. For now. Certainly in the next couple of years I'm expecting to butt heads with him more and more frequently."

"Butting heads with a teenager is wonderfully normal," she replied. "What are your thoughts about dogs?"

He blinked at the rapid change of subject. "I don't know. I don't think about dogs often. Should I?"

"Charlie has been talking about maybe getting a dog."

"I think he'd be just as happy with a Jimmy."

Jessie laughed. "Definitely. How do you think Jimmy would feel about having a Charlie permanently in his life?"

"He's fine with the idea. He told me on the way over here he'd even share a bedroom with the kid as long as Charlie doesn't snore or mess with his stuff." Jake placed a hand on top of hers. "It's going to be fine. We're going to be fine. We're going to have a wonderful life growing old together and watching our boys grow into men."

"I want that. I want you."

His eyes flashed with a hot darkness that shot a trembling breathlessness through her. "If you keep talking like that to me, I'm going to sweep the pizza off this table and take you right here."

"I think the puppets might be shocked."

"Screw the puppets," he replied. "They all look half demented to me."

She laughed shakily as a rush of sweet anticipation overwhelmed her. "Thursday night." The words were a promise. "I want to fall asleep in your arms and wake up in the same place in the morning."

He shifted positions in the booth and gave her a pained look. "Stop it. Just thinking about it is making my pants too tight." He picked up his soda glass and took a deep drink.

She loved the fact that she had the power to arouse him just by talking to him. She loved that he'd seen her scars, knew her body intimately and wanted her still. "I told Chris I'm not coming into the station Thursday night."

"Did he ask why?"

"Yes, and I told him I had some personal matters to take care of. He wasn't thrilled, but he'll survive."

Jake's expression darkened. "He's a worm."

"Not really. He's just young and full of himself and ambition."

At that moment the two boys returned to the table, and any conversation about sex and murders halted.

He was in.

It had been incredibly easy to breach the lock on Dr. Jessie's back door. He stood in the kitchen and breathed in the essence of her.

The need in him was huge. A clawing, tormenting need he couldn't ignore. He'd thought about taking another woman off the street, but had decided he was tired of appetizers. It was time for the main course.

Tonight he would finish what he'd begun so long ago. Tonight he would complete the ritual that had needed to be completed for so many years.

The house was silent. The only sound he could hear was the hum of the refrigerator and the sound of his own breathing.

He knew she was gone. He'd watched her drive away a half an hour ago. He had no idea when she'd be home, but he'd be ready for her. He knew it was possible she'd go directly to the station from wherever she'd gone now. That was fine with him. He could take her after midnight or he could take her before. But one way or another, tonight she would be his.

Inside the latex gloves his hands trembled. But first he needed to check out the house. He wanted

to know the layout. He liked to know his surroundings when he was at work.

It was a rare experience, to be in the dwelling of
one of his victims. Even when he'd lived in California he'd never taken a victim from her home. The
streets had been his hunting grounds. Easy pick-
ings.

This was a new experience, being able to see how
she lived, to touch her things. It heightened his
hunger in a thrilling way.

The other thrill came from the fact that she was
seeing the detective in charge of the other murders.
Small world, he thought. detective Jake Merridan
had been in the paper several times, assuring the
public that the KCPD was on the job and an arrest
in the murders was imminent.

"Imminent, my ass," he muttered. They didn't
have a clue. Detective Jake Merridan didn't have a
clue. Merridan might be smart, but he was smarter
than all of them. He'd left a string of victims in his
path and the cops had never even gotten close.

He walked down the hallway, peeking into bedrooms as he went. The housekeeper's room was
neat and tidy, decorated in pale yellow and with
pictures of the Virgin Mary on the walls.

Charlie's room was typical little-boy, with toys
spilling out of a painted box in one corner and the
bed covered in a spread with a baseball motif.

The last room he entered was Jessie's. The trembling that had possessed his hands swept through
his entire body. He looked around with interest.

A night-light burned in a socket next to her bed, and a paperback novel sat on the nightstand. The top of the dresser held a bunch of perfume bottles, a jewelry box and a stack of eight-by-ten glossies of the good doctor.

He stretched out in the center of her bed, breathing deeply of the scent of her.

He knew he was leaving behind hairs and fibers, but when the police investigated the death of Jessica Langford any DNA evidence they might find would do them no good. They'd have nothing to match it with. He'd never been arrested, wasn't on file with his DNA.

He grabbed her pillow and buried his face in it. Tonight she would no longer haunt him. Tonight he would complete what he'd tried to do so many years before.

His cock was hard. . . . Harder than he could ever remember. It wasn't the thought of raping Jessica that made him hard. He'd already had her that way and felt no need to have her again.

No, what made him so hard, what made him ache with sweet, tormenting desire was the need to put her in the ground and shovel dirt on top of her.

What aroused him the most was the idea of her terror as the dirt fell on top of her, slowly suffocating her to death.

Chapter 23

It was almost eight when Jessica pulled up in Larry's driveway to drop off Charlie. She hated this. She hated the fact that things were such that her son wasn't sleeping in his own bed in her house.

"Jimmy said we might be brothers if you and Jake get married," Charlie said. He remained buckled in the passenger's seat as he looked at his mother for confirmation.

"What would you think about that?"

He smiled, the freckles on his cheeks dancing with the gesture. "I think it would be totally awesome, except Jimmy told me if we share a bedroom I can't touch his stuff."

"And what did you say about that?"

Charlie shrugged. "I told him that he couldn't touch my stuff either. But I'd let him if he wanted to."

Jessie smiled and opened her car door. "Come

on, my little man, it's time for you to get settled in for the night."

As they walked up to the front door, Jessie once again wondered if Larry was responsible for the things that had been happening to her. Was he trying to scare her back into his arms? She knocked on the door and was surprised when a blond woman answered.

"Hi, you must be Jessica. I'm Trisha," the woman said with a warm smile.

"Hi, Trisha," Charlie said. "Where's Dad?"

"He's on the deck." Charlie raced away, and Trisha once again smiled at Jessica. "It's so nice to meet you. I've heard so many things about you."

"Good things, I hope," Jessie replied. Instinctively she liked this woman, who appeared not to be threatened in the least by her presence.

"Great things," Trisha assured her. "Please, come in. I know Larry will want to speak with you."

As Jessie followed the attractive Trisha through the living room, any doubts she might have had about Larry fell away. Why on earth would he want her back when he had Trisha?

"Hey!" Larry stood from a deck chair as the two women stepped outside. "I guess you two have introduced yourselves." He sat back in the chair.

"We did," Trisha replied.

"I was just asking Charlie how it went at the pizza place," Larry said.

"I told him it was cool. I made two baskets when we were playing hoops," Charlie said.

Larry looked relaxed, more at ease than Jessie had ever seen him, and she wondered if that was Trisha's influence. If so, then the new woman in his life was good for him.

"Would you like something to drink?" Trisha asked. "Maybe a glass of iced tea?"

"No, thanks. I'm not staying," Jessie said.

"Mom, guess what?" Charlie's features danced with excitement.

"What?"

"Dad said that tonight we're going to stay up really late, like midnight, and have a movie marathon. Aren't we, Dad?" Charlie moved over to his father and looped an arm around his shoulder.

"That was our deal," Larry agreed, then looked at Jessie. "I finished up a big case today and I'm not going into the office tomorrow, so we agreed that tonight we'd have a special celebration. It's just one night, a little break from routine."

"Popcorn, ice cream and Disney movies," Charlie exclaimed.

"Sounds like big plans," Jessie said. "Come here and give me a kiss, and I'm out of here so you can start your big night."

Charlie ran to her, planted a quick kiss on her cheek, then hurried toward his bedroom with an announcement that he was going to gather up the movies.

"Jess, I know you probably don't approve," Larry began the moment Charlie had left the deck. She and Larry had agreed early on that the rules needed to be the same at both houses, that routine and consistency were vital for Charlie's well-being.

Jessie held up a hand to stop him. "It's fine, Larry. An occasional late night won't kill him."

"No, but it might kill me," Larry joked.

Jessie turned to Trisha. "It was nice meeting you. And now I'll get out of your hair so you can get on with your evening plans."

Larry walked with her to the front door as Trisha went to help Charlie make his movie selections. "She seems nice, Larry," Jessie said.

"Yeah, she is. She doesn't take any crap from me."

"All the more reason to hang on to her."

"I'm going to do my best."

Jessie grinned at him. "You'd better do better than your best."

Minutes later, as Jessie drove from Larry's toward the radio station, she suddenly remembered the photos she'd left at home.

"Dammit," she muttered. Chris had called her earlier in the day to ask her to bring in a stack of her publicity head shots. She'd pulled them out and placed them on her dresser, then had promptly forgotten them.

At least she had time to swing by home and grab them. As she drove, her thoughts, as always, turned to Jake. Two more nights and he would be in her bed. Two more nights and she'd have him all to herself. Unless there was another murder. Unless she had a crisis with a patient.

She shoved these thoughts from her mind. She could only hope that the serial killer haunting the area would remain unheard from for a while longer and all her patients stayed stable. She wanted, needed that night with Jake.

For the first time in a very long time Jessie looked forward to the future. In her heart of hearts she'd never imagined life might hold a man like Jake for her. In her soul of souls she'd never imagined there could be so much happiness in her life.

She pulled up into her driveway and got out, hurrying toward the front door. She'd grab the pictures and take off again. There were several things she wanted to do at the station before her show began. Busy work that needed some attention.

As she walked through the front door she paused in the foyer, an unexpected inner alarm ringing in her head. She frowned and stood as still as a statue, trying to identify the reason for the apprehension. She heard nothing to give her pause, saw nothing that would produce the edge of disquiet that rose up inside her.

She took a step into the living room and looked around. Everything was as she'd left it. She saw absolutely nothing that should alarm her. She shook her head, as if to shake the bad feeling away.

She shouldn't be surprised that a faint chill seemed to be riding her shoulders. It was that time of year when she always struggled, when her brain received false fear signals as distant memories surged upward. Always in the days leading up to the anniversary she was more tense, more prone to unexpected bursts of uneasiness.

Walking toward the bedroom she told herself she was being silly. There was nothing wrong here. No reason for the chill of trepidation that clutched at her.

Still, in the bedroom the chill intensified. Again she looked around the room. Nothing out of place, nothing amiss. She grabbed the photos from the dresser, then turned to leave the room, deciding she was just being silly and on edge.

She didn't relax again until she was back in her car and headed for the radio station. Silly. She was being silly. She knew better than anyone how dangerous listening to false fear signals could be.

If you listened to the false ones, you might miss the very real signals that could save your life.

"Come on, Dad. We've hardly spent any time together lately, just the two of us," Jimmy said. "Just a couple of games."

Jake was exhausted. He'd been burning the candle at both ends between the lily murder investigation and his concerns for Jessie. After eating too much pizza all he wanted to do was hit the hay. But Jimmy asked for so little, and it didn't seem fair that the person who got shortchanged in Jake's life was his son.

"All right." He roused himself from the sofa and stood. "Just a couple of games. Nickel and dime, limit of three raises and nothing wild."

Jimmy's eyes gleamed as he sat at the kitchen table and shuffled the cards for a couple of games of poker. As he dealt the cards, Jake tuned the radio they kept on the kitchen counter to the station that played *Are You Afraid of the Dark?* with Dr. Jessica Langford.

"We'll play until the show is over, then I absolutely have to go to bed," he told his son.

"Deal," Jimmy agreed.

Over the next two hours Jimmy took him for every bit of change he had in his wallet, plus several dollar bills. As they played Jake listened to the sound of Jessie's voice soothing callers, speaking with infinite patience and laughing when laughter was warranted.

Pride swelled his heart. She was so good at what she did. He heard the desperation in some of the caller's voices, and when Jessie was finished speaking with them the desperation was replaced with calm.

None of the callers could know the dear price she'd paid for her knowledge and expertise in the emotion of fear. They wouldn't know that she'd learned it not just from books and research but rather from a life experience few would ever know.

One thing was certain: she'd never, ever spend another anniversary of that horrible night without him.

He'd thought about taking her when she'd come into the house earlier, but instead he'd hid in her closet and watched as she took the photos and left again.

The rush he'd gotten from hiding in the shadows of her clothes, glimpsing the sweet sight of her through the closet door that was open a crack, had been awesome.

It would have been easy to take her then. She'd been alone and had stood for a moment with her back to the closet. But after all the years he'd waited, after all the time of anticipating and desiring, he'd held back.

He'd let her have one more show. It was a shame she didn't know that tonight would be her final radio hour. If she'd known she might have said a fond farewell to her fans, given her son an extra-special kiss and whispered a sweet, loving good-bye to Detective Jake Merridan.

She'd be home just after midnight. He'd be waiting. Yes, he had big plans for a dramatic end. He anticipated high drama in the final hours of the life of the woman who had been the bane of his existence.

Chapter 24

It had been a good show. The callers had been livelier than usual and the problems more interesting. When she finished with the last caller she pulled off her earphones and shot Chris a thumbs-up through the window.

She gathered her purse and keys and walked out of the booth. "Great show," Chris said. "Baby, you were on tonight."

"It was good, wasn't it?"

"Better than good. It was great."

A few minutes later as Jessie got into her car to head home, she not only felt the warmth of a job well done but also the exhaustion of a woman who hadn't been sleeping enough in the last couple of weeks.

Usually it took her a while to unwind after a show, but tonight she had a feeling she'd be asleep the moment her head hit the pillow.

As always she kept her eyes not only on the road in front of her, but also on the rearview mirror,

checking to make sure nobody suspicious was behind her.

On a Tuesday night just after midnight there was
little traffic on the streets, and nothing to cause her
any sense of unease.

She'd better get a good night's sleep tonight and
tomorrow night, for she had a feeling she'd get pre-
cious little sleep on Thursday night if Jake had anything to say about it.

A thrilling shiver filled her as she thought of Jake
and the way his dark, gorgeous eyes had promised
a night of passion.

She tried to remember if it had ever been like this
with Larry, but she knew that it hadn't. Larry's
lovemaking had been like a whisper. Jake's was a
roar of intensity and passion that deafened her to
anything else but his voice, his gaze, his touch.

As she drove into her driveway she hit the button that would raise the garage door, and pulled inside. Sleep. That's what she needed more than
anything.

She dragged herself from the garage and into the
kitchen, her exhaustion multiplying tenfold with
each step. She dropped her purse and keys on the
counter, turned off the lights and walked through
the living room.

She left a small lamp burning in the living room
as she did every night, then went down the hall to
her bedroom. She kicked off her shoes just inside
the door and headed for the bathroom.

Fifteen minutes and I'll be asleep, she thought as

she took off her makeup, then brushed her teeth. The slacks, blouse and bra she'd worn to the station hit the laundry basket. She sighed with pleasure as she pulled her soft, fabric softener–scented night-shirt over her head.

There was nothing better than 100 percent cotton against your skin when you were ready to sleep, unless maybe it was something silky and sexy.

She eyed her reflection in the mirror over the bathroom sink. She'd never owned a piece of sexy nightwear. Mostly because she'd never felt sexy.

She thought of Jake's hot, hungry eyes as he gazed at her, and she wanted silk. She thought of the two of them lying in her bed on Thursday night, and she wanted satin and lace.

Black or red? She frowned thoughtfully. No, blue. Jake had told her blue was her color. Tomorrow on her lunch hour she'd go shopping for something incredibly sexy and exciting in a shade of blue to match her eyes. She smiled. She couldn't wait to see Jake's eyes when she pranced, wearing a blue wisp of nothing, in front of him.

After shutting off the bathroom light she stumbled toward the bed. It took only minutes of watching the shadows from the night-light dance on her ceiling for her eyelids to grow so heavy that they closed and she drifted into a dreamless sleep.

She awakened suddenly, heart pounding, mouth dry. She had no idea what had yanked her from her sleep, but opened her eyes and gasped.

Dark.

Pitch-black.

No night-light.

"Oh, God." She shot up to a sitting position. When was the last time she'd changed the bulb? Last week? The week before?

Bad things happened in the dark. Terrible things happened in the dark. Her chest heaved as in a panic she fumbled for the lamp on the nightstand, desperately needing light.

Her fingers found the lamp switch and she turned it. Nothing. No explosion of brilliance. No rays of illumination.

The dark remained.

Impenetrable.

Frantic, she turned the switch again and again, and still nothing. The hair on the nape of her neck jumped to rigid attention.

The odds. What were the odds of both bulbs burning out at precisely the same time? Her mind exploded in sheer panic.

Half wild with fear, she grabbed for the phone and gasped in relief as her fingers closed around the receiver. She picked it up and nearly wept. No dial tone. Dead.

She rolled across the bed, functioning on sheer instinct alone, her mind no longer able to process. When she reached the edge of the bed she slid off and hunkered on the floor. The trembling that took possession of her body made it impossible for her to move.

Her throat closed, forcing her breaths to come

from her in gasps. Her heart thundered so loudly she thought it might drive her insane.

What was happening? Why hadn't the lights worked? Why was the phone dead? There could only be one explanation. Somebody was in the house. Somebody was in her room.

She heard it then, a rustle of movement that told her she was not alone. She wanted to scream. She wanted to cry. But her throat constricted as a panic attack screeched through her.

"Dr. Jessica," a low voice whispered softly out of the black nightmare she'd fallen in. "Are you afraid of the dark?"

Chapter 25

Jake had just closed his eyes when his phone rang. Oh, God, no, not another one, he thought. Phone calls after midnight could only mean bad things. It could only mean the lily killer had struck again. Another body had been found. More work, more frustration.

He flipped on the lamp next to the bed and reached for his cell phone. Dammit. He hoped the call wasn't an announcement of another body found. He didn't recognize the number on the caller ID.

"Merridan."

"Uh . . . Detective Merridan, my name is Larry Langford," a deep voice said. "We haven't met yet, but I got your number from Charlie, who got it from his mother."

"What's up, Mr. Langford?" Why on earth would Jessie's ex-husband be calling him at this hour of the night?

"It might be nothing. You probably know Charlie has been staying here with me for the last couple of days. Tonight we had a movie night. We let Charlie stay up late and watched a couple of Disney movies."

Jake fought back a growl of impatience, wondering where in the hell this conversation was headed.

"Anyway," Langford continued, "Charlie decided to give his mom a call a few minutes ago to tell her good night. He was all excited because he's never talked to her after her radio show before. Anyway, the point of this call is that she didn't answer the phone."

Jake frowned and looked at his clock radio on the nightstand. Twelve forty-five. "Is it possible she got held up at the radio station?"

"Well, that's the thing," Larry said, and the rich concern in his voice was evident. "I called the station and Chris told me she left immediately after the show. Her place isn't that far away from the station. She should have been home a half an hour ago."

Jake's heart raced a little bit faster. "Maybe she's sleeping so soundly she didn't hear the phone."

There was a long pause. "She doesn't ever sleep that sound. Look, I might be overreacting, but with everything that's been going on in her life lately, I just thought I should talk to you. Frankly I'm worried."

Frankly so was Jake. "I'll try to give her a call, and if I don't get an answer I'll head over there and check things out."

"I think maybe we'll head over there too."

Before Jake could tell him that maybe that was a bad idea, Larry hung up.

Jake refused to panic. There wasn't any real reason to assume that something was wrong. Maybe she'd been in the shower when Charlie had called. Maybe she really was sleeping so soundly she hadn't heard the phone.

"Dad?" Jimmy appeared in Jake's bedroom doorway. "Is everything all right?"

"Probably," Jake replied as he punched in Jessie's phone number.

"Is it about the murders?" Jimmy asked as Jessie's phone rang and rang. Why didn't she answer? Why wasn't her answering machine picking up?

"No, I'm just trying to get hold of Dr. Jessie," Jake said as a rising sense of disquiet swept through him. Don't panic, he told himself.

He hung up his phone in frustration, then stood and reached for his jeans. "I've got to ride over to Dr. Jessie's house." When he had his pants on he grabbed his phone once again and punched in his neighbor's phone number.

A sense of urgency ignited inside him as Mrs. Crawford's phone rang without answer. "Doesn't anyone answer the damn phone anymore?" Jake grabbed his shirt. Even if he managed to wake the old woman, it would take her too long to get dressed and get over here.

With every minute that ticked by the sense of

disquiet in his stomach was growing into something bigger, something darker.

"Dad, if you're calling Mrs. Crawford, she's not home. Don't you remember? She told you yesterday that she was leaving to spend a couple of days with her sister. Dad, I can stay here by myself," Jimmy said. "If you need to go, I'll be fine."

Jake wasn't comfortable with that. His name had been in the paper concerning the lily murders. He'd practically taunted the killer in print. He couldn't leave his son here alone, not knowing what that madman might be capable of.

"I can't let you do that." Jake grabbed his keys and his gun from the nightstand. "Go get in the car. You can take the ride with me."

Jake knew it wasn't the best alternative, but it was the only one he had at the moment. He needed to get to Jessie's house.

"When we get to Dr. Jessie's house, you stay in the car. If you leave the car I will ground you for a month, you got that?" Jake said tersely as they left the house.

"Got it," Jimmy said.

As he and his son got into his car, Jake hoped to hell he'd get to Jessie's house and find her sound asleep in bed. He hoped like hell they were all concerned for nothing.

"Dr. Jessie, it's time," the voice whispered in the darkness.

That voice. She knew that voice but she couldn't

place it. The panic attack intensified as she searched the floor around her for something that could be used as a weapon. Nothing. There was nothing.

"Time for you to fulfill your destiny." The voice seemed to be moving closer to her.

Escape. She needed to escape but had no idea where to go, couldn't figure out how to get away. She felt herself sinking into a dark place, a place much darker than her surroundings.

"Jessie, it's time to finish it, the ritual that got broken so many years ago."

She jumped at the nearness of the voice that she suddenly recognized. "Daniel?" The name croaked from her in shock. Daniel the security guard at the radio station? It made no sense. What was he doing here? In her bedroom?

Before she could process this new shock, a sharp prick hit her in the arm. She screamed, a half-strangled cry of terror, then whimpered as instantly a dizzying wave of drowsiness weakened her limbs. Drugged.

"Are you afraid now, Dr. Langford?"

Those were the last words she heard as consciousness slipped away.

When Jake pulled up in front of Jessie's house Larry was already parked in the driveway. Charlie and a blond woman were also in his car. He got out with a grim frown on his face.

"We've knocked and knocked, but she's not answering. I've got a key, but I was afraid to go inside until you got here."

Jake nodded and held out his hand for the key. "You mind if Jimmy sits with Charlie in your car?" he asked.

"No, that's fine."

Jake motioned for his son to get out of the car. "Sit with Charlie," he instructed. "And you," he said to Larry. "Wait here."

He pulled his gun as he approached the front door, hoping that this was a bad case of overreaction on everyone's part. His hand trembled as he fitted the key into the lock.

The minute he opened the door he knew something was wrong. The house was dark. No lights shone anywhere. Jessie would never allow the darkness in her home. His heart filled his throat as he flipped on the living room light.

"Jessie?"

No reply. Not a sound. Not a whisper. The house held the stillness of empty space devoid of human life.

As much as he wanted to storm through the house and find her, his police training kicked in. He needed to make sure nobody else was in the house. He couldn't be much help to Jessie if, as he walked down the hallway to her bedroom, somebody shot him in the back.

He headed for the kitchen and turned on the bright overhead light. It took him only moments to clear the room. Nobody hiding in the pantry; nobody in the laundry room. He checked the garage, a cold horror claiming him as he saw her car parked there.

So she'd made it home from the station.

Despite his need to run, he walked back through the living room with coolheaded, deliberate movements. There were no signs of a struggle, nothing to indicate anything bad had happened, except the fact that there was no Jessie.

Maria's room, then Charlie's, then the main bathroom; he checked each and found nothing to cause the tremendous rush of adrenaline that was half nauseating.

Fear. He'd felt it before in his life. When his old man had come at him with eyes blazing and fists raised. He'd known fear when Jimmy had been two and had suffered a bad case of strep and his fever had spiked.

But nothing had prepared him for the fear he now felt as he approached Jessie's bedroom. He reached his hand inside first and turned on the ceiling light.

He whirled inside with gun ready. In the first sweep of the room his head catalogued impressions. A struggle had occurred here. The phone was on the floor, the cord cut. The shade on the bedside lamp was askew, and still there was no Jessie.

At least she wasn't lying dead on the floor, he told himself. At least there didn't appear to be any blood anywhere in the room.

He did a cursory check of the bathroom, then

stepped back into the bedroom and saw what he had missed on his first glance.

"No." The word erupted from him as if he'd been kicked in the gut. He stared at the object in the center of the bed and tried to make sense of it.

A plastic white lily.

Just like the ones left on the murdered victims.

A screaming panic sliced through him, a panic he knew he couldn't afford to indulge. He had to think like a cop, not like a man. But the terror that flooded through him made any rational thought momentarily impossible.

He tried to remember everything he'd ever heard Jessie say about battling fear. Worse-case scenario. He grabbed on to the notion, then swallowed hard against rising bile.

The worst-case scenario in this instance didn't work, because if he went down that path, the worst-case scenario was that Jessie was already dead.

Chapter 26

It took less than thirty minutes to transform Jessie's place from a home to a crime scene. As the technicians moved from room to room, collecting evidence and dusting surfaces, Jake stood in the kitchen, barking orders to whomever would listen to him.

He'd gone to a cold place, a place where his emotions were unreachable. It was the only way to survive. He'd already dispatched half a dozen officers to various locations, checking the alibis of people who had been on Jessie's list, canvassing the neighborhood for anyone who might have seen anything.

Larry and his girlfriend sat at the kitchen table, as did Charlie and Jimmy. Charlie's little face was white, making his freckles appear to stand out from his skin.

The sight of the boy shot a wave of despair through Jake. We'll find her, he wanted to tell Charlie. No matter where she is, no matter who has her, we'll find her. But Jake knew he couldn't make any promises. His only hope was that the killer stayed true to his habits. All the victims of the lily killer hadn't been murdered immediately after their disappearance.

Jake didn't even want to think about the fact that if Charlie hadn't decided to call his mother in the middle of the night, nobody would know she'd gone missing until morning.

While he was grateful she couldn't have been missing for more than thirty minutes when he'd burst into her house, he was afraid those thirty minutes would haunt him for the rest of his life.

"Tell me again who was on that list," Monica said, distracting him from his painful thoughts.

Jimmy knew something bad had happened. Something terrible. He'd heard the officers talking about a plastic lily that had been found in Dr. Jessie's bedroom, and that it appeared to be the same kind left with all the murder victims.

He felt sadder now than he had when his mother had left. He remembered the way Dr. Jessie had finger combed his hair, just like she was his real mom. His dad had been so happy with her. They were all going to be a family, and it wasn't fair that this had happened.

He glanced over at Charlie and noticed that his lower lip was trembling and his eyes were too big as he stared at the table in front of him.

The kid was wearing SpongeBob SquarePants

loose pajamas, for crying out loud. How lame. Now Jimmy would probably never get the chance to make the kid cool.

At that moment Charlie looked at him. Tears spilled from his eyes and he hurriedly swiped at them with the back of his hand, as if embarrassed that Jimmy would see him cry.

Even though Jimmy would never admit it to anyone else in the whole world, he thought he might love the kid just a little bit.

He scooted his chair closer to Charlie's and threw an arm around his shoulder. "It's okay, Charlie. My dad is the best, smartest cop in the world. Don't worry, he'll find your mom."

Charlie didn't answer, but he leaned his head against Jimmy's shoulder, and for just that moment in time Jimmy felt like he had a family.

"Detective Merridan," an officer called from the front of the house. "There's somebody here who insists he talk to you."

Jake hurried toward the front door and eyed the officer with impatience. "Who is it?"

"He won't give me his name. He says he has information and won't talk to anyone but you."

Jake stepped outside the front door and saw a tall, dark-haired man standing between two uniformed cops. The street in front of the house was lined with cruisers, cherry lights flashing. A growing crowd had gathered and was being held back by a handful more of uniforms.

As Jake approached, the man shifted from one foot to the other, as if gripped by some nervous energy.

"I'm Detective Merridan. Who are you and what do you want?" he asked tersely.

The man's cheeks flushed with the hint of color. "Who I am isn't important. I saw the man take her."

Jake grabbed the man by his upper arm and pulled him closer. "If you're fucking with me, I'll bust you up." Jake released him.

"I'm not, I swear."

"Talk now and talk fast."

The man's gaze slithered away from Jake's. "I was parked just down the block. I was sitting in my car and I saw a car pull up in her driveway, and a man went inside her house."

Jake didn't know whether to believe the man or not. At every crime scene there was always a nut in the crowd who had seen the crime, knew the criminal or confessed to every crime that had occurred in the area in the past fifty years. The proof was always in the details.

"What kind of a car?"

"I think it was a Ford. Silver or beige. He disappeared into the house and a few minutes later he left. He opened the trunk and put something inside, something big, but I couldn't see exactly what it was." His gaze met Jake's once again, and there was torment there. "It was her, wasn't it? He put her in that trunk."

"Did you recognize the man?" Jake held his

breath. This was when he'd know if the man was credible or not. Please, God, please give us a break, he prayed. He narrowed his eyes. "And if you're wasting my time, I'll see you in jail for a long time to come."

The man nodded. "I was too far away to be sure, but I think it looked like one of the security guards down at the radio station where she works."

A million things went through Jake's head. Like what this guy was doing parked outside Jessica's house, like how he knew what the security guards at the station looked like. He wanted to ask why he'd waited to contact anyone. But he didn't have time for answers. This was the only lead they had and he needed to move fast.

"Take this man into custody," he said to the nearest cop. "Get his identification and hold him as a material witness." He yelled the order as he raced back to the house, where Monica stood at the door waiting for him. "Get on the phone and call the radio station, get a list of all the security guards who work there, names and addresses. And for God's sake, hurry."

Chapter 27

Déjà vu.

Consciousness returned in bits and pieces, and when it claimed her fully Jessie realized she was in the trunk of a car, just as she'd been eighteen years ago. Duct tape bound her hands, her feet, and her mouth. But her eyes weren't covered this time.

The trunk wasn't completely dark. She could see a faint illumination coming from the rear car lights. She had no idea what he'd drugged her with, but whatever it was it was wearing off fast.

She worked without success to free her hands, then strained to break free of the binds that held her legs, but found the duct tape impossible to break. Her chest ached from trying to breathe through her nose when what she needed to do was draw in deep lungfuls of air through her mouth.

Daniel. The security guard at the station. She didn't even know his last name, but she knew he was the boogeyman who had haunted her, the faceless killer she'd thwarted by surviving his night of horror so long ago.

He'd win if she lost hope, but it was difficult to sustain any kind of hope at the moment. Nobody knew she'd been taken from her bed in the middle of the night. Nobody would miss her until she didn't show up at the office the next morning. By then it would be too late.

She squeezed her eyes tightly closed as tears seeped from her eyes. Charlie. Her heart cried his name and in a flash of memories she thought of the night of his birth, his first toothless grin, his first toddling step.

So many firsts she'd shared, but so many she would miss when she was gone. His first baseball game, his first date. Graduation, prom, his wedding. The thought of her loss sent sharp grief through her.

And Jake. Sweet, sexy Jake. She had been going to buy a silky nightgown just for him. The tears slipped faster down her cheeks and she tried not to cry, knowing that if her nose got stuffed she wouldn't be able to breathe at all.

They had been going to share a future together. They had planned to be a family and build memories of love and caring and passion.

She'd cling to those thoughts, to thoughts of Charlie and Jake, as she faced the next few minutes or hours of her life. She'd let Charlie's smile carry her through the torture, she'd keep Jake's face in her mind as she breathed her last breath.

Worst-case scenario . . . she was going to die. He could rip her belly with a knife, he could do whatever he wanted to her body, but he couldn't touch the shining brightness of the love that filled her heart.

When she'd been sixteen she'd had nothing to cling to, no thoughts to distill the horror of what he did to her. Things were different now. Unless she could figure a way out of this, she knew she was going to die. But it gave her some measure of comfort to know that in death she'd still love Charlie and Jake.

"Daniel Bannister," Monica yelled to Jake. "Called in sick tonight. First time in the three months he's been working for the station."

"Got an address?" Jake asked. When she nodded he was already out the door and headed toward her car. She hurried to follow behind him.

"Five-one-two-oh Ague Road," Monica said, as Jake pulled away from the house. "It's up north, off 169. It's all farmland up there." Three cars followed Jake's to provide backup.

"What's the story on this Bannister? Did you get anything on him?" Jake needed conversation to quiet the screaming voice in his head. Had he brought this danger to Jessie? With his high profile in the lily murder case, had he brought the lily killer directly to her door?

"Moved here from California three months ago. No arrests on record. According to Jessie's producer he's a nice guy but keeps to himself. Usually works the seven-to-three shift."

Jake frowned. "Most of our victims were picked up just after three in the morning. So if this is our guy, he works the night shift, then on his way home he picks up a little perverted pleasure. Some men stop for doughnuts and coffee. He picks up women."

He slammed his fist on the steering wheel, an explosion of impotent rage. "Only he didn't pick up Jessie on the street. He went after her because of me. I brought him to her."

"Jake, don't go there," Monica warned. "Don't do that to yourself. You can't know what set him off with her."

"We were so damned worried that the T and B killer might be after her again. I didn't even consider she might be a target for the lily killer."

"I've got to tell you, none of this makes sense. And who the hell is the guy who just happened to be sitting in his car in the middle of the night down the street from Jessica's house?"

"Trust me, when this is all over I'm going to know everything there is to know about that guy. Something about him isn't right. Just do me a favor." He shot Monica a bleak look. "Pray that we're going in the right direction, and pray that we're not too late."

"Already done," she replied softly.

Number 5120 Ague was indeed in the middle of farmland. As the police cars pulled up in front of the small ranch house, Jake realized it was the perfect place for killing women. The nearest neighboring house wasn't even visible in the distance. Nobody would hear a woman's scream here.

Besides Jake and Monica six other officers advanced on the dark house. Two went around back, two went to each side and Monica and Jake took the front. There was no sign of a vehicle anywhere around, but there was a large barn in the distance.

"I don't suppose I should mention to you that we probably should wait for a search warrant," Monica said softly as they approached the front door.

Jake exploded forward, putting all his weight, all his rage into the shoulder that sent the front door off its hinges and imploding inward. "Search warrant delivered."

They went in like a SWAT team, covering each other's asses as they checked room after room for occupants. Each light that went on in each room indicated that this wasn't a home, but rather just a place to stay, as impersonal as a motel room.

It took only minutes to clear the place and begin the real search for anything that might lead them to Jessie and her whereabouts.

The living room was sparsely decorated, holding only a recliner sofa and a television. "We know he doesn't entertain much unless his guests sit on the floor," Monica observed.

The bedroom was the same. It contained only the basic bed and nightstand and a closet full of casual clothes and neatly pressed uniforms. The spare bedroom was completely empty.

Jake slammed his fists against one of the kitchen cabinets. "Nothing," he said, his voice hollow. "There's nothing here to help us." He leaned weakly against the cabinet, his despair such that he could speak no more.

"Detective?" A young uniform walked into the kitchen.

Jake frowned at him, trying to remember his name but without luck. He was fried with grief.

"We found some kind of a cellar on the west side of the house. It's got a padlock on it. Do you want us to . . . " He stopped speaking because Jake was past him and out the door.

"Looks like an old root cellar," Jake said, staring at the slanted door that appeared to lead into a small hillside.

"Why would anyone want to lock up a root cellar?" Monica asked.

"Because there's something to hide." Jake didn't wait for anyone to pry off the lock. He pulled his gun and fired at the lock, the *ping* of metal on metal piercing the silence of the night.

He yanked off the lock and saw about a dozen wooden stairs leading down into pitch darkness. He pulled his flashlight and started down the stairs.

Jake's grandmother had had a root cellar, but it hadn't smelled like this. Hers had smelled of sweet onions and new potatoes. This smelled like death.

No, Jessie. Please, don't let Jessie be in this dank, dark place.

When he hit the bottom step his light flashed on a wall switch and he flipped it, illuminating the area in the brilliance of several lightbulbs. And in that illumination he gasped and stumbled backward, wanting to escape.

"Jake?" Monica called from the top step. "Are you all right?"

He cleared his throat, swallowed against the bile that had risen. "You better call for the crime-scene guys."

"I'm coming down."

He knew Monica had reached his side when he heard her gasp. "My God," she said, her voice filled with the sickness he felt.

The area wasn't large, no bigger than an average room. Chains were cemented into the walls, earthen walls stained with the rust of old blood. A vase of plastic white lilies stood in one corner.

"This is his killing place," Jake said. He smelled the blood, the death, and could hear the cries of all the women who had been guests in this chamber of hell. The one voice he didn't hear was Jessie's.

"Where is she?" He turned to stare hollowly at Monica. "Where in the hell has he taken her?"

"Maybe the answer is there." She shone her flashlight on a metal file cabinet in a corner. Together she and Jake hurried toward it. Files were inside. Files with newspaper articles about the murders, and each file held a city map with a bright red dot depicting where he'd dumped the body.

They pulled out half a dozen of the files, scanned them, then tossed them aside for more. Jake frowned as he read the articles in one manila folder. "This one is about a serial killer in California. Four victims, each raped and left at dump sites around the Los Angeles area, four maps with tiny red dots."

"I can do better than that." Monica's hands trembled as she held out a file.

Jake took it from her and stared at the news articles clipped from the Kansas City papers years ago. Eighteen years ago.

Had Daniel Bannister clipped these articles because he'd been a fan of another serial murderer? Or was the answer something darker, something more sinister? Was it possible that the lily killer and the T&B killer were the same man? Was Jake's monster the same as Jessie's monster?

"I think I know where she is." Jake dropped the file on top of the cabinet and headed for the stairs.

As he and Monica jumped back in his car, the crime-scene van arrived. Jake knew they'd be busy for days processing everything in Daniel Bannister's cellar.

"Where are we headed?" Monica asked, as he started the engine and roared away from the small farmhouse.

"If I'm right in my thinking, then he's our lily killer. A year ago he was Los Angeles's nightmare.

And I think eighteen years ago he was the T and B killer. He liked to bury his victims alive, and if he's come back for Jessie as his unfinished project, then he'll revert to his old patterns."

"He'll bury her alive." The words seeped from Monica with an underlying tone of horror.

"So we're headed to the Hillside Cemetery." He didn't want to think about the pattern Daniel Bannister might have once again embraced, the pattern of rape and slicing. He told himself if that happened, then Jessie could survive. She had before and she would again.

What she couldn't survive was being put in the ground and having dirt shoveled over her while she struggled for air.

When the car stopped, Jessie's heart thundered painfully hard. If he did what he had done the last time, then he'd brought her someplace where he could rape and cut her up.

Even though her heart banged an uneven rhythm, she was surprised to realize her fear wasn't all consuming. She'd been through this before. She knew she could survive the violation of rape and the sharp point of a knife.

And with every moment of life, she prayed that somehow, someway a miracle would occur to save her. The miracle last time had been a group of teenagers. She couldn't imagine what form a miracle might take now.

The whole time she'd been in the trunk she'd

tried to think of ways to get out of this, knowing that she couldn't expect a bunch of partying teenagers to save her this time.

Nobody else knew she had been taken from her home. If she was going to be saved, then it was going to be up to her to do something. But what?

If he cut the tape from her ankles to rape her, then she'd kick him as hard as she could. Years ago she hadn't done that. She'd submitted meekly to his rape. At that time she'd been young and blind-folded and so sure that he'd let her go when he'd finished with her.

This time she knew better. She was certain death awaited her, but until she gasped her last breath, she'd fight him any way she could.

The trunk lid opened and in the faint light of the moon spilling down from overhead she saw him for the first time. Daniel, the security guard. Daniel, whom she would have trusted with her life.

Her monster had been close to her every night for the past three months and she'd never known, had never sensed his evil presence.

He picked her up as if she were nothing more than a bag of potatoes, and when she left the dark-ness of the trunk and saw their surroundings, the visceral fear that hadn't been present before came crashing in.

The cemetery. He'd brought her right to the cemetery.

"I've been waiting a long time for this, Dr. Jessie," he said as he carried her away from the car.

She struggled in his arms, twisting her body and arching in an effort to get away.

"You might as well stop it." He held her tight. So damned tight. "Even if I drop you, what are you going to do? You can't run."

He was right. She might as well conserve her energy for when she had the potential for some kind of success.

"I never forgot you. Of all my victims in all the various states, you were the one I never forgot." His voice was conversational, like he was having a discussion over a nice dinner with a date.

She closed her eyes, but once again the sense of déjà vu struck her with a haunting force. She could smell the flowers, sweet lilacs and powerful honeysuckle. She could hear his footsteps in the lush grass as he carried her to her grave.

"It was fate that brought us back together," he continued. "I heard you on the radio one night, and after doing a little bit of checking discovered that Dr. Jessica Langford was little Jessie Clinton, the girl who'd gotten away. Imagine my delight when I applied for the position of security guard at the station and was hired."

His fingers bit into her skin painfully. "You ruined things. Now it's time to make them right."

He was silent for a few minutes and she kept her eyes closed, praying for strength, praying for rescue, praying for a swift and painless death.

"Unfortunately the final resting place I'd picked out for you years ago has since been filled. But the good thing about cemeteries is there's always a grave waiting to be filled."

She opened her eyes then and their gazes met. He smiled, the pleasant smile she remembered from so many nights at the radio station. There was no madness in his eyes, no glittering signal of disease or evil.

Why? she thought. Why this? What had happened to this man to transform him into a cold-blooded killer? He must have seen the question in her eyes.

"I like it," he said, his voice softer, lower. "That's why I do it. I'm not reenacting a trauma from my past. I'm not working through mother issues. I just like killing women and burying them in the ground."

Thrill killer. They were the worst of all. She'd read enough to understand that they were sociopaths, without conscience, without guilt. But it didn't matter what label he wore; he was death.

"The ones that came after you, I couldn't put them in the ground after you got away. You screwed up the ritual for every woman that came after you." He stopped walking, and the blood in her veins iced as she saw that they stood beside an open pit. A shovel was on the ground nearby.

This time she struggled for her life, twisting and turning, knifing her knees and trying to claw at his face with her bound hands.

Without warning he dropped her. The fall was brief, and she hit the ground in the bottom of the grave hard. Her breath whooshed out of her and she saw stars.

Then she saw the stars, the real stars, winking down on her from their place in the sky. Far away. So very far away. Her head ached with nauseating intensity, and any hope of survival she might have entertained seemed as distant as the stars overhead.

The sound of a shovel against dirt.

The scent of earth all around her.

She screamed against the duct tape, screamed until she felt as if her throat had been ripped raw. But she knew there was nobody to hear her cries.

The first of the dirt hit her in the chest. Get up, her mind screamed. Stand up and he can't bury you. She tried to sit up but pain ripped through her back and she knew the fall had hurt something.

The second shovelful of dirt struck her on the face. She twisted her head back and forth to dislodge it. At that moment she heard it, the sound of whistling. As the strains of "Amazing Grace" filled the air, more dirt hit her. Then more. Then more.

Chapter 28

"We go in quiet," Jake said as he parked his car on the street just outside the tree-laden Hillside Cemetery. "He probably has a weapon. I don't want to alert him and have him use it on Jessie."

"This place is huge," Monica said. "It could take us an hour to find somebody in here."

"I know where he'll be. It's on the north side of the cemetery. The headstone will read CAMERON JACKSON." By this time he and Monica were out of the car and moving through the darkness of the night.

Jake led, gun drawn and heart pumping. So much time had slipped by since they'd discovered Jessie gone. Too much time.

If it's too late, I don't know how to survive, he thought. He'd promised Jessie a life of happiness and love. He'd promised her that nobody would ever hurt her again. If she didn't survive this night he didn't know how he'd live with his grief, with his guilt, with the loss.

Although he didn't know the specific gravesite that held the headstone that read CAMERON JACKSON, he did know the general area from the description of Jessie's rescue in the paper.

They moved silently, quickly. It would have helped had there been a full moon to illuminate the grounds. But the moon was just a sliver in the sky, not giving them much help.

He didn't want to use flashlights, didn't want to draw attention. He didn't want Bannister to get away, because if the man had killed Jessica, then Jake intended to kill him.

When they reached the area where Jake was sure the grave should be, a wave of sick helplessness struck him. There was no sign of anyone. Was it so late that Bannister had already buried her and left?

Had she already gasped her last breath of air and suffocated in a grave? Too late. Too late. The words taunted him in his head as a faint night breeze brought him the scent of flowers.

Monica gripped his arm tightly and she leaned close to him. "I thought I just heard something," she whispered. "A whistle."

A whistle? Jake's head flashed with the memory of Jessie telling him that as the T&B killer had buried her, he'd been whistling. "Where?"

The dark despair vanished beneath an electric surge of new energy. Monica frowned, then pointed toward a stand of trees in the distance. "There, I think."

Jake ran, possessed by a wild need that threw

caution to the wind. He broke through the trees, and in the faint moonlight stood a man with a shovel.

He must have made a noise, for the man turned toward him, his eyes wide with surprise. He threw the shovel and took off running.

"I'll go after him," Monica yelled.

There had been no choice in Jake's head. He'd never intended to purse the man. Rather he raced to the side of the grave where Bannister had been standing and looked down.

"No," he moaned. There was nothing to see but dirt. Wild and possessed, he threw himself on the ground. Fingers scrabbled at the dirt.

Digging.

Scooping.

The sound of frantic grunts filled the night, grunts mixed with deep, wrenching sobs, and someplace in the very back of his mind he knew he was making those sounds.

"Jessie! Jessie!" Her name ripped from his throat over and over again.

Hair. His fingers touched hair. He was like an animal burrowing into the earth. Forehead. The pale skin of her forehead appeared and he worked to uncover her nose, her mouth.

"I'm here, Jessie." He sobbed as he continued to seek the rest of her face, her too-pale, still face.

He heard a gunshot and hoped to hell Monica had killed Bannister. He hoped she'd put a bullet through his sick, twisted brain.

Too late. As her face came clear of the dirt his heart cried in anguish. Too late. "Jessie. Breathe. Breathe, Jessie," he screamed.

Monica appeared at his side, and as she worked to free the rest of Jessie, Jake jumped into the pit and pressed his mouth to hers and tried to force air into her lungs.

Chapter 29

It was an odd kiss. Too much air and it tasted like tears. She couldn't imagine why Jake was kissing her like that. He was usually such a great kisser.

She opened her eyes to brilliant sunshine and white walls. Heaven? She hadn't expected walls. She tried to sit up but pain shot through her. Pain in heaven?

Then she heard it. The faint, deep snore. As the last of her dream faded from her mind, she sought the source of the noise and saw Jake sleeping in a chair next to her hospital bed.

She wasn't dead. She was alive, wonderfully alive. The last thing she'd remembered was drawing her final breath and tumbling into a darkness too profound to escape.

Jake's eyes snapped open and in that unguarded moment of a gaze she saw all his emotions shining in the depths of his eyes. Exhaustion. Fear. And love.

He leaned forward. "Jessie?" The word was a hoarse whisper.

"I dreamed you were kissing me," she said, surprised to discover her voice was a husky rasp. "I dreamed you were kissing me badly."

Relief swept over his features. "Obviously a nightmare."

Tears shone in his eyes as he reached for one of her hands. He grabbed it and held tight, as if it were his lifeline. "You're okay. We weren't sure. We don't know how long you were without oxygen."

"Charlie?"

"Is fine. He and Jimmy are with Larry and Trisha."

She started to sit up once again, but he stopped her. "Don't," he said. "You strained your back pretty bad."

She squeezed his hand as memories rushed toward her. Daniel. The grave. The sounds of "Amazing Grace." No air. Just dirt. "It was Daniel, a guard at the station."

"We know. He's dead. My partner shot him as he tried to run away. We managed to kill two birds with one bullet. Daniel Bannister wasn't only the T and B killer, he was also responsible for the murder cases I've been working on."

"Thank God. Thank God he's dead."

She must have fallen asleep, because when she opened her eyes again the sun slanted through the windows in the purple hues of twilight. Jake was still beside her and he smiled at her. "Hi again."

"Hi."

"How are you doing?"

"I must be better, because I think I'm hungry."

"I'll see about getting the nurse to bring you something. But before I do that, there's somebody here who is desperate to see you."

"Charlie?" she asked.

Jake shook his head negatively. "No, but I think you'll find this interesting." He got up from his chair and disappeared from the room for a moment. When he returned, Mark Smith was with him.

"Mr. Smith," she said, and looked at Jake in confusion.

Mark Smith stepped closer to her bed. "Dr. Langford." He looked ill at ease, and Jessie tried to make sense of his presence here. What did he have to do with all of this?

"Uh, my name isn't really Mark Smith. It's Mark Cappa," he said.

"Cappa?" Jessie knew that name. A picture of Adam Cappa, the detective who had originally been in charge of the T&B killer case, filled her head.

"Adam Cappa was my brother," he said.

"Was?"

Sadness darkened Mark's eyes. "Adam committed suicide two years after he dug you out of that grave."

"I'm so sorry," Jessie said. "He was very kind to me."

"He was a good man." Mark jammed his hands

into his pockets and looked both ashamed and embarrassed. "I'm the one who's been following you."

"Why?" Did he blame her for his brother's death? If so, why had it taken him so long to act on it?

Mark stared at the wall behind her head. "Adam and I were close, really close. But the T and B case got hold of him and wouldn't let him go. He became obsessed. He pulled away from all of us and buried himself in the case."

He looked at her once again. "When we were younger we had a plan. We were going to retire the same year, move to Florida and start a fishing business. This was the year we were going to do that. I thought I'd dealt with his death, but when the date arrived that we were going to retire, I guess I went a little crazy."

"Crazy?" She glanced at Jake, then back at Mark.

"I suddenly needed to know about you, about your life. It was like I needed to know that Adam had counted for something, and the last thing he did that meant anything was dig you out of that grave. I'm sorry. I never meant to scare you. I just . . . I just needed to be around you." He flushed with color.

"If it hadn't been for Mark, we wouldn't have found Daniel and you wouldn't be here now," Jake said to Jessie. "He was parked down the street, watching your house, when Daniel went in to get you."

"At first I didn't understand exactly what I was

seeing. I didn't know I was watching a crime occur. It wasn't until all the cop cars pulled up in front of your house that I realized something terrible had happened."

Jessie tried to digest all the information. "Then I guess I owe two Cappa men my life." She held Mark's gaze for a long moment. "Your brother did count. I'm sorry if I had anything to do with his suicide, but he was my hero and his friendship and support after that night helped keep me alive."

Mark pulled his hands from his pockets and raked one of them through his hair. "You didn't have anything to do with Adam's suicide. I never blamed you for that. Adam had some problems with depression before the T and B case."

He drew a deep sigh, as if relieved that he had come clean. "I won't be following you anymore. Whatever craziness possessed me passed last night. It's time that I go back to my wife and the life I had before all this. I'm going to retire and move to Florida and open that fishing-guide business. And I hope you have a wonderful life."

He didn't wait for her reply, but turned on his heels and left the room. For a long moment Jessie said nothing, then she looked at Jake. "Life is definitely strange, isn't it?"

He moved to sit in the chair he'd recently vacated. "From now on I'm hoping life is going to be wonderfully mundane."

He leaned closer and stroked a strand of her hair away from her face, his features haunted and stark.

"I came so close to losing you," he whispered. "When I got to that cemetery and realized you were under that mound of dirt, I think I went more than a little crazy."

She reached her hand up and laid it on the side of his face, felt the sweet warmth of his skin, the faint scratch of whiskers. "I'm quitting my job at the radio station." She surprised herself with the words. She hadn't realized it was a thought in her head until she'd spoken it aloud.

"Why?" His eyes clouded in confusion.

"Because life is too short to work two jobs. Because I don't want to be in the public eye anymore. I've got my private practice, and I'm hoping soon I'll have a husband and two boys to raise."

"I don't need raising," Jake said, the cloudiness in his eyes clearing as joy shone through.

"No, you just need loving," she replied.

"I love you, Jessica Langford," he said, and his voice held a passion and promise that filled her heart, filled her soul.

"And I love you, Jake Merridan," she replied. She just barely got the words out of her mouth before he leaned forward and kissed her. It wasn't the odd kiss of her earlier dream. It was a magnificent kiss that spoke of sweet beginnings and happy endings.

Epilogue

The wedding was a small, intimate affair with only close friends invited. There were no bridemaids or groomsmen, only two ring bearers who walked side by side down the aisle to deliver the rings that would bind Jake and Jessica forever in matrimony.

When the ceremony was done, Jimmy stood with Charlie as they waited for everyone to head to Tony's for a celebratory meal.

It had been two months since the night that Dr. Jessie had been kidnapped, and those two months had been busy ones. They'd bought a new house, one where Charlie and Jimmy could have their own bedrooms.

Jimmy liked the house. It was a two-story with trees in the backyard, and his dad had promised that after the wedding he'd help the two boys build a tree house.

Maria had her own room there too. She'd be living with them, and that was cool with Jimmy. She cooked a million times better than Mrs. Crawford. Besides, Maria wasn't really like a babysitter, but more like family.

Tonight they were eating at Tony's, and tomorrow morning they were getting on a plane for Colorado for a weeklong stay at Lake Vallecito. They were gonna fish and ride horses and have more fun than Jimmy had ever had in his life.

He glanced over at Charlie, who was scratching under his arm like a monkey. The kid was still lame, but Jimmy had the rest of his life to teach him how to be cool.

It was going to be a tough job, but Jimmy figured if his dad could save Dr. Jessie's life, then the least Jimmy could do was make Dr. Jessie's son not be a dork.

At that moment his dad and Dr. Jessie walked up to them. "Are you ready for some of Tony's lasagna?" Jake asked.

"I'm ready," Charlie replied. "I'm starving."

Jimmy elbowed him. "You're always starving."

Dr. Jessie leaned down and straightened Charlie's bow tie, then she moved to Jimmy and did the same with his. When she was finished she smiled at him, and it was a mother kind of smile.

A family. He looked at his dad, at Dr. Jessie, then at the helplessly lame Charlie. His family.

Happiness swelled in Jimmy's chest, such happiness that he felt a sting of tears burn his eyes. He swallowed hard and quickly swiped his eyes. He wasn't about to cry. He couldn't cry, not from happiness, not in front of Charlie.

That would be totally lame.

**Read on for a preview of
Carla Cassidy's next book.**

She was supposed to be in school, but eight-year-old Molly Ridge had awakened with a sore throat that morning and her mom had kept her home.

Two slices of French toast and a glass of milk had somewhat eased the sore throat, and now Molly ran down the hallway in the house as her mother counted from the kitchen. "... three ... four ... You'd better find a good place to hide, my little lollipop, because when I find you I'm going to eat you up! Five ... "

Molly stifled a giggle with her hand as she careened into her mother's bedroom. The closet? No, her mom would find her there for sure. Behind the curtains? Her feet would stick out, and besides the curtains were kind of see-through with the late morning sun shining in.

"Six ..."

Panic ripped through her as her mother's counting continued. When she reached ten, she'd come looking for Molly. She looked around the room and finally slid beneath the bed, ignoring the dust on the wood floor and the pinch of the metal springs against her back.

"Seven . . ."

Beneath the bottom of the bright yellow dust ruffle she could see the bedroom doorway and she held her breath as she waited for her mother to come find her.

"Eight . . ."

A loud knock on the front door interrupted her mom's counting. Molly sighed, hoping whoever was at the door would go away fast.

"Hi! What's up?" Her mother's voice drifted down the hallway from the living room. "Wait! Oh my God. What . . . what are you doing?"

A scream pierced the air.

Molly froze, her heart pounding frantically. A crash resounded, followed by the sound of glass breaking. A bang. More screams.

Something was wrong.

Something awful was happening.

In horror Molly watched as her mother appeared in the bedroom doorway. Bright red splashed her white blouse, and she staggered across the room and fell to the floor next to the bed.

"Mommy?" Molly whispered.

Monica Ridge turned her head and saw her daughter beneath the bed. "Shush, lollipop. Don't move. Don't make a sound." The words were slurred and barely audible. Molly stuffed a fist in her mouth as she heard footsteps coming down the hallway, and her mother tried to get up.

"No. Please," Molly heard her mother say as Molly squeezed her eyes tightly closed.

More noise.

Scary noise. She opened her eyes once. A flash of blue. A knife slashed downward. She quickly squeezed her eyes closed again.

Then silence.

She had no idea how long she remained, eyes tightly closed, listening to the silence. When Molly opened her eyes once again, she saw her mother lying on her back nearby.

Blood. It was everywhere. On her mommy, on the floor, on the walls.

Mommy? She wasn't moving, but her eyes were wide open and staring at the ceiling. Her hand was stretched out toward where Molly hid, and Molly wanted to reach out and grab her mommy's hand and tell her to get up and to stop staring like that.

Molly screamed inside her head as she shoved her fist harder against her mouth.

Shush. Don't move. Don't say a word.

Shush. Don't move. Don't say a word.

F   Cassidy, Carla (Carla
CASSIDY Bracale)
          Are you afraid?